Penguin Books

TRANSGRESSIONS

Don Anderson was born in Sydney in 1939, and has always lived there, apart from the odd year in other great cities – London and New York. He is Senior Lecturer in English at the University of Sydney, where he teaches Renaissance and Modern Literature, and Textual Theory. He has regularly reviewed Australian, American and European books for the *Age*, the *Age Monthly Review*, the *National Times* and the *Sydney Morning Herald*. Don Anderson writes a monthly column in the *National Times* on Australian writing, 'On His Selection', and also contributes to the ABC radio programme, 'Books and Writing'. His articles have appeared in *Meanjin*, *Quadrant*, *Southerly*, *Southern Review* and *Westerly*.

TRANSGRESSIONS

Australian Writing Now

Edited by Don Anderson

Penguin Books
Published with the assistance of the
Literature Board of the Australia Council

Penguin Books Australia Ltd,
487 Maroondah Highway, P.O. Box 257
Ringwood, Victoria, 3134, Australia
Penguin Books Ltd,
Harmondsworth, Middlesex, England
Penguin Books,
40 West 23rd Street, New York, N.Y. 10010, U.S.A.
Penguin Books (Canada) Limited,
2801 John Street, Markham, Ontario, Canada L3R 1B4
Penguin Books (N.Z.) Ltd,
182-190 Wairau Road, Auckland 10, New Zealand

First published by Penguin Books Australia, 1986

Publication assisted by the Literature Board
of the Australia Council, the Federal Government's
arts funding and advisory body

Typeset in Palatino Roman & Palatino condensed by 15% by Leader Composition
Made and printed in Australia by Dominion Press-Hedges & Bell

CIP

Transgressions.

ISBN 0 14 008393 6.

1. Short stories, Australian. I. Anderson, Don, 1939-
II. Australia Council. Literature Board.

A823'.0108

CONTENTS

INTRODUCTION

This book was conceived as a sequel and companion-piece to Frank Moorhouse's anthology of contemporary Australian short stories, *The State of the Art* (Penguin, 1983). At the risk of sounding like Vladimir Nabokov advising his readers to buy *two* copies of his novel, *Pale Fire*, to make their reading of it easier, I suggest that this volume carries on a dialogue with Moorhouse's, and that they may profitably be read together.

Our books share only seven authors out of a total of seventy-five stories. Together, you will find the two volumes present sixty-seven authors of contemporary Australian short fiction. I think this book continues Moorhouse's high standard, but that it is significantly different enough in authors and editorial preferences to be of interest in its own right. *Transgressions* is selected from stories, fragments, texts, writing, published or written in Australia in the period since Moorhouse's volume appeared – though it is worth noting that some were written a considerable time before they were published.

Commenting on the perhaps notorious absence of Elizabeth Jolley from *The State of the Art*, Gerard Windsor observed that Moorhouse's anthology was 'tendentious (allowably so no doubt)'. An anthology would necessarily fail if it were *not* tendentious. It might be duly and dully 'representative' (of what?), but the strengths of *The State of the Art* came from the personal nature of Moorhouse's choice. His book had a homogeneity of vision that reflected his own concerns. It had all the compelling vigour of obsession. I trust that this volume shares those qualities.

Elizabeth Jolley *is* represented in this volume. I want, however, to thank Frank Moorhouse for his invaluable advice that I should publish 'the best stories' from the last two years – that I should choose stories, not authors. So 'The Bathroom Dance' is here because it is a fine story, not because it is by Elizabeth Jolley.

Not that Frank Moorhouse's advice was by any means easy to follow. There are very strong sectional interests demanding representation in Australian writing, and they deserve a sympathetic as well as a critical ear. Some writers and their unions hold that men and women ought to be represented in equal numbers in any anthology (this is not so here, though the numbers are close). Minority groups, such as Aborigines and various migrant groups, are demanding space or separatist publications. This raises, among other things, the spectre of ghetto cultures. Aboriginal and migrant writing is represented in this anthology, but not because it belongs in those categories. It is chosen because it meets the standard of 'the best stories', at least in the eyes of this editor. To discover the best, I read all the short fiction in Australian little magazines from April 1983 to April 1985. Unlike Moorhouse, I did not invite submissions, except from authors whose work I considered indispensible, though word did get around, and some that I received are included here.

One of Moorhouse's contributors, Michele Nayman, has written that 'a good short story has an internal logic, a completeness, a gem-like quality.' The Hungarian critic, Georg Lukacs, has asserted that the short story is the most purely literary form. It is the narrative mode which pinpoints the ambiguity and strangeness of life, and which expresses the ultimate meaning of all artistic creation as mood. While both these categorisations of the short story inform my selection, I must point out that not all the pieces in this volume can be called 'short stories'. For example, one appeared in the 'Poetry' section of a magazine; another appeared in an art criticism journal; others appeared in the comment columns of newspapers. Which is simply to say that the 'short story' does not exhaust the range of short prose being published in Australia today. It is more satisfactory to regard some of the contributions to this volume as 'text', or as 'writing'.

In this and other senses, then, I hope that this is a transgressive volume. Some of the contributions are generically transgressive; several come from small presses, and thus transgress the hegemonies of major publishing houses or established journals; many, I hope, transgress what Moorhouse has characterised as a dominant drift in Australian writing – 'platitudinous humanism'. There can be no doubt that the Australian short story today is under the dominance of a drab realism that smacks of mindless conservatism. My editorial soul thirsted for 'experimental' writing, for the fresh, the new; for the 'experimental' that had its own voice and did not display mere dependence on, say, Beckett or Stein.

There is an unexamined realist orthodoxy in Australian short fiction. Most stories chronicle childhood and development towards a responsible maturity; celebrate domestic virtues and examine families; laud rural verities or mythicise The Land; most are Humanist with a capital 'H'. They are as formally conservative as they are ideologically so. If this volume to some extent subverts that dominant pattern, then it will have succeeded. Which is not, of course, to deny that there are fine realistic short stories between its covers.

This volume is also informed by a more abstract and embracing notion of writing as transgression. I have in mind the observations of Roland Barthes, à propos de Sade:

The transgressions of language possess an offensive power as least as strong as that of moral transgressions, and that 'poetry' [writing] which is itself the language of the transgressions of language is thereby always contestatory.

I would be happy if much of the writing in this volume were found to be 'contestatory': of dominant rhetorical and structural patterns in writing no less than of dominant social and political ideologies. I accept that this volume, no less than *The State of the Art*, endorses Frank Moorhouse's observation that political life as a narrative site is hardly evident (though this cannot be said of his own contribution or of Patrick Cook's satirical Homericisms). But writing that is not located in the political-as-content may be no less subversive in that, as a mute transgressive text, it voices protest against the prison house of language while exploiting that very language as the vehicle of its protest. If that sounds paradoxical, it is because truly contemporary writing cuts against the *doxa*, cuts across received opinion. To subvert dominant literary structures and dominant linguistic and rhetorical patterns is also to subvert dominant ideologies.

I have divided the volume into six sections. While there is always something necessarily arbitrary about such divisions (I would be happy for any reader to rearrange the book in imitation of Richard Lunn's story), they do display something of the current concerns and obsessions in Australian society. There is also a covert, at times ironical, structure in the order and juxtapositions of the stories. The 'Overture' is intended to sound the principal themes of the volume; but I confess that I think the 'Finale' keeps the best for last.

Don Anderson
The University of Sydney
June 1985

OVERTURE

OVERTURE

Richard Lunn

MIRRORS

1

A couple. A man and woman standing silent, as if framed in a
camera lens. Nothing moves. There is no wind here to feather
the smooth auburn of her hair. The blue ice of his eyes seems
flawless, unmeltable. Behind them is a wall of smoky glass,
with hints of further walls and chambers beyond its dark
translucency. Two low archways, one on the left and one on the
right, are open at the corners of this wall. Another couple stand
inside the room, a man and woman. They too are still, facing
the first couple as if framed in a camera lens. Behind her darkly
glinting hair, and unobserved by his blue gaze, a wall with two
doorways grants shadowy glimpses of further corridors and
compartments. The two couples stand, almost touching, separated by a veneer so thin it might not be there. Yet this surface,
transparent as air, is the plane dividing two realities, or rather,
dividing reality from illusion. It is a mirror, for as one couple
turn to face each other, so too do their images. But which is the
living reality and which the reflection? Each woman turns to
face each man, each man turns to face each woman. Their eyes
meet quickly, watchfully, and yet they might be strangers.

If they speak, go to 2.
If they don't speak, go to 3.

2

The man of each couple smiles. 'A frog he would a-wooing go,' they laugh. 'We haven't been a-wooing, Ruth. We've been amazing.' Their face becomes more serious. 'You've been amazing.'

Now it is the woman of each pair who laughs. 'Naturally,' they say pertly. 'So now you must obey me. It's time to go outside and get some sun.'

'Amazing,' the man intones, mock-reverent. And all four figures leave the room, but only two escape the mirror-maze to amble through the sunlight of the patterned garden. Behind them is a tall Palladian facade, its pilasters and pediments grafted to the stones of a more ancient manor. They stroll together hand-in-hand down pathways of heraldic topiary, past cooing columbaria, submerged in the scent and regimental finery of the serried flower-gardens. As if assembling piece by piece their own vignette, they sit beneath a beech tree and kiss with the easy intimacy of established lovers.

'Gerald wouldn't like that,' he says primly, then kisses her once more.

'Gerald wouldn't like a lot of things we've done this afternoon,' she replies.

He performs a pantomime of lechery, but grows suddenly reflective. 'The maze is quite a place for making love. All those mirrors, hundreds of you. I was literally beside myself.' She groans and then his smile turns mischievous. 'I'll bet Gerry never does it there. The sight of the countless flabby bums of countless paunchy Geralds would have to be too much for even his conceit to stand.'

'You might be surprised. Besides,' she adds, eyebrows echoing his archness, 'Gerry's rather superstitious and there are some odd stories connected with the maze.'

'Of course, it's haunted!' and he claps his hands with glee. 'Why didn't you tell me, Ruth? All those voyeuristic ghosts getting the lowdown on my sexual style.'

'Well, alright, one of the stories does say it's haunted.' Her tone seems slightly defensive, as if she feels a sudden loyalty to her legends-in-law. 'It's something about a woman and her lover being trapped in the maze by the woman's husband, an old robber baron or some such thing. They're supposed to be walking endlessly round and round. But sooner or later, no matter where they . . .' Yet here she pauses for a moment as a white Rolls Royce pulls up at the gates. 'But sooner or later . . .' And again she peers towards the gates.

If the car backs up and drives away, go to 5.
If the car drives in, go to 6.

3

Silence amplifies the momentary shock of meeting. In her eyes there is confusion, a tense distraction, and he breaks away. He walks toward the door upon the left, she to that upon the right. He glances back across his shoulder, curious perhaps, or with a hint of recognition. They enter the low archways. Four figures disappear from the chamber.

If his path leads out, go to 4.
If his path does not lead out, go to 5.

4

He strolls from the recess that conceals the mirror-maze, heading for the gardens at the front of the house. More buses are pulling up, disgorging streams of sightseers. A coachload of Norwegians and a minibus of Japanese form ranks round their respective guides. Daytripping armies sprawl across the lawns, their infant skirmishers pillaging the flowerbeds, while tourists with tripods take aim at statues. He watches them stream through the portico, dwarfed by its towering Palladian columns. Vandals and Visigoths, he decides with a smile, and continues in the direction of the gardens. Pebbles crunch underfoot, endorsing the silence, while a story suggested perhaps by a distant glimpse of symmetrical, pruned mazes, starts tugging at his thoughts. He follows its thread down the pebbled path, now wishing he'd brought his notepad and pen, and arrives at the foot of a tall beech tree.

If he decides to sit under the tree, go to 9.
If he continues up the path, go to 10.

5

But sooner or later, no matter where they begin, they invariably return to the place from which they started. They are caught like foxes run to ground, trapped by the vengeance of her husband. His jealousy is cruel and circular, like one of his prize falcons rushing from his glove. For the maze in which he's shut them is a series of connected spirals, divisions of yet greater involutions which constitute, in turn, the sections of a single pathway. They run down tunnels lined with mirrors, each anguished gesture, each desperate change of direction, echoed in the walls about them. Their images grow slowly into spectres, the walls reveal the dying process. Their dread, now etched upon their faces from within, begins to overwhelm them.

If they keep trying to discover a pathway leading out, go to 7.
If they finally attempt to smash their way out, go to 8.

<u>6</u>

'It's Gerry,' she says, her frown betraying her anxiety. 'He was supposed to be down south for at least another day.'

'So what?' he chuckles. 'Big Bad Gerry's nothing to get the willies about.' Then he stares at her, a look of comic horror on his face. 'Or is he? Ruth, give it to me straight. He's the one who locks lovers up in mazes, isn't he? Come on, baby, you've got to level with me.'

'Oh shut up, Rob,' and he notes that she isn't laughing. 'I know he seems harmless enough, but he can be a very suspicious person. And if you knew the way he does business you'd realise he can be pretty vindictive. I mean, it isn't as if he's weaponless. If he suspects anything, I wouldn't put it past him to cut me off with as little as he could, and that wouldn't do either of us any good. It'd probably be a good idea if you made yourself scarce for a few days.' She watches him quizzically, but he returns her gaze with a blank stare. 'Damn,' she says, 'I've left my shoes in the maze.'

If he decides to leave, go to 10.
If he decides to stay, go to 11.

<u>7</u>

They career through their glittering, closed cosmos, reflections fluttering about them like panic-stricken birds. The cycles of their fear are mirrored by the swiftness of their flight. They run, then walk, then run again, diverging through the branches of the maze, then meeting some time later in alarming flurries of reflection. As days pass they grow distant, each becoming to the other a single moving image amongst a plethora of moving images. The consciousness of each begins to doubt where it resides among the multitude of selves. Then suddenly they'll meet and hug closely for comfort. They'll walk together slowly, and then run . . .

If they keep trying to discover a pathway leading out, go to 5.
If they finally attempt to smash their way out, go to 8.

8

At last, through desperation more than anger, they begin to break the mirrors. They beat the flat, deceptive glass with their bare fists, watching their dismembered selves collapse about them, until finally, as if an act of sheer strength might break them through to the sky and lawns and depths of air, he lunges at a mirrored wall. His image flies toward him, converges in a sudden fragmentation, and he is dying in a pool of bleeding glass upon the floor. She mourns him briefly, sitting by his body for a time, until a sense of hoplesslessness begins to overwhelm her. But she determines to renounce despair till every mirror in the maze is broken.

Go to 12.

9

He reclines against its aged, grey bole and watches the intaglios of leaves and twigs imprinted on his eyelids by the sun. He imagines the driveway empty of buses, the stillness of the house devoid of tourists. The woman in the maze distracts his thoughts. Her face, it seems, is one of those that tease the mind with some insistent, yet elusive quality. For a moment he opens his eyes and, in a sudden dazzle of light, pictures himself once more before a mirror that contains the figures of a man and woman. Before these figures stand a pair of perfect reproductions. He sees the faces of each couple turn. He sees each man begin to smile. The outlines of a plot are growing clearer in his mind. But he has now become accustomed to the glare, and with the sun's hot weight upon him, feels disinclined to puzzle out a story. In many ways a further exploration of the path seems more inviting.

If he continues with the story, go to 2.

If he decides to walk further, go to 10.

<u>10</u>

He walks briskly down the pebbled path towards the rear of the house, somewhat surprised at the relief he feels to get away. Sunlight warms him as he walks, alternately drenching him with heat and dappling his dark suit with changing leopard-spots. Invisible birds disturb the foliage about him, or boast aloud of their security, while he too disappears amongst leaves and increasingly unkempt hedges. He strolls between the columns of a crumbling stoa, where ligatures of crimson bougainvillea coax blood-drops from the stone. The pathways twist and thin, inevitably suggesting the configurations of the maze, each leaf a mirror shining in the sheets of light. Nor can he stop thinking of the woman. Despite the pleasure of escape, her image remains with him. Paths branch without a hint of which will lead him to the postern gate. Leaves shimmer with a hard metallic lustre. Her beauty, dark and vulpine, fills his thoughts until a sudden, seemingly quite random fantasy suggests itself to his imagination. He sees her, as he walks, running through a mirrored labyrinth. With hosts of hurtling counterparts she races along corridors, stumbling in the sun-bursts of reflected bifurcations. He imagines the rhythms of her slow despair, the sudden rushes slackening to methodical investigations of each pathway, then lunging faster as she sees there is no way that ends beyond the maze. Until at last, maddened by the grotesque anguish of the faces that stare at her from every wall, she throws herself against the glass. She leaps back, watching her reflection and its flat world shatter, watching for the sudden depths beyond, the sunlit garden, pale clouds, blue sky. But there is only her facsimile staring from a mirror in a further chamber, already reflecting her determina-tion to renounce despair till every mirror in the maze is broken.

Go to 12.

<u>11</u>

He follows her towards the house. 'Look, Ruth, I think you're overreacting. I've done business with people like Gerry. They're just not tough-minded enough to hurt you if you handle them properly. That silver spoon in the mouth blunts

8

their teeth. Anyway, what's he got to be suspicious about? He's hardly been here in the last few months.' She slows her pace a little, purses her lips doubtfully then smiles.

'Well, I'd still better get my shoes,' she says not quite convinced enough to forget the impression her appearance might create. However, as they reach the deep-set recess at the side of the house, where the doorway leading to the maze seems always to be open, the Rolls glides to a stop beside them. She is surprised to find that Gerry isn't in it, but only the wizened, snail-paced chauffeur he insists upon retaining. 'Where's Mr Sheldrake?' she inquires. But before he can answer she beckons him to follow them into the maze. As they enter its gleaming tunnels, his voice, now coming from outside, echoes leadenly across the space behind them: 'Mr Sheldrake's had a heart-attack, Mrs Sheldrake.'

If she is genuinely concerned for him, go to 13.
If she feels no real concern for him, go to 15.

12

A slow, cold anger takes hold of her and hurls her like a stone through corridors of glass. A mirror crazes round her fist and breaks apart. Another follows, then another, but hunger and exhaustion too are fists, which beat inside her as she moves until, as if she were a shattering reflection amongst a host of shattering reflections, she stumbles to the floor. Unconscious hours pass in which her memories fragment and merge with fantasies, as multiple reflections might break apart and merge into reality. For when she wakes there is no past that she recalls, no thought or feeling but the anger that hurls her down the corridors. Emptied of memories, devoid of fear or regret, she marches through the gleaming chambers. Her images swagger beside her, raise bloodied arms and smash themselves to tinkling shards. She lies on floors in jagged puddles of reflections and rushes up glass tunnels in a headlong herd of selves. She feels at times as if she's nothing but a moving consciousness, a disembodied, many-bodied anger, nowhere and everywhere, conquering whole armies of herself. Her body streams with red medals. She lifts her fist to smash a mirror. It tinkles into splinters and reveals a man face down upon the floor.

If she recognises him, go to 13.
If she doesn't recognise him, go to 14.

13

She pauses, seems confused and then remembers, at first quite distantly, as if a dream had broken, how once upon a time they'd ventured to investigate the mirror-maze, embracing in a ballroom crowd where every couple was the same. With sharp, regretful mourning she recalls that long ago they grew confused, perhaps only for a moment, until there was . . .

Go to 1.

14

She bends towards him, inspects the cold perfection of his features, touches his soft hair. Her fury cracks then crumbles to reveal, like the sandgrain at the centre of a pearl or the first cell of a cancer, the hopeless isolation that exists within. A surge of loneliness breeds dreams, a welling hope, a fantasy, until it seems she had divined his history and sees him rise before her, tall and beautiful, a figure from some old romance. He laughs and takes her hand to guide her through the maze. They saunter casually, chattering and giggling like two children, making faces in obliging mirrors. They explore the branching paths, turn patiently in twisting helices and smile, confident that labyrinths have exits. Yet slowly, as they circle through the tunnels, their smiles grow fixed and grin grotesquely at them from the walls. Their words become less frequent, their pace increasingly hurried, as they trace the mirrors' spirals.

Go to 5.

15

Instinctively she clutches at Rob's sleeve. 'Why didn't you telephone?' she cries, realising that the old man must be several corners behind her. It seems ludicrous to have to raise one's voice in such a situation. Yet she does. 'I could have flown down and been with him already.'

'But, Mrs Sheldrake, he's only in the town.' His words are muffled with mirrors.

'In town? He was on business in the south.'

'No, Mrs Sheldrake,' the old cracked voice insists from back along the maze. Is he in or is he out? she wonders. 'He was seeing Mr McEwan.' And already her thoughts are racing back across the months now gone, the weeks, the past few culpable hours. The memories of events that have rushed her to this moment whirl about her brain, while the voice drones on. 'Something about his will, I think.' And with this, though perhaps it's only in her mind, she hears a door click shut, a lock snap home, and she is seeing . . .

Go to 1

Elizabeth Jolley

THE BATHROOM DANCE

When I try on one of the nurse's caps my friend Helen nearly dies.

'Oh!' she cries, 'take if off! I'll die! Oh, if you could see yourself. Oh!' she screams and Miss Besser looks at me with six years of reproach stored in the look.

We are all sewing Helen's uniform in the Domestic Science room. Three pin-stripe dresses with long sleeves, buttoned from the wrist to the elbow, double tucks and innumerable button holes; fourteen white aprons and fourteen little caps which have to be rubbed along the seam with a wet toothbrush before the tapes can be drawn up to make those neat little pleats at the back. Helen looks so sweet in hers. I can't help wishing, when I see myself in the cap, that I am not going to do nursing after all.

Helen ordered her material before persuading me to go to the hospital with her. So, when I order mine it is too late to have my uniform made by the class. It is the end of term, the end of our last year at school. My material is sent home.

Mr Jackson tells us, in the last Sunday evening meeting, that he wants the deepest responsibility for standards and judgements in his pupils, especially those who are about to leave the happy family which is how he likes to think of his school. We must not, he says, believe in doing just what we please. We must always believe in the nourishment of the inner life and in the loving discipline of personal relationships. We must always be concerned with the relentless search for truth at whatever

12

cost to tradition and externals. I leave school carrying his inspiration and his cosiness with me. For some reason I keep thinking about and remembering something about the reed bending and surviving and the sturdy oak blown down.

My mother says the stuff is pillow ticking. She feels there is nothing refined about nursing. The arrival of the striped material has upset her. She says she has other things in mind for me, travelling on the continent, Europe, she says, studying art and ancient buildings and music.

'But there's a war on,' I say.

'Oh well, after the war.'

She can see my mind is made up and she is sad and cross for some days. The parcel, with one corner torn open, lies in the hall. She is comforted by the arrival of a letter from the matron saying that all probationer nurses are required to bring warm sensible knickers. She feels the matron must be a very nice person after all and she has my uniform made for me in a shop and pays extra to have it done quickly.

Helen's mother invites me to spend a few days with Helen before we go to St Cuthbert's.

The tiny rooms in Helen's home are full of sunshine. There are bright yellow curtains gently fluttering at the open windows. The garden is full of summer flowers, roses and lupins and delphiniums, light blue and dark blue. The front of the house is covered with a trellis of flowers, some kind of wisteria which is sweetly fragrant at dusk.

Helen's mother is small and quiet and kind. She is anxious and always concerned. She puts laxatives in the puddings she makes.

I like Helen's house and garden, it is peaceful there and I would like to be there all the time but Helen wants to do other things. She is terribly in love with someone called David. Everything is David these few days. We spent a great deal of time outside a milk bar on the corner near David's house or walking endlessly in the streets where he is likely to go. No one, except me, knows of this great love. Because I am a visitor in the house I try to be agreeable. And I try to make an effort to understand intense looks from Helen, mysterious frowns, raised eyebrows, head shakings or noddings and flustered alterations about arrangements as well as I can.

'I can't think what is the matter with Helen,' Mrs Ferguson says softly one evening when Helen rushes from the room to answer the telephone in case it should be David. We are putting up the blackout screens which Mrs Ferguson has made skilfully to go behind the cheerful yellow curtains every night. 'I suppose she is excited about her career,' she says in her quiet voice, picking up a little table which was in Helen's way.

Everyone is so keen on careers for us. Mr Jackson, at school, was always reading aloud from letters sent by old boys and girls who are having careers, poultry farming, running boys' clubs and digging with the unemployed. He liked the envelopes to match the paper, he said, and sometimes he held up both for us all to see.

Helen is desperate to see David before we leave. We go to all the services at his mother's church and to her Bible class where she makes us hand round plates of rock cakes to the Old Folk between the lantern slides. But there is no David. Helen writes him a postcard with a silly passionate message. During the night she cries and cries and says it is awful being so madly in love and will I pretend I have sent the postcard. Of course I say I won't. Helen begs me, she keeps on begging, saying that she lives in the neighborhood and everyone knows her and will talk about her. She starts to howl and I am afraid Mrs Ferguson will hear and, in the end, I tell her, 'All right, if you really want me to.'

In the morning I write another card saying that I am sorry about the stupid card which I have sent and I show it to Helen, saying:

'We'll need to wash our hair before we go.'

'I'll go up first,' she says. While she is in the bathroom using up all the hot water, I add a few words to my postcard, a silly passionate message, and I put Helen's name on it because of being tired and confused with the bad night we had. I go out and post it before she comes down with her hair all done up in a towel, the way she always does.

Mrs Ferguson comes up to London with us when we set off for St Cuthbert's. Helen has to dash back to the house twice, once for her camera and the second time for her raincoat. I wait with Mrs Ferguson on the corner and she points out to me the window in the County Hospital where her husband died the year before. Her blue eyes are the saddest eyes I have ever seen. I say I am sorry about Mr Ferguson's death, but because of the uneasiness of the journey and the place where we are going, I know that I am not really concerned about her sorrow. Ashamed, I turn away from her.

Helen comes rushing up the hill. She has slammed the front door, she says, forgetting that she has put the key on the kitchen table and will her mother manage to climb through the pantry window in the dark and whatever are we waiting for when we have only a few minutes to get to the train.

David, unseen, goes about his unseen life in the narrow suburb of little streets and houses. Helen seems to forget him easily, straight away.

Just as we are sitting down to lunch there is an air raid warning. It is terrible to have to leave the plates of food which have been placed in front of us. Mrs Ferguson has some paper bags in her handbag.

'Mother! You can't!' Helen's face is red and angry. Mrs Ferguson, ignoring her, slides the salads and the bread and butter into the bags. We have to stand for two hours in the air raid shelter. It is very noisy the ARP wardens say and they will not let us leave. It is too crowded for us to eat in there and, in any case, you can't eat when you are frightened.

Later, in the next train, we have to stand all the way because the whole train is filled with the army. Big bodies, big rosy faces, thick rough great-coats, kit bags, boots and cigarette smoke wherever we look. We stand swaying in the corridor pressed and squeezed by people passing still looking for somewhere to sit. We can't eat there either. We throw the sad bags, beetroot-soaked, out onto the railway lines.

I feel sick as soon as we go into the main hall at St Cuthbert's. It is the hospital smell and the smell of the bread and butter we try to eat in the nurses' dining room. Helen tries to pour two cups of tea but the tea is all gone. The tea pot has a bitter smell of emptiness.

Upstairs in Helen's room on the Peace corridor as it is called because it is over the chapel, we put on our uniforms and she screams with laughter at the sight of me in my cap.

'Oh, you look just like you did at school,' she can't stop laughing. How can she laugh like this when we are so late. For wartime security the railway station names have been removed and, though we were counting the stops, we made a mistake and went past our station and had to wait for a bus which would bring us back.

'Lend me a safety pin,' I say, 'one of my buttons has broken in half.' Helen, with a mouthful of hair grips, busy with her own cap, shakes her head. I go back along the corridor to my own room. It is melancholy in there, dark, because a piece of blackout material has been pinned over the window and is only partly looped up. The afternoon sun of autumn is sad too when I peer out of the bit of window and see the long slanting shadows lying across unfamiliar fields and roads leading to unknown places.

My school trunk, in my room before me, is a kind of betrayal. When I open it books and shoes and clothes spill out. Some of my pressed wild flowers have come unstuck and I put them back between the pages remembering the sweet wet grass near the school where we searched for flowers. I seem to see clearly shining long fingers pulling stalks and holding bunches. Saxifrage, campion, vetch, ragged robin, star of Bethlehem, wild strawberry and sorrel. Quickly I tidy the flowers – violet, buttercup, King cup, cowslip, coltsfoot, wood anemone, shepherd's purse, lady's slipper, jack in the pulpit and bryony
. . .

'No Christian names on duty please,' staff nurse Sharpe says, so, after six years in the same dormitory, Helen and I make a great effort. Ferguson – Wright, Wright – Ferguson.

'Have you finished with the floor mop – Ferguson?'

'Oh, you have it first – Wright.'

'Oh! No! By all means, after you, Ferguson.'

'No, after you, Wright.'

Staff nurse Sharpe turns her eyes up to the ceiling so that only the whites show. She puts her watch on the window-sill saying:

'Quarter of an hour to get those baths, basins and toilet really clean and the floors done too. So hurry!'

'No Christian names on duty,' we remind each other.

We never sleep in our rooms on the Peace corridor. Every night we have to carry our blankets down to the basement where we sleep on straw mattresses. It is supposed to be safe there in air raids. There is no air and the water pipes make noises all night. As soon as I am able to fall asleep Night Sister Bean is banging with the end of her torch saying 'Five thirty a.m. nurses, five thirty a.m.' And it is time to take up our blankets and carry them back upstairs to our rooms.

I am working with Helen in the children's ward. Because half the hospital is full of soldiers the ward is very crowded. There are sixty children; there is always someone laughing and someone crying. I am too slow. My sleeves are always rolled up when they should be rolled down and buttoned into the cuffs. When my sleeves are down and buttoned it seems they have to be rolled up again at once. I can never remember the names of the children and what they have wrong with them.

The weeks go by and I play my secret game of comparisons as I played it at school. On the Peace corridor are some very pretty nurses. They are always washing each other's hair and hanging their delicate underclothes to dry in the bathroom. In the scented steamy atmosphere I can't help comparing their clothes with mine and their faces and bodies with mine. Every time I am always worse than they are and they all look so much more attractive in their uniforms, especially the cap suits them well. Even their finger nails are better than mine.

'Nurse Wright!' Night Sister Bean calls my name at breakfast.

'Yes Sister,' I stand up as I have seen the others do.

'Matron's office nine a.m.,' she says and goes on calling the register.

I am worried about my appointment with the matron. Something must be wrong.

'What did Matron want?' Ferguson is waiting for me when I go to the ward to fetch my gas mask and my helmet. I am anxious not to lose these as I am responsible for them and will have to give them back if I leave the hospital or if the War should come to an end.

'What did Matron want?' Ferguson repeats her question, giving me time to think.

'Oh, it is nothing much,' I reply.

'Oh, come on! What did she want you for? Are you in trouble?' she asks hopefully.

'Oh no, it's nothing much at all,' I wave my gas mask, 'if you must know, she wanted to tell me that she is very pleased with my work and she'll be very surprised if I don't win the gold medal.' Ferguson stares at me, her mouth wide open, while I collect my clean aprons. She does not notice that one of them is hers. It will give me an extra one for the week. I go to the office to tell the ward sister that I have been transferred to the theatre.

> Had I the heavens' embroidered cloths,
> Enwrought with golden and silver light.

O'Connor, the theatre staff nurse, is singing. She has an Irish accent and a mellow voice, I would like to tell her I know this poem too.

The blue and the dim and the dark cloths
Of night and light and the half light,

In the theatre they are all intimate. They have well-bred voices and ways of speaking. They look healthy and well-poised and behave with the ease of movement and gesture which comes from years of good breeding. They are a little circle in which I am not included. I do not try to be, I wish every day, though, that I could be a part of their reference and their joke.

In a fog of the incomprehensible and the obscure I strive, more stupid than I have ever been in my life, to anticipate the needs of the theatre sister whose small, hard eyes glitter at me above her white cotton mask. I rush off for the jaconet.

'Why didn't you look at the table!' I piece together her angry masked hiss as I stand offering a carefully opened and held sterilised drum. One frightened glance at the operating table tells me it is catgut she asked for.

'Boil up the trolley,' the careless instruction in the soft Irish voice floats towards me at the end of the long morning. Everything is on the instrument trolley.

'Why ever didn't you put the doctors' soap back on the sink first!' The theatre is awash with boiled-over soap suds. Staff nurse O'Connor, lazily amused, is just scornful enough. 'And,' she says, 'what in God's Holy Name is this!' She fishes from the steriliser a doll-size jumper. She holds it up in the long-handled forceps. 'I see trouble ahead,' she warns, 'better not let Sister see this.' It is the chief surgeon's real Jaeger woollen vest. He wears it to operate. He has only two and is very particular about them: I have discovered already that sister is afraid of the chief surgeon, consequently I need to be afraid of her. The smell of boiled soap and wool is terrible and it takes me the whole afternoon to clear up.

Theatre sister and staff nurse O'Connor, always in masks, exchange glances of immediate understanding. They, when not in masks, have loud voices and laughs. They talk a great deal about horses and dogs and about Mummy and Daddy. They are quite shameless in all this Mummy and Daddy talk.

The X-ray staff are even more well-bred. They never wear uniform and they sing and laugh and come into the theatre in whatever they happen to be wearing, backless dinner dresses, tennis shorts or their night gowns. All the time they have a sleepy desirable look of mingled charm and efficiency. War time shortages of chocolate and other food stuffs and restrictions on movement, not going up to London at night for instance, do not seem to affect them. They are always called by pet names, Diamond and Snorter. Diamond is the pretty one, she has a mop of curls and little white teeth in a tiny rosebud mouth. Snorter is horsey. She wears trousers and little yellow waist coats. She always has a cigarette dangling from her bottom lip.

I can't compare myself with these people at all. They never speak to me except to ask me to fetch something. Even Mr Potter, the anaesthetist, who seems kind and has a fatherly voice, never looks in my direction. He says, holding out his syringe, 'Evipan' or 'Pentothal', and talks to the others. Something about his voice, every day, reminds me of a quality in my father's voice; it makes me wish to be back at home. There is something hopeless in being hopeful that one person can actually match and replace another. It is not possible.

Sometimes Mr Potter tells a joke to the others and I do not know whether I should join in the laugh or not.

I like Snorter's clothes and wish that I had some like them. I possess a three-quarter length oatmeal coat with padded shoulders and gilt buttons which my mother thinks is elegant and useful as it will go with everything. It is so ugly it does not matter what I wear it with. The blue skirt I have is too long, the material is heavy, it sags and makes me tired.

'Not with brown shoes!' Ferguson shakes her head.

It is my day off and I am in her room. The emptiness of the lonely day stretches ahead of me. It is true that the blue skirt and the brown shoes, they are all I have, do look terrible together.

Ferguson and her new friend, Carson, are going out to meet some soldiers to go on something called a pub crawl. Ferguson, I know, has never had anything stronger than ginger beer to drink in her life. I am watching her get ready. She has frizzed her hair all across her baby-round forehead. I can't help admiring her, the blaze of lipstick alters her completely.

Carson comes in balancing on very high-heeled shoes. She has on a halo hat with a cheeky little veil and some bright-pink silk stockings.

'What lovely pink stockings!' I say to please her.

'Salmon, please,' Carson says haughtily. Her hair is curled too and she is plastered all over with ornaments, brooches, necklaces, rings and lipstick, a different color from Ferguson's.

Ferguson looks bare and chubby and schoolgirlish next to Carson.

Both of them are about to go when I suddenly feel I can't face the whole day alone.

'It's my day off too,' I say, 'and I don't know where to go.'

Ferguson pauses in the doorway.

'Well, why don't you come with us,' Carson says. Both of them look at me.

'The trouble is, Wright,' Carson says kindly, 'the trouble is that you've got no sex appeal.'

After they have gone I sit in Ferguson's room for a long time staring at myself in her mirror to see if it shows badly that I have no sex appeal.

I dream my name is Chevalier and I search for my name on the typed lists on the green baize notice boards. The examination results are out. I search for my name in the middle of the names and only find it later at the top.

My name, not the Chevalier of the dream, but my own name is at the top of the lists when they appear.

I work hard in all my free time at the lecture notes and at the essays 'Ward Routine', 'Nursing as a Career', 'Some Aspects of the History of Nursing' and 'The Nurse and her Patient'.

The one on ward routine pleases me most. As I write the essay, the staff and the patients and the wards of St Cuthbert's seem to unfold about me and I begin to understand what I am trying to do in this hospital. I rewrite the essay collecting the complete working of a hospital ward into two sheets of paper. When it is read aloud to the other nurses, Ferguson stares at me and does not take her eyes off me all through the nursing lecture which follows.

I learn every bone and muscle in the body and all the muscle attachments and all the systems of the body. I begin to understand the destruction of disease and the construction of cure. I find I can use phrases suddenly in speech or on paper which give a correct answer. Formulae for digestion or respiration or for the action of drugs. Words and phrases like 'gaseous interchange' and 'internal combustion' roll from my pen and the name at the top of the lists continues to be mine.

'Don't tell me you'll be top in invalid cookery too!' Ferguson says and she reminds me of the white sauce I made at school which was said to have blocked up the drains for two days. She goes on to remind me how my pastry board, put up at the window to dry, was the one which fell on the headmaster's wife while she was weeding in the garden below, breaking her glasses and altering the shape of her nose for ever.

My invalid carrot is the prettiest of them all. The examiner gives me the highest mark.

'But it's not even cooked properly!' Ferguson is outraged when she tastes it afterwards. She says the sauce is disgusting.

'Oh well, you can't expect the examiner to actually eat all the things she is marking,' I say. Ferguson has indigestion, she is very uncomfortable all evening because, in the greedy big taste, she has nearly the whole carrot.

It is the custom, apparently, at St Cuthbert's to move the nurses from one corridor to another. I am given a larger room in a corridor called Industry. It is over the kitchens and is noisy and smells of burning saucepans. This room has a big tall window. I move my bed under the window and, dressed in my school jersey, I lie on the bed for as long as possible to feel the fresh cold air on my face before going down to the basement for the night. Some evenings I fall into a deep and refreshing sleep obediently waking up, when called, to go down to the doubtful safety below.

Every day, after the operations, I go round the theatre with a pail of hot soapy water cleaning everything. There is an orderly peacefulness in the quiet white tranquillity which seems, every afternoon, to follow the strained, blood-stained mornings.

In my new room I copy out my lecture notes:

. . . *infection follows the line of least resistance* . . .

and read my school poetry book:

Through the thick corn the scarlet poppies peep,
And round green roots and yellowing stalks I see
Pale pink convolvulus in tendrils creep:
And air-swept lindens yield
Their scent . . .

I am not able to put out of my mind the eyes of a man who is asleep but unable to close his eyes. The putrid smell of wounded flesh comes with me to my room and I hear, all the time, the sounds of bone surgery and the troubled respiration which accompanies the lengthy periods of deep anaesthetic . . .

Oft thou hast given them store
Of flowers – the frail leaf'd, white anemony,
Dark blue bells drench'd with dews of summer eves
And purple orchises with spotted leaves . . .

. . . and in the theatre recovery ward there are fifteen amputations, seven above the knee and eight below. The beds are made in two halves so that the padded stumps can be watched. Every bed has its own bell and tourniquet . . .

St Cuthbert's is only a drop in the ocean, staff nurse O'Connor did not address the remark to me. I overheard it.

Next to my room is a large room which has been converted into a bathroom. The dividing wall is a wooden partition. The water pipes make a lot of noise and people like to sing there, usually something from an opera.

One night I woke from my evening stolen sleep hearing two voices talking in that bathroom. It is dark in my room; I can see some light from the bathroom through a knot hole high in the partition. The voices belong to Diamond and Snorter. This is strange because they live somewhere outside the hospital and would not need to use the bathroom. It is not a comfortable place at all, very cold, with a big old bath awkwardly in the middle of the rough floor.

Diamond and Snorter are singing and making a lot of noise, laughing and shrieking above the rushing water.

Singing:

Give me thy hand O Fairest
 la la la la la la la
I would and yet I would not

laughter and the huge bath obviously being filled to the brim.

Our lives would be all pleasure
 tra la la la la la la
 tra la la la la la la
 tum pe te tum
 tum pe te tum

'That was some party was it not!'
'Rather!' their rich voices richer over the water.
I stand up on my bed and peer through the hole which is

about the size of an egg. I have never looked through before though have heard lots of baths and songs. I have never heard Diamond and Snorter in there before – if it is them.

It is Diamond and Snorter and they are naturally quite naked. There is nothing unusual about their bodies. Their clothes, party clothes, are all in little heaps on the floor. They, the women not the clothes, are holding hands, their arms held up gracefully. They are stepping up towards each other and away again. They have stopped singing and are nodding and smiling and turning to the left and to the right, and, then, with sedate little steps, skipping slowly round and round. It is a dance, a little dance for two people, a minuet, graceful, strange and remote. In the steam the naked bodies are like a pair of sea birds engaged in mating display. They appear and disappear as if seen through a white sea mist on some far-off shore.

The dance quickens. It is more serious. Each pulls the other more fiercely, letting go suddenly, laughing and then not laughing. Dancing still, now serious now amusing. To and fro, together, back and forth and together and round and round they skip and dance. Then, all at once, they drop hands and clasp each other close, as if in a private ballroom, and quick step a foxtrot all round the bathroom.

It is not an ugly dance, it is rhythmic and ridiculous. Their thighs and buttocks shake and tremble and Snorter's hair has come undone and is hanging about her large red ears in wispy strands.

The dance over they climb into the deep hot bath and tenderly wash each other.

The little dance, the bathroom dance, gives me an entirely new outlook. I can't wait to see Diamond and Snorter again. I look at everyone at breakfast, not Ferguson, of course (I know everything there is to know about her life) with a fresh interest.

Later I am standing beside the patient in the anaesthetic room,' waiting for Mr Potter, when Snorter comes struggling through the swing doors with her old cricket bag. She flops about the room dragging the bag:

And on the beach undid his corded bales

she says, as she always does, while rummaging in the bag for her white Wellington boots. I want to tell Snorter, though I never do, that I too know this poem.

I look hard at Snorter. Even now her hair is not combed

properly. Her theatre gown has no tapes at the back so that it hangs, untied and crooked. She only has one boot on when Mr Potter comes. The unfairness of it all comes over me. Why do I have to be neatly and completely dressed at all times. Why do they not speak to me except to ask for something to be fetched or taken away. Suddenly I say to Snorter: 'Minuet du Salle de la Bain,' in my appalling accent. I am surprised at myself. She is hopping on one foot, a Wellington boot in her hand, she stops hopping for a moment.

'De la salle de bain, surely,' she corrects me with a perfect pronunciation and a well mannered smile, 'also lower case,' she says, 'not caps, alters the emphasis.'

'Oh yes, of course,' I mutter hastily. An apology.

'Pentothal,' Mr Potter is perched on his stool at the patient's head. His syringe held out vaguely in my direction.

Angelo Loukakis

PARTYING ON PARQUET

He sat there on the edge of the bed, now gazing down at his new boots, now staring in the wardrobe mirror. Only a half an hour before people were supposed to arrive, and he was beginning to feel sort of paralysed. All these questions kept coming up, like the one with which he was currently grappling – one candle or more than one candle. Of the necessity for candles he was certain; but as to how many, he had no idea.

He wished he could ring someone. Theo maybe, yes Theo who had been going to East Sydney Tech for years – he was someone who would have been to a million parties of the kind he was about to throw. Too bad that right at this minute Theo was somewhere in Cyprus on holidays with his parents.

He was new to this business of holding his own parties; there were a million other questions he would have liked answered for him at this moment. For instance: how much grog do people drink? He had bought some – beer and cask wine – but was it enough?

Then there were the dips. Because these seemed to be a pretty regular thing at parties, he had bought some from David Jones earlier in the day. He remembered that they had still to be taken out of their packets, and the crackers too. This practicality worked to mobilise him at last, and he got up to go to the kitchen.

On his way there, he pulled himself up in the hall at the doorway of his little living room and looked in.

It all seemed so bare. He had been renting this place for six months or so, had even accumulated a few pieces of furniture and so on, but this room still felt so empty. As did the whole flat really. Here, another little flame licked up around him, the fear that he might never be able to make it look or feel right, like a home that is.

But, as his father had said, if you leave your parents, you're on your own. Tonight, that was exactly how he felt.

He went on to the kitchen and opened the fridge. The six different dips in those little plastic containers with the houndstooth check took up most of the top rack – and what with the three wine casks on the bottom, and a few bits and pieces like sliced cheese and some carrots and a bottle of Coke, the mini-fridge was practically full. This food-buying caper was something else he wished he could get on top of.

He took the dips out and lined them up on the kitchen table. Using a teaspoon, he began emptying them into the soup bowls, the ones his mother had given him when it had finally sunk in with her that he was actually going away, leaving home.

They said he would get lonely, but he didn't feel himself to be *that* alone. He had made a few friends since moving out; it was they who were supposed to start arriving soon – Marina and Pavlos, and Penny. Penny – who was tutoring him in HSC English – had asked when he had rung to invite her if she could bring her friends, Jan and Phil. So there was every chance that he would soon be making some more.

He arranged the dips up his arms and headed for the living room. Once again, he stopped at the doorway and looked around. Was this the place to hold a party? It was so small; how many people could you fit in here? But these aside, the one question for which he desperately wanted an answer in advance was – would Penny like it?

Crossing into this room, he suddenly found his boots making a God almighty clatter on the parquet. He put the dips down quickly and sat on the edge of the sofa to inspect their soles. What was wrong? – these R.M. Williams' had cost top dollar. There was nothing to see but, annoyed at this new development, he put the boots back on the floor and began to test them for noise again. The soles weren't the problem, it was the heels. Weird, because even though they didn't have metal tips or anything, they still made a sharp racket.

Back at the job in hand, he turned to moving the dips around on the side table, trying to find the best arrangement. And yet he couldn't help thinking about the floor. He had never noticed it to be so noisy – but then no one had ever walked across it in big heels before.

The only solution he could think of was a rug, but it was too late to go looking for one now. He should have sorted this one out earlier. But how could he have known? This was the premiere outing for these boots. The only other way he might have found out was if he'd had a girl wearing high heels in here some time in the past. But this evening in fact would be the first time that chicks, booted or otherwise, had ever crossed his threshold.

What the hell. Penny was a uni student; she probably wouldn't give a stuff about such a silly detail. He chided himself for being so neurotic. As for Marina and Pavlos, they were only dumb ethnics like himself whom he had met at Greek dancing class; they wouldn't even hear the noise.

Again, he checked himself. There was no point in being defensive. This was his – this flat in a three storey block – and it was more than a lot of twenty-year-old guys had. What's more, how many of them had their own private coach, paid for out of their own wages? He felt a smirk take over his face, but then there was guilt.

With the good-looking Penny, whose ad in the local paper he'd answered at the beginning of the year, and for whom he was paying – when he cared to admit it to himself – almost a quarter of his accounts clerk wages, he was rapt. He was well and truly gone on her, but it was, just the same, one big secret. It was a secret he had done a great job of keeping, even from her.

It was the first thing they said. The very bloody first thing. Penny and her friends had already arrived and were sitting there on the sofa. Pavlos walks in, with Marina right behind, Marina in *clogs*. And she says, 'Jeez your floor's noisy!'

Then Penny says, 'Actually, I was wondering about that myself.' And then she turns to Jan and gives her a knowing look and says very quietly, 'we're partying on parquet tonight, folks.'

And Jan starts giggling and says, 'Very swish.'

As for Phil, Phil who turns out to be a sarcastic bastard, he just starts making snorting noises.

He was pacing around the living room. He'd already taken all the left-over junk and dirty glasses into the kitchen, but was putting off the washing up. He couldn't help going over the things that had happened, playing them through his head over and over again. How could it have turned into such a fucking disaster?

Someone then said, he couldn't remember who exactly, 'Hey! Where's the grog?'

So he went and got two of the casks, a red and a white, and the glasses as well. He put them down on the floor where Penny and friends were now sitting (Why did they do that? It seemed like a low-class thing to do), and Phil says – 'Christ, how many were you expecting?' Then Jan looks at Penny and then his way and hits him with, 'They're a bit big for wine, aren't they?'

The smart-arse Phil then asks, 'They're not from your Dad's milk bar are they, Steve?'

This, *everyone* thinks is funny, even Marina and Pavlos, and they all start to laugh like idiots.

Penny's friends turn out to be not the sort of people you can feel comfortable with; Marina and Pavlos never exactly relaxed with them, that was for sure. But after they've had this laugh, Marina, stupid Marina, gets up a bit of courage; she never usually talks out of place, why tonight? – and says, 'So this is your tutor, ay Steve? Very nice. Very nice. Does your father know she's a girl?'

Jan started raising her eyebrows and doing funny things with her eyes. But Penny pretended – he just knew she pretended – that she didn't hear what Marina had just said. Pavlos, good old Boilermaker's Certificate Pavlos, has to ask, 'How much do you cost? Like if I wanted to come to you, how much would you cost?'

What he felt like doing at that point, he didn't do; and he was hating himself for it now. He wanted to tell them to shut up. He could have said, 'Why don't you embarrassing ethnics just shut up?' But he didn't, and that was that. Maybe if he had, they wouldn't have gone on. Maybe they, Pavlos that is, wouldn't have started talking about parents.

'How come your old man puts up with you, mate?' he said. 'I mean, if I moved out, he'd shoot me. What does he say about it?'

'Wow, Steve, you're brave I reckon,' Marina tells him.

Hearing this stuff got Penny started, worst luck. God how it got her started. Thinking about it now was actually making him feel peculiar in the guts. She said something about how it must be very difficult living in a patriarchal family set-up, with a father of that typical kind or something. And then she had a gentle look on, and even touched his leg.

28

But at least he could see how he had got it all wrong. She just felt sorry for him – that's all it was. He should have worked it out from the way she just went straight on talking, even after she had touched him and he'd tried to get a bit closer to her there on the floor, with all that uni type language and stuff about sex roles. If he'd seen then that she was only taking pity on him, he probably wouldn't have gone on to make a fool of himself later in the kitchen.

What followed all this stuff? Oh yes, everyone sitting around looking at each other and not speaking, until Phil asks if there is any music.

'Music?' he could hear himself replying, sounding surprised. The most obvious thing in the world for a party, and he, dopey Steve, had forgotten all about it. 'No, not really. Only the cassette radio. It's in the bathroom, hang on, I'll got and get it,' he had said.

But Phil said, 'Don't bother. We'll probably have to go soon anyway.'

He finally stopped the pacing and threw a punch in the air, imagining that bastard was there to collect it. It was just after midnight and enough was enough. He made himself head for the kitchen, with an idea that washing up would get his mind off the crap that went down here tonight.

He squirted detergent in the sink and watched the suds grow as he filled it with hot water. He wasn't very good at blocking things out anymore. Used to be, when a stuff up happened, he would forget it straight away, just rub it out and keep moving. But as he got older, things seemed to hang around longer.

Piling the dirty glasses into the water, he knew it would take him weeks to stop thinking about what happened in here.

Still, he tried to go easy on himself and put his behaviour down to the grog he had drunk. He had got the wrong idea earlier, and the grog had just helped to make everything worse. What other reasons were there for cornering her in here, and blurting out that she was really great, and trying to grab hold of her.

The way she pushed him off – he hadn't expected her to be that angry, or that strong.

So what more did he expect?

The fact was, he realised, he was always expecting too much. And assuming too much as well. He hardly even knew her, for Christ's sake; it was just too soon to have done a big number, any sort of number for her.

'It's not on this level, Steve. I mean you're a nice guy and all that, but as far as I'm concerned, I'm helping you with your HSC English and Maths. Right?'

'Right,' he'd said. 'Right, right . . . ' and backed away and bumped his head on the cupboard.

He pulled the glasses out of the water and put them into the rack. The rest of it could all wait until tomorrow. Wiping his hands on his trousers first, he turned the light off in the kitchen. But before he left there, he grabbed a glass. He would have a last drink to help him go to sleep; whatever he had drunk this evening had stopped working long ago.

In the living room again, where he stood filling his glass from the cask still on the side table, he changed his mind. What he really felt like doing now was to take shower. His clothes stank from the cigarettes they had all been smoking, but that wasn't the reason. Something about washing it all away – if he could just wash everything away . . .

He threw his clothes off there and then, and went straight to the bathroom and into the recess. Unlike at home, here you could have a shower without worrying about leaving water for somebody else – and there was no doubt he was going to let the water run right through tonight.

He turned the knobs and got into position.

It was magic, just letting the water run down his body – the best thing that had happened all night. No soap, no nothing; he leaned against the tiles and watched the steam begin to slowly fill the room.

Yes, living on your own had a lot of things to it unlike home.

For all that tonight had been such a mess, there was no way he could ever go back. You didn't have to get in early at night. You didn't have your crazy father waiting for you to come in, and giving you a look up and down.

And smelling you.

Baba's trick of coming over and smelling around him, searching for something. Grog? Perfume?

What would he have done if he'd ever found anything?

There was no use in even mulling over it. That part of it was all over; what he had to do was learn how to cope with this new deal.

Well, at least one problem could be solved, the Marina and Pavlos problem. That was simple – they were out. Finished. No more. He didn't need people like them to make him look stupid.

And he would apologise to Penny.

As for Phil and Jan, the only way he would ever be able to get on top of smart arses like them was to beat them at their own game. He would study hard and get into uni. He would throw that stuff of theirs back at them so hard, they wouldn't know where to duck . . .

After a few minutes, the heat started to get to him, exaggerating his tiredness, making him sleepy.

He looked at his skin, going red in different patches on his shoulders. The steam had got so thick, he could hardly see a thing. He stared up at the ceiling. It was hanging there like a mist, a fog, with the light shining through; and it was his for as long as he wanted.

Kris Hemensley

THE BOOK
(CHEZ CLAUDE MAURIAC)

(a)

The Book is a backwards & forwards affair. One may only ever flick thru it, backwards & forwards, backwards & forwards, dealing with it as if it were alive. It is made in the images of Life, it is made of Life's images, if one flicks thru it fast enough the images live. Now i am he, as once i was me, & then, & then. And there is no book, & 'but there is no book'. It always remains to be written. And since i am always somewhere else, as he is, & she is, & you are, & they in all probability, always somewhere else doing something else, this is the most i can offer you. You have me here as one who always puts you off. These off-putting passages are the shadows the critics require, they recall what might have been inside & outside of the book, but what might have been was never ever on so long as the writer was i. Either you have me or you employ someone else. Either you have this or you gather something else someplace elsewhere. Here you are reading 'me' 'this' 'a' 'the'. You are reading 'here' & 'now'. This is an in-between-times reading written in-between-times. The Book is a tax upon time. There is never something for nothing.

(b)

B visits a whore ('the'). Come with me, he says to us. What should we wear? is on the tips of our tongues. Just feel your best, he says, be well within yourself. Wear what you wish, similarly shoes. Empty gestures won't wash in this neck of the woods. Hog-wash; one's inclined to scoff the sophisticate's advice. Carbolic soap was what i wanted to hear! There's no physical preparation necessary, says B, & if you're already anticipating remedy dont even advance a metre from your bunk. Either this is a matter of course & all up to the mind to fulfil, or it's a chore. This uncle's one who cares! Imagine us there, A, B, & C, fed & aired, all butterflies so dispersed no one'd know they were ever there. We pass a woman on the stairs, who bargains for a bigger note than the one proffered, which she duly receives & secretes, it seems, in the elastic of her protruding woollen underwear.

(c)

And we remember her oh so well, from De Mandiargues' *The Margin*, his four-nights-running pied a terre, the selfsame concierge. We say to one another, it's Mauriac who passes De Mandiargues on the stairs & pays him generously. To retrieve the past (as memory, as recollection does) is a little miracle. De Mandiargues not opening that letter for all the time he is in Spain, the letter that bears the gravest news, that he is cut adrift, the sole survivor of the family (child drowned, self-blaming wife suicided), is kith & kin of Mauriac postponing the writing of this book thru all four sections of *Femmes Fatales*, a writing that's never written (so we imagine with him the book he might write). There's another kumrad, a third musketeer, Marlon Brando, in Bertolucci's film *Last Tango in Paris*: in the room he denies to the world, the room in which he & Maria Schneider are not to question one another. That room is indicated by a short coloured sequence in Bertolucci's black & white masterpiece *Before The Revolution*. All of these references drift in space (in time). They conceive space & suspend it, not writing, not reading, not opening. Each one is hidden in 'colour'. This camouflage ensures that the ostentatious reveals least. But in another suburb of grand buildings, Vargas-Llossa's *The Green House* eludes the rule's proscription. His design's originality isn't contended. But one day i stumbled across Machado's short story *The Psychiatrist* in which he tells of a doctor of vision & good will who built a madhouse in the most prosperous street in the city, inspired by a Persian tale in which Allah made some people mad so as to protect them from sin & to keep their visions pure. Some of his patients had been driven mad by love. Machado's madhouse is called 'The Green House'. I feel i have been here before. As Mauriac passed her on the stairs i instantly knew that i had. And of course four times with Sigismund in *The Margin*. B pays her generously. It is De Mandiargues himself, nodding off. The plaster is painted green: i have to pinch myself that this isnt the old council swimming-baths. It has a green door-mat. We scuffed our shoes upon it religiously. B merely dropped a spent match on it. Someone ran down the stairs & skipped up the corridor towards us. A local boy. He had just lit up too. He also dropped a spent match upon the doormat. He wore a mallard-green poloneck sweater. The place assumed the aspects of a YMCA. Are you going to stand in the foyer all day? B asked in an extravagant Irish accent. We laughed at our backwardness & joined him on the stairway. We ascended, hearts in our mouths (A later confirmed). We passed a lady in a chair, nodding off. It's alright, said B, I've paid her. This could go on all day. It doesnt for reasons external to the running of this house. Simply, we dont belong here, we're inmates of another place. And so we go, 'all three', that is we'll go, he comes & goes as he chooses, ineluctably his own boss, now the two of us, cast off, fast home.

(d)

Yeah! Chirpy, yeah! There's books & books. I'd've written one if you'd let me. Some of the chapters are done & if they can avoid the fate that befell our friend's manuscripts (the most jealous Dearly Beloved's mattresses for binders) then we'd all be lucky. But i'm taking the wrong tack (i almost said 'sonny'). One book was the commercial success all provincials dream of. Another was too though i hadnt intended it. Another, as serious as that one, fell flat on its face. One that amuses me bemuses everyone else. The memory of another one overwhelms me with, at first, catch-breath excitement, then gradually with nostalgia & sentimentality, & finally with the insidious asphyxia of sadness & remorse – for it has gone & will never return. Only by retracing the words one by one could i begin again, & small chance of that, seventy-one thousand facets of young blood's shining face, at this stage of the race beyond reach. Another is one that makes me squirm. If only i could eat my words! And one that's yet to be written, i don't care if it's the defaecation of that other one, regurgitation of the one long gone, or something

new (as they say). One, just one last go at it before i'm thru –
and i'm not asking, i'm telling you – it's what i've set my heart
upon. (I like the sound of that!) And that's that.

John Clarke

FARNARKELING: A TYPICAL REPORT

The victorious Australian Farnarkeling team returned home in triumph last night with the bevelled orb safe in their keeping until the challenge round in late July Australian time.

Team members were fulsome in their praise of the running of the championships and are approaching the government to get an arkeling grommet of international standard built in Canberra so overseas teams can provide much needed competition here during the northern summer.

The heavily-bandaged Dave Sorensen, who aggravated a thigh injury with a heavy fall from the aircraft while deplaning before the ramp was in position, reacted strongly to suggestions that corporate sponsorship is poised to take farnarkeling into commercial television.

Proposals are already with the governing body to introduce a solid program of one-day farnarkeling fixtures under lights with edited highlights between the warbles and a viewer competition tentatively called 'Classic Arkels'. Major manufacturers have already come up with what they claim is the definitive farnarkeling shoe and T-shirts and initiatives in fast food are already in the pipeline.

The well-credentialled Sorensen said he would have nothing whatever to do with what he described as 'A ridiculous farnarkeling circus' which he claimed would turn the game into some kind of joke. Although he did admit he had been approached.

It will be very unfortunate for arkelophiles if Sorensen's assault hearing coincides with the exhibition match in Perth next Friday.

THE
WAR
BETWEEN
THE
MEN
AND
WOMEN,
FAMILY
LIFE

Craig McGregor

THE HERALDRY OF THE BODY

His arm, crossing her body diagonally just above the navel, signified Possession.

Did she object? If she objected, she wouldn't be here now. Correction: if she objected enough. It comforted her. The arm was muscular, with thin wrists, and wiry sporls of ginger hair. The torso to which it was attached was naked. It had an underlay of freckles. Beneath that again, pale skin so unlike her own. He burned easily. So did the children.

The children, like her, were his.

Almost.

The other arm was tucked under the torso, elbow bent, for safekeeping. Like a child who slept with its hands between its thighs. Baby. He depended on her. Somehow that entrapped her too. As her therapist friend Francoise explained, she had come to depend upon his dependence. When that was threatened, she found the original relation reversed: she, not her husband, became the child.

Either way she lost out.

Francoise was into masturbation. From maleness to maleless: the retreat of the wounded. Francoise had an epistemological justification for masturbation. Self-knowledge preceded everything else. In the Whitney Centre, once, two naked women and a naked man masturbated inside a rope square while the art patrons walked admiringly around the outside. Hours: 9 to 5, with a one-hour break for lunch and a trip to the loo. So what? Even epistemology had its exhibitionists.

Her friend Francoise was heavily into Berne. But she herself didn't like the idea of reducing everything to transactions. He's good value, a friend would say at a dinner party. She's good value. There was something commercial about it. You ended up turning relationships into another capitalist commodity.

Stuff Berne.

On her dexter wrist a silver bangle, locked, against a field argent of fleur-de-lys. On his sinister hand a wedding ring, gold, inscribed with his name. They represented Bondage.

He gave her the bangle. She gave him the ring. AC/DC. Sado-macho. While waiting for his next erection, de Sade invented ways of ravishing his mother. In London a bonded homosexual was found, gagged, throat cut, hanging upside down in a coat cupboard. Her mother, thrice married, fat-fingered, who gave them their wedding sheets, wore only her three engagement rings.

A precaution?

Sexual encounters were easy to come by. In the laundromat, the art class, the pub. She avoided them, voluntarily, and expected her husband to. Someone – who was it, Berne again (surely not)? – believed in serial sex, each encounter preparing the individuals for and giving way to the next. Like the Green Hornet, in 39 episodes. There was a logic to it; but how did you fit the rest of your life into such a progression? It didn't make allowance for children, work, non-serial love, or friendship beyond the sheets.

The ring.

You led a bull by a ring through its nose. You led a man by a ring around his finger. The act of slipping the ring over the finger was clearly coitus, paraphrased. Why then, when they married, had it been his ring, her finger?

She clearly hadn't made her mind up about marriage.

His left leg, entwined betwixt her flaunches, both or, signified Desire.

Hers too. Though his (leg) was bandaged, from above the ankle to the mid-way calf, with her Woolworths cotton roll and fastened with one of the baby's super-size nappy pins. Brushooking the lantana at the bottom of their quarter-acre block, he had sliced at his leg as well. 'Self-inflicted wound', he had explained. And laughed. 'Also an act of symbolic castration. I deserve it.'

It wasn't so funny.

Ice to stop the bleeding. From the shinbone, and the marrow

of the heart. If you don't hurt me, I won't hurt you. It's a bargain. (Transaction.) But sometimes bargains were bent, or betrayed. 'There's been a change in the weather, a change in the sea / And from now on there'll be a change in me,' sang Jimmy Rushing. Funny how the songs you heard when you were a teenager stayed with you for the rest of your life. Imprinting. Adolescence was where everything counted. Give me your child for the first six years, and I will really foul her up. Give me my own child from ten to sixteen, and I will do the same.

Her husband had had a classic ocker childhood. Smokes behind the dunny wall. Prick-pulling in the gym. Furtive gropes on front porches. The girls saying No but Yes. Feminists thought rape was unmistakeable: she remembered it as indistinguishable. Everything illicit. Nobody ever got enough, her husband said, until they got married. But by then the pattern was set, and only the illicit excited . . .

Maybe she should give him a good kick on his sore leg.

His side, invected, was laid, contiguous, along her breast, cupolad.

Yin, yan. Positive, negative. The segments of the Whole.

Bullshit.

'I'm an Aries,' he had apologised, 'I can't help it, it's my nature.' More bullshit. Linda Goodman, Krishnamurti, and the entire Eastern Consciousness Revival had a lot to answer for. So did Jehovah. For years she believed women had one less rib than men. Never occurred to her to count them. Until, once, she held him in her canting arms.

Her husband had six ribs per side. There was a hollow beneath his narrow chest. It protected but engulfed her. She was the classic figure of Renaissance cartography, X-shaped, encased within a circle, arms and legs outstretched, straining to stop the perimeter closing in on her. In sketchbooks, the figure was always male. But in her mind it was always female.

There was something remorseless about circles.

Against a field paly, and twice-crossed pillowslips, his profile, hurt.

She examined it discreetly. In the visible earhole, a faint fuzz of ginger hair. The sidelever, serrated, from years of misuse of the rotary razor she gave him for their anniversary. The forehead, cretaceous, drawn vertically to the hairline, recessive. The disarming nose. The eyelid, closed. The mouth, slightly open. His breath smelt of beer, the garlic bread she had cooked with dinner, and a faint fetid familiar odour, like a fox's burrow, from his belly. From their lovemaking.

His breath moved her.

Not so his genitals, unrampant, against her hip. She had once had to apologise to her mother for him: 'He's not always like that!' she said, as he levered himself, shivering out of the rock pool in the Carthage Ranges. Her mother believed in the theory of the Supermasculine Menial; she would have liked Eldridge Cleaver as a tame stud. Maybe that's why her daughter, in perverse contradistinction, had ended with a grown-up version of Ginger Meggs!

Oh well.

Some women felt complimented by detumescence. Not so she. (The white swan, ducally gorged and chained.) For all his special pleading, the gift felt . . . soiled. Secondhand. I have been given the wet worm of remorse.

But else beside.

Their bodies, parallel, signified History.

Together, but apart. Separate, but conjoined. Two lines ruled across the years: the Arms of husband and wife, impaled and quartered. Never quite touching. That's how he wanted it. 'Oneness is a confidence trick,' he said. She thought: 'Oneness is a confidence trick' is a husbandtrick. And yet there was something she respected about it. Like Hume's philosophy, a cold and cheerless comfort.

She hated paradoxes.

Her foot, naked, supported a sable instep, resplendent, with ankle superior.

The bandaged ankle was heavy. Every now and then she retracted the muscles in her foot to prevent it going to sleep. When she did, it pressed against him. She could almost feel the impulse travel the entire length of his body, upwards, like a nervous tremor. She only had to move herself, minutely, and his whole being shuddered.

Which was, perhaps, the sole sublimity of marriage.

In the heraldry of the body, the foot and ankle, crossed, signifies Content.

She thought.

SWOON

It was like a swoon.

When he came to, the sun had moved around and the bamboo blind threw stripes across their bed. It was too early for the heat to become oppressive. Down the hill, near where the creek emerged from a rot of lantana and crofton weed and tree ferns, he could hear a mournful hooting, note after note, ascending the scale in measured intervals. A wood dove. Or pigeon. He had never identified it. What the Readers Digest book of birds needed was a soundtrack.

The children were at school.

He should be working.

But suspended, trance-like, he allowed his insubstantial body to drift and thought:

of Virginia Woolf, who also watched a beam of light flood her body with ecstacy, before ivy choked her neck in a garden at Rodnell;

of photographs, contra lumiere, which told real lies;

of flesh;

of camphor laurel schoolyards, and bubblers, and therefore Bruce Dawe, glass monuments and intimations of mortality;

of desks;

of children, and how they must separate;

of how, instead of his father's son, which he had been for as long as he could remember, and liked to be, he was now his son's father, and even that on God-given lease;

of wives and wifedom.

Such words were suspect. People were defined, it was said, by their individuality, not by their relationships. But he didn't believe in essences, Platonic or otherwise. Relationships made people what they were. Where the thin complex of cobweb lines crossed, a knot called . . . character?

Karik-ter: an old-fashioned concept they used to write short stories about.

When he was away from her he became maudlin. The sentimentality of country-and-western songs became infinitely moving. The platitudes of barmaids became charged with wisdom. People became ineluctably noble. Strangers smiled. The world became, like Baudelaire's landscape, a forest of symbols; nothing was merely what it was, but became significant. His love for her swelled and ballooned, encompassing everything and everyone.

At school, he had failed dismally to make anyone love him. Tried too hard, perhaps? Later he had failed again, but succeeded in other ways. Some of the women had lain there like blobs of jelly. Some over-acted. Some had huge breasts and tiny pink nipples; some were olive everywhere. Some, after they had generously consented to him on blankets at North Head (in the cold) and in the front seats of cars (with difficulty) he had been embarrassingly incapable of making love to at all. That worried him, until later he came to realise his reaction was irrelevant: though he may have been unable to love them, others would, and did, which was their irrefragable triumph; his role was but to stand back and cheer.

These days, however, even 'wife' was role-playing, and therefore unacceptable.

He listened.

This is what Humphrey (Here Comes) Everybody heard:

The pigeon, or dove, coo-cooing in its repeated cadences, like a milkbottle rocking on its heavy base, the notes perfectly regular and irritatingly repetitious.

Another answering it.

A distant plane.

A shrill of cicadas which swelled and died like a wave in slow motion.

A car somewhere up Gibraltar Road.

A dog's toenails scratching the lino outside the door.

An unidentified sound.

A blench of sunlight, windless, all over the gullies and creeks and hillsides of The Risk.

'Men are so easy to make love to,' she had said earlier, laughing. 'They're so *available*.'

She had strong wrists, and when she made love to him with her mouth she lifted his body (and his heart) against her. She was unembarrassed to suck greedily at him, and swallowed everything she drew out. He was possessed.

And, swoon-like, his body dreaming, unfocussed, the universe displaying an unaccustomed perfection, he thought:

I admired you most, perhaps, when you were least beholden to me; when you were least conscious of me, and unsullied by my demands. Because then you were most yourself. And though I was jealous of your independence, and callous enough to want to suppress it, you were then at your purest.

Purity?

Now, years later, with that chance at perception irrevocably lost . . . now, with all those compromises and misunderstandings that were lined in her face, and that he had forced upon her (and himself), all subsequences become consequences . . . now he understood he loved her more, for all that she had
    forsaken

and accepted
and suffered
and wrongly endured
and graciously given
and sometimes graciously taken
and had fully vouchsafed
and less fully received
and had consummated
and had made him, at last, learn to consummate
and thus
had taught to love
unselfishly
She was asleep.

She slept with her mouth open. It showed the squared-off ends of her teeth, which he had always cherished.

Sometimes, at night, he could hear her catch her breath, and move slightly, and resume her suspended lifefulness.

He was careful not to wake her. Instead, he put his hands under his head, and looked at the bamboo blinds, and listened vainly for the first morning wind in the hoop pines, and tried to imagine what rain would sound like on the iron roof, and wondered whether, when he was dead, the mortal copy of happiness he now felt would endure.

Time enough, later, for her to wake.

And for them to resume their entwined opposition.

THE BANGLE

Around her right wrist she was wearing a silver bangle. Her skin was freckled. On the third finger of her right hand, he noticed, she was wearing two rings.

One was their wedding ring.

The other, he assumed, was for decoration.

She had a black dress on, and when she leaned forward against the restaurant table he could just discern, through the black linen dress, her skin. It was a very conservative dress, as became a wife or widow.

She had hair which was almost ringleted. She was what other people called middle-aged. She had a straight, almost severe nose, an erotic mouth and a breath which, he knew from experience, turned his stomach and his soul.

However, she loved someone else. Possibly. But did nothing about it.

He did not love anyone else . . . and did something about it.

She found this hard to bear. Whereas he found her unfaith-fulness, whether enacted or not – that is, her generalised affection, her generosity, her willingness to love – insufferable.

Out of goodness, her own personal righteousness, she stayed with him. This turned what he found insufferable into mere suffering. She slept with him, warmly, in their innerspring bed each night and sometimes she fucked him. They ate breakfast together each morning. Sometimes they ate dinner together at a restaurant.

However, she could/did/had/would get love from someone else. What made it worse was that the someone else was worth loving. Whereas: was he? This is how it seemed to him then, anyhow, despite the memory of skin and the handlaced tablecloth.

'I don't care what your friends or Foucault or anyone else says', she said. 'You believe in something where everyone can reach their fullest potential . . . without hurting anyone else . . . or it's a fake. And so are they.' She leant forward. 'Anything which hurts people hurts us all.'

She had the stem of a red wine glass between her fingers. He noticed the rings again. She had the honesty and loveliness of the princess before . . . before the frog began croaking in the pond. He also noticed that, as she leant forward, her breasts seemed to swell beneath the linen dress. The skin thickened. Any man who loved her, he knew, would find that ravishing.

'Easy to say,' he said.

'Are you being cynical?'

'No. Just sceptical.'

The tablecloth glistened.

'Not for dishonourable reasons,' he said quickly. 'Finding out how to do what you *know* to be right is where the hard thing starts.'

'Politics,' she said.

'Yes.'

'You know I agree with you about that.'

'Yes,' he said. 'But you've got the morality straight. Everyone else forgets.'

Once, another woman said to him:

'Do you like my gappy teeth?'

'Yes,' he answered, truthfully.

'Do you think my tits are too big?'

'No,' he lied.

He had given up lying, and he didn't give a damn about

46

gappy teeth and big tits. Or small tits. Or Marilyn Monroe. Or Norman Mailer. Or necrophilia, necromancy, or San Francisco silicon chips-and-titsburgers. He had given up forecasts. He had given up nostalgia. He had never even taken up existentialism. He had a daughter who had Adam & the Ants posters on the wall, a son who played him Mastermind, and he knew precisely where he was.

Her breath, even across the table, reached him. There were small, fine lines along the edges of her fingers. They had grown old together. He could not imagine the world continuing to exist after she had ceased to.

If her lover had been there, he would have told him so.

'How can you respect someone who goes around hurting people,' she said.

'I hurt people too.'

'Perhaps you don't mean to.'

'Everybody hurts people.'

She was silent.

'Loving is a political act,' he said. 'Everything is a political act. I understand that. I've got the politics worked out; the other thing's harder.'

'Tell me about her,' she said.

'There are some people,' he began, 'who continually need to have their own worth restated. Like Catholics, they seek eternal ... reassurance. Sexual, I attract, therefore I am.' He felt, suddenly, a rush of pity, almost tenderness, for such people. 'They're children. They continually seek confirmation of their own being. I don't know why. Some childhood hurt. It doesn't matter.'

'Are you talking,' she said, 'about yourself?'

He looked at her.

'I hadn't thought of that.'

'Why should you provide it?'

'Provide what?'

'Provide the confirmation?'

She was right, of course. Anyone could provide it. How explain that, in the past, he had felt that to refuse such a request was ignoble?

Even as he thought it, however, he realised the sentiment was self-serving. She deserved better. She deserved better than him.

'Look,' he joked. 'I'm giving it up, I'm not Bobby; I'm not confused.'

47

'I don't want you to give it up for me,' she said. 'I want people to be generous. I want their politics to be generous too. I don't want them to talk feminism and be manhaters and womanstealers. I wish Shulamith and the others would understand that.'

'Their minds are dirty but their hands are clean,' he paraphrased.

She laughed. On her right arm, the bangle. It had slipped further towards her elbow. From her grandfather, sepia-brown eyes in a photograph on an upright piano. Her closest friends were a continent away. He would hug them, one of these days, because they knew her.

A blind mole, or skin cancer, disturbed the line of her left upper lip. She had a gap between her front teeth.

He began again.

Outside, the wind blew a fine crust of salt against the car windscreens. A sweet French chansonnier sounded through the speakers. Jean-Luc Godard, Resnais. But these, these real lives, were too important for art.

He stopped writing.

We try, in what we do, he thought, to gain the slightest, faintest suggestion of what is true. We never succeed. But . . . we are at our best in our failures.

'My love for you,' he said, 'is the most honourable thing about me. It is the thing I do best.'

On her hand, the two silver rings.

In her mouth, red wine.

In her heart, love for many.

In his head, jealousy.

In his wallet, a girl's school photograph.

Behind his ribcage, in what passed for a heart, was a dead father, an unposted letter from a mother, a childhood he had long left behind, a bloody and ugly death which rushed towards him, and a manhood he was still struggling to achieve.

SELFLESS

When he was into his late middle age, his heart faltered.

It was no ordinary heart attack. The specialist looked worried. That worried him too.

He told his family.

Later, the close friend of his youngest daughter said:

'I had a funny dream last night. Really weird. I dreamt your father banged himself on the heart.'

48

Of course.

Of course he had banged himself on the heart. Through remorse, and guilt . . . and sorrow.

The only question now was, would he survive at all? Selfless?

Carolyn van Langenberg

AN UNFINISHED HEAD

I am having trouble grappling at the mind's extent. My arm is thin. It can pass through the visceral tissue of brain without damaging the delicate grey matter. It can reach the soft centre where the nerves no longer govern the doing. My arm can brush against memory. Against light. Against dark. But when it passes through monotony, the diligent sweep of bureaucratic concern, the librarian's muddle, the careful management of home, this thin arm aches. Would it disappear into an erotic embrace with Jules, flaying madly either the air or his back or rounding between rump and balls. Sometimes the arm will reach a finger into his arsehole. Then the brain imagines a dream lover and, locked in that embrace, the arm forgets skill and learns abandonment. But it aches. This thin arm. Aches. It will not, cannot, disassociate from the function of the brain. Sweated from sex, the arm lies still, the brain composing letters, rearranging the alphabet with method to form words that hang in the morning air, listless, wanting paper. The mass of brain slips. Agonises with the arm. Its several parts insist the arm can never regain strength if it is passive to the power of its reasoning, continuing to do all that is practical. Nor should it indulge whim. To skid on impulse requires the ability to control direction. This thin arm loosens the grip. Appears reckless. Meaning flies away. A nuance leapt over, a new barrier of knowledge crashed through. And the body. Rolling, rolling, down a rough slope, the brain passive to imaginings the arm is too thin to grasp. Memories of beautiful exploits break over the body with the clarity of dawn. But the arm and the brain must measure with paltry measure the boundaries of a minimum strength. Rest. Idle. Escape, this dulled body. Smells death cold. Beyond and below its edge with life where it lies mirrorless and black. It rejects this thin arm, this weakening piece of flesh.

... no sign no clue no lump burning pain troubling the nerves governing the soft centre against blood rushing blackening memory and, lightless, terrorising the movement of a single finger ...

Body frees, body limits. Body cannot or will not do. Body shudders. Or body is composed, a drover's wife, a madonna, a darling child, its hairless face redeemed, radiating forgiveness. But it aches. This hairless face. Aches. Gone stiff with memories slipping, light colliding against light fading dark. Beautiful exploits. And abuses too terrible for literature. Rolling rolling down rough years, cascading over the body. Dawn clarifies. Morning filters light, establishing the grey darkening that grey wall is a chair. Is a wardrobe. Is a dressing table. Is a painting. Is a woman on the wall bending over her foot. Always. Scrubbing. Always. Washing. Her cleansing her pleasure. With two sure hands languid in the morning air. Taking up the hairbrush. The fingers no longer curl around the handle. Listless, or in pain. Grasping a white square, paper folded. Neat. And letters thick, words refusing flight, no nuance intended. Brain swings high, cannot escape words squared by felt pen, meaning crashing through. Arm struggles, brain slips, fumbling with a minimum strength. Appears reckless. Boundaries, haphazardly mea-sured, capsize, leap away from knowledge, Jules ... *cannot cope ... cannot do all ... cannot will not ... stay ...Brain seethes within its skull, Jules! forgiving Jules!* too fragile to grapple anger, the hairless face too thin, serene ...

... sometimes
there is no sign no lump Jules read it for the television news just ter-rible pain dragging with it life rucking across day and night ...

skids on impulse. This arm. Controls direction. Through its pain. Loosens the grip. Appears reckless. Body. Rolling rolling in a rough bed disappearing erotically beneath his back. Hairless face radiates. Jules loves Jules cannot cope. Jules cannot push a vacuum cleaner, chop carrots, scrub feet. Neither arm nor Jules has any imagination for pain. Body aches. For love of him. Arm aches. Arm. Aches. It will not, cannot, forget skill and learn abandonment. Sweated, this arm lies still, disassociated from the brain imagining the tumult these fingers once played through Jules. Memories of beautiful exploits break over the body. Dawn clarifies. Jules swings his legs over the edge of the bed. This thin arm vaunts whim. I reach to touch his back, to caress the breadth of shoulders and round over his upper arm. But the brain measures with paltry measure the boundaries of a minimum strength. Rest. Idle. Watch Jules wordless pull on trousers. The mass of brain slips, *no lump no sign*, through a loop, knows time. Shivers for strength, the woman I am forlorn in the soft dark centre of brain where the nerves no longer govern the doing. She lights memory, those first vital days with Jules . . . ; a schoolday sweated in grey serge . . . ; listening to the drone of bees one bright infant day. She arranges my face to be free of pain, of any condemning expression. Jules slams the door.

smash shut
smash shut
smash shut the gate

Chases meaning round the streets. Skids on impulse. Cherishes whim . . . *pain white burn no sign no lump no withering* words in the newspapers, words he spoke to the television camera. Information. For workers. Not for her, words. Rolling rolling with his face buried in her soft flesh, Jules, clear in the dawn, words knotting them in the bedsheets. The thin arm brushes against memory, against beautiful exploits, rounding between rump and balls. Aches. This thin arm. Bound by monotony, the brain composing skill, never discovering abandonment. Aches. Under his body, spry and hard and athletic. The words spoken by his mouth printed on his flesh by her weakening hold, her diminishing strength, her listlessness. The mass of brain slips. Agonises, waiting for the arm to regain strength and indulge whim. Meaning flies away. Brain smashes ambiguities against its skull, words, and words smash. Smash open the door and watch the sheen of her hairless face as she chooses words to explain her trouble, Jules

no sign no clue nothing visible the report said no lump paining he read it into the television eye read it in the journal article read it on her medical report . . .

The arm is thin. It can forgive the visceral tissue of brain its delicacy, ignore the librarian's muddle, and live with light breaking
through dark, through all day night. It can imagine memory
and hotly embrace the words etched in the flesh of its life as it
weakens, not taking hold, always listless and forgetting its
meaning. Reaching the soft centre where no one else may
follow. Retreating to silence. Entering the dark centre where
Jules has no place.

. . . grappling at the mind's extent . . .

And Jules tears a leaf, tears it to bits, the stalk, the veins, the fila-
ment, tears the fragments of heart he composes round his
resilient self. He throws shredded leaf at the wind . . . *fly away,
eye.* Sweats. At the temples. Trembles. Fearing aloneness. Being
without her. Fidgets. Hair, buttons, cuffs, pockets. No time to
hesitate. No time to chew rage. No time to struggle back to a
better memory . . . *fly, time, away, with meaning.* Jules flings
open the door.

smash
smash open clues
smash open signs
smash open
words smash

Silence dripping from the furniture. Chills. Muffles his shouts.
And he presses his crying mouth into her flesh. Into his words.
And her head and limbs fall away from his arms. And eyes
moist with hurt, his brain seethes within its skull protesting her
hairless face concealed too well her pain her fears so that he
could not know what to do, how to act.

Jean Bedford

CAMPAIGN

I'd been on a binge with Iris for most of the week. Now I woke up in the hot morning still drunk. Somehow I'd pulled up the quilt in the night and I was sweating.

My daughter Sarah looked in at me with one of her fifteen-year-old looks. She was home studying but I noticed *Dune* under her arm and gave her one of my forty-year-old looks. It hurt when I laughed.

'I thought you were going out to lunch?'

'I am.' I looked at the clock; I was already half an hour late. 'Get me two Panadol. Quick.'

I showered and dressed. I don't usually wear too much makeup but now I needed heaps. Too old to drink all night, I decided. Time to dry out. I rang the restaurant and left a message for Harry, then I rang a cab. The walk up the road to hail one was too daunting.

Harry was going to introduce me to a Yugoslav attache, so I could get invited to Belgrade. My friend Iris said he was my type. Iris was in love, she thought I should be, too. I thought I didn't want to fall in love again; but if I did, I said to Iris and Harry in the wine bar one night, this time I wanted it to my exact specifications.

'A French diplomat,' I'd said. 'Preferably half Jewish. Married once, perhaps been gay. Rich, sophisticated, a lot older. He'll take me to Paris for holidays and buy heaps of champagne.'

'I can do you a Yugoslav,' Harry said. 'At least he might get you invited to the Belgrade festival.'

'That'll do. Love's fucked, anyway.' We all laughed – our young friend Moira was going through a phase of telling us that everything was fucked just then.

Harry was at his usual table, with people I didn't know. I was the only woman. Then I noticed Tom and sat beside him. I don't like to be at Harry's table with just strangers, they always intimidate me, talking politics and corruption with Harry.

'He didn't come,' Harry said. 'Perhaps I should have rung him back. I don't understand Yugoslav protocol.'

I'd forgotten the Yugoslav, so I laughed and went on talking to Tom, drinking the first glass of wine quickly to stop the shakes. It was one of Harry's lunches; he's famous for them. Eclectic and jovial, socially, politically, intellectually omnivorous, Harry collects very good lunches.

There was a retired American colonel canvassing for the Australian Democrats; there was his shadow from *Newsweek*; there were a couple of men who were probably lawyers or politicians, another whom I knew to be a judge. And Tom, an old friend. I was pleased to see him and catch up on gossip. There was also a youngish man beside Tom but he didn't talk much, and I only got glimpses of him when Tom leaned forward to pour another drink. Most of the talk was of the election, now a fortnight off.

Tom paid for my lunch and cashed a cheque for me and we thought we might all go somewhere and have a palate-cleansing ale, Harry's expression that he said he'd got from Ernest. The youngish man invited us back to campaign headquarters – he was working for a Victorian politician. I remembered I'd met him before, he'd said he liked my book. He looked tired. His name was Tony something, I thought.

So we had our beers there while Tom called clients in Perth and Melbourne and Harry called other people. I was bored with the election, I wondered why I was there, but it was pleasant drinking cold beer a long way above the hot city, with the storms starting again. I thought idly that if this had been America we'd have all been rich.

Tom left and Harry and I decided to share a taxi back to our suburb. He got up to go and I groaned at the thought of more travel.

'Don't go,' Tony said to me. 'Have another beer.'

Harry waited, and I thought, why not?

'You coming Sal?'
'No, I'll stay.'

On Monday morning I went into Iris's office. She was on the phone as usual. It was nearly lunchtime so I waited while she harassed publishers, dealt patiently with clients.

'Well,' she said in the wine bar. 'Are you going to Belgrade?'

'Nah,' I said. 'Belgrade's fucked. But . . .' I poured the wine, 'I think I'm falling in love.'

Iris laughed. I always said that at first and then the next day, or the next week, I'd deny I ever said it.

'Who with? Do I know him?' Iris knows it's always a him.

I told her and we settled down to girl talk. I wondered if I usually said, 'This is different. I feel it.' I didn't think so, I didn't think I'd had this for years. It was starting to obsess me. I was even getting interested in the election.

'Tactics,' I said. 'I've never been good at them, but I need some now.' I didn't really think I did. I felt confident.

'I even took him down to the beach house,' I said. 'That'd show him. Kids and dogs and ex-husbands everywhere, and a party where all my com mates put shit on him. That'd show what he was made of.'

I thought I was beginning to know what he was made of. I'd found his verbal reticence off-putting at first, wondered if I was bored, if it had been a mistake to invite him to the beach. I thought he was very tense and uncertain, I wondered if I intimidated him. But I'd seen him fence with my coastal friends, watched his smile when people got illogical or brought out cant. I'd liked the way we stood squeezed together all night, feeling each other up like teenagers. I'd laughed at my friend Mary's sardonic disapproval. Mary doesn't believe in being in love, especially, she said, with a State apparatchik. I'd liked the way, when we were lying on the beach, he had stroked the hair on my neck.

I said something to Iris about feeling vulnerable again.

'I don't know if I remember how you do it,' I said.

'No. You've got guarded.' She laughed. 'Don't tell him I told you, but Alec said once that you hardly ever kissed him.'

'No.' I was struck by that. 'He's right. I hardly ever did. It's like whores, isn't it? Alright to fuck and suck and everything else, but kissing's too intimate.'

'It lets them into your head,' Iris said.

'I don't think I've kissed anyone properly since Robert,' I

said. 'Oh, well. Tactics are fucked, too. He knows where to find me.'

Well, he found me; we found each other, I thought. I started to learn to kiss again, and stare at someone's eyes. He brought champagne and presents. I bought him red roses. My kids told him he looked spunky in his suit. My darling Leo told him it was sickening to see me so happy. We had our jokes, we watched videos, we drank, fucked, talked. I did no work, I waited the days through to see him. I didn't believe it, but I wanted it to be true. I didn't think of the future, the future's fucked, I said to Iris. We scandalised the waiters at my favourite restaurant. 'Wanton behaviour,' said the nice fair one, with pursed lips. He'd often poured us out at 3 a.m. after rowdy drunken dinners, but no one approved of love.

'I'm worried about your expectations,' he said.
    'I've got none. Really.' Just – let this go on.
    'I can't handle it. It's my fault. I didn't mean to let it happen. It's dangerous and I can't go on with it.'
    I knew about his marriage, of course, but it was in another city. I only wanted what we had, I wasn't interested in the rest.
    'But to stop. So suddenly.'
    'It happened suddenly.'
    'Straight in, straight out?' I watched his impatience at my bitchiness.
    'We can be mates still.'
    'Can we?' I stared at him. ''Is this how you make *all* your friends?
    He stared back. 'No,' he said. 'No, it's not.'
    I'd intended not to talk about it at all, to be gallant, give in gracefully. Now I had all sorts of pride, hurt, defensiveness struggling out of me. I'd had too much to drink, I was confused. I couldn't help trying to fight for myself. Even though I knew fighting for yourself is fucked, when the other has already left the field.
    'I don't know,' I said, 'if I can be your friend,'
    It gave me some satisfaction that this seemed to hurt him. He was tired, as usual, I really didn't want to hassle.

'Did you ever tell him you were in love with him?' Iris said. 'Perhaps that would have helped.'
    'No.' I said. 'It would have made it worse. I think. I tried to

cover myself in the end. I can't *make* him want me if he doesn't. I bloody wish I could, but.'

'Well, you can cry on my shoulder,' she said. 'It might not really be over.'

'No. It's over. And I don't feel like crying on shoulders.'

We're friends now, I suppose we always were. We sometimes send each other postcards with lighthearted messages. I cut out obscure newspaper paragraphs that I think will interest him and he sometimes rings just to say hello. When he is in this city we meet for drinks, buy each other lunches, sometimes dinner – but not often, because the night time is dangerous and besides it is to spend with the one you love.

Sometimes we are both at one of Harry's lunches. I never think – this is where we met. We gossip, I ask about his work, he asks about mine. I try to amuse him, I show off and am illogical, animated. He doesn't seem to mind – he likes me. We're fond of each other. He is his reserved self and I like that. I like his eyes and the way the smile breaks in his dark tired face. I like his honesty and his clear mind. It's good to have a friend like him.

I wrote him a poem recently but I haven't sent it. It's meant to make him laugh. It goes: If you're ever free/To fall in love with me/Please can I be/The first to know?

I'm going to say on the postcard, if I send it, 'This is a line from a short story I once wrote.'

Rosemary Creswell

EPITHALAMIUM

It was after Sal and Peg planned Iris's wedding that things between Iris and Phillip really went wrong.

Iris and Sal and Peg were idling away a few hours at the wine bar one night. Iris and Sal had been idling away the afternoon at the wine bar since lunchtime and Peg had joined them on her way from visiting a spiritualist. Peg was writing another book and they were discussing whether the narrative should be in the first or third person.

'The first, I reckon,' said Sal whose own books were a mixture of persons.

'The trouble with that,' said Peg, 'is that I always get it muddled up with myself.'

'Who *is* talking?' asked Iris.

'Well I don't know. I'm writing this book backwards. I know what she does, but I don't know who she is because I'm not up to the first chapter, which is last, in my head.'

Iris talked about that not mattering and people being defined by their actions and not having any central persona, which she vaguely remembered from first year philosophy twenty-five years ago, but she couldn't remember which philosopher.

None of them could remember anything much that week. They were having a lot of trouble with nouns, especially proper ones. Only that morning Iris had needed to look up something in the shorter OED but couldn't find the dictionary. She had asked Peg, who lived with her, if she had been using it and Peg had said no, but then when she was making her bed she had found one of each volume under each of her pillows as though the words were going to seep into her head in the night.

They worried about this failure to remember substantives. Peg, who was a nursing sister, referred to the problem as dealing only in connective tissue not with muscle and bones. Sal said it was caused by drinking but as Iris pointed out only she and Sal drank a lot, not Peg, but Peg had just the same problem. Iris was annoyed that Sal said it was drinking.

Sal then thought it was the full moon.

'Well, even if I don't quite know who she is, she's got to have a certain age and appearance and so on, and a name I suppose.'

'That's immaterial,' said Sal.

'As a matter of fact it's very material,' Peg snapped. She was having trouble with this book.

Iris tried to explain the doctrine of Nominalism to them – she was in a philosophical frame of mind – but she couldn't remember much about that either.

They were silent for a while and Iris squeaked the wine glass by running her finger around the rim.

'Phillip asked me to marry him last night,' she said.

'What,' Sal screamed, animated, leaning forward. 'Why didn't you tell us before?'

'I forgot.'

'When is it?' asked Peg.

'Oh, I'm not going to. It was just drunken talk at 5 a.m., but even if it was sober I'd have said no.'

'You will say yes,' said Sal, 'you are going to get married. It's your duty. We need an uplifting human emotional event for 1985, and your marriage will be it. All of Sydney needs an uplifting event for the rest of this century, and your wedding is it.'

Peg agreed. 'Absolutely,' she said. 'All of Australia. Don't be selfish.'

'Harry will give you away,' said Sal, 'he likes ceremonies, and Peg and I will be the bridesmaids; no I mean matrons of honour.'

'And Jenny and Carol will be bridesmaids,' said Peg, 'because they are nearly sixty and will enjoy it.'

Sal said it should be colour co-ordinated, and thought of red because Phillip was left-wing.

Peg felt that was too garish for such a subtle event, and such a significant one. 'Harry should wear a mauve suit,' she said, 'and Phillip will wear a mauve shirt and tie with a white suit. White for peace.'

'And mauve lace over white satin for us,' said Sal. 'And bonnets, mauve bonnets.'

Peg thought matrons of honour shouldn't wear bonnets.

'Big crownless picture hats is what we'll have,' she said.

'With mauve cabbage roses on them, said Sal.

'And sweetheart necklines,' said Peg

'And white lace over mauve satin for the bridesmaids,' said Sal.

(Later, when they explained the colour scheme to Jenny, Jenny said she wanted pink. Sal got annoyed with her for wrecking the co-ordination but Peg said it was alright; Jenny and Carol could have pink tulle kick-pleats in their mauve and white dresses.)

'And in the derro's park opposite Kinselas with the reception in Kinselas,' Sal went on.

'Absolutely,' said Peg. 'With the honeymoon at the Marxist Summer School.'

'Yellow for your going away outfit,' said Sal. 'Mauve and yellow and white will be the colours, with a dash of pink for the bridesmaids.'

'A lemon linen suit, with a pill-box hat and a half veil,' said Peg.

'Mauve and yellow and white with a dash of pink will become the fashion colours of the decade,' said Sal. 'Jenny Kee jumpers, Maggie T. shirts, Prue Acton dresses, Stuart Membery jackets. We'll patent the colour combo.'

'And lemon patent-leather high heel court shoes,' said Peg.

'And I'm going to write a long epithalamium,' said Sal, 'which will be read at the reception. With rhyming couplets in Old Norse at the end of each verse which will be recited by the guests.'

Peg felt this would take some of the spontaneity out of things, but Sal explained that great events have to be planned or they get out of hand, so Peg said, 'Absolutely.'

'Don't just sit there, Iris,' yelled Sal. 'Take notes or something. It's going to happen and these things have to be prepared and co-ordinated.'

Iris was embarrassed. It *was* getting out of hand. Even though Phillip was drunk and it was a silly idea it was a gesture of love. And she did love him. She explained this to them.

'We're not knocking it, Iris' said Sal. 'We're celebrating love in the last fifth of the twentieth century. We are giving thanks to love in a loveless world.'

'I think Phillip's very brave saying that,' said Peg. 'I mean I don't mean brave because he said it to *you*, not brave because he wants to marry *you*, just brave for saying it. Like a knight in the Middle Ages or something.'

'Yes, courtly,' agreed Sal. 'He's courtly. *Fin amour.*'

And gradually Iris was drawn into it and they planned it over four bottles of Dom Perignon which Sal couldn't afford but she bought on Bankcard because she said it was worth it. And they laughed a lot and in the end all the customers in the wine bar were drawn in and Louise the proprietor wanted exclusive rights on catering for the shower and kitchen teas, and the guitarist wanted to be a troubadour at the wedding reception and Peg said there should be ten, and Sal said Marlboro could sponsor it, and Peg wanted to organise the sale of the film rights and Sal said should would write the book of the film. It was a great night.

It had all seemed very funny at the time, but when Iris told Phillip he was not amused. He was much more than not amused. He was very angry.

It was the following night and they were at the movies, at *The Big Chill*. Iris tried to explain that they had not been mocking his emotions, they had been celebrating them. They had been toasting love in a cynical world. It had been a eulogy to love between a man and a woman. An epithalamium, a *chanson d'amour*. A testament to his honest courage. A paean to the institution of marriage in the twentieth century.

He was unconvinced and angry. He told Iris he would never reveal his emotions to her again. He said that she and her woman friends were dedicated to trivialising all male feelings. That they were interested only in drinking and the emasculation of men. That they didn't deserve love. That it was no wonder Sal's and Peg's husbands had divorced them years ago. That it didn't suprise him that no one had ever married her. No matter how Iris tried to defend the planning of the wedding it just made things worse.

She felt wretched.

Alone in bed that night, she wondered if she shouldn't have said yes.

Susan Hampton

CONRAD'S BEAR

Behind us a voice on the video was announcing that breast feeding is the most natural and fulfilling thing in the world. The voice continued with a description of how the sucking action is healthy for baby. A groan shivered along the queue. An Aboriginal kid began bashing a stick on the only empty chair. Every time his stick hit the red vinyl, it made a plastic *squwach*.

I gave the receptionist the letter from my doctor, and she told me to wait in the line for the Breast Clinic. Two women who knew each other were talking quietly. 'Last night,' the tall one said, moving her bracelets up her arm, 'I dreamt that when they opened up my breast, it was made of wood. Music came out from my insides, from my pipes and tubes. And glands. The doctor couldn't work it out. After a while I regained consciousness, and they'd taken a baby out of my breast. Tiny and coloured, like a Russian doll,'

The queue had moved on and I was at the desk again. The same woman gave me some forms to take down a corridor to the X-ray clinic. A doctor rushed toward me, opening the plastic flap doors against my arm. 'Sorry,' she called, 'emergency.' There was a swell of jittering and shushing noises behind me.

The waiting room for the X-ray clinic had wood panelling like a railway carriage. I sat on a long bench seat, facing cubicles numbered 1, 2 , 3.

Three other women were staring at the cubicles already: a small one, who wanted a cigarette; a large one with a handbag upright on her lap; and a European lady surrounded by shopping bags, who was reading a book written in Spanish. The small one couldn't stop talking. She came from Narrabeen, she said. I took out a book also, and that left the large lady with the handbag to respond. She turned sideways and frowned politely.

'Northern beaches,' the small one said. 'When I squeezed my breast this morning, blood came out of the nipple.'

I looked down at the cover of my book; *Para-criticisms: seven speculations of the times.* I opened it in the middle and began to read.

> Beckett, we recall, ends *How It Is* by confessing that it wasn't.
>
> 'Joyce's last novel is not an end but a start. The argument for its position in a literature of silence, in a tradition of anti-literature . . .'
>
> Here the Speaker stops, dismayed by intimations from his audience, and before he can resume, a voice interrupts.
> THE VOICE
>
> Pedantry and peeling plaster. Tradition is a cushion, a chair, a construct.
>
> The issue is still symbolism, i.e., the crisis of forms, i.e., the re-making of human consciousness.

'Blood?' the large lady said, 'you must be very worried.'

'I am, a bit. Do you live in Sydney?'

The large lady laughed, and opened her handbag. She took out a photo and held it out.

'This is where I live. Wee Waa.'

And getting no response, she said, 'Cotton country. That's our farm.'

'Very dry, isn't it?' the other one said.

The large woman laughed again, 'Not now it isn't, it's flooded now,' she said. 'The roads are cut off.'

'Oh dear,' the small woman said. She turned the photo over in her hand, as if she expected to see the flooded cotton appear on the back, and then returned it. The clasp on the handbag snapped shut and the large lady leaned back and closed her eyes.

I began to read again..

> There is a curious music in the wood: the dream of the longest night of the year. Joyce says: 'I have put the language to sleep.'

... But still Nora frets: 'Why don't you write sensible books that people can understand?'

The small woman is hoping it's a blocked milk duct. Her daughter came in last year for a lump; her daughter is twenty-four. Now the small woman turned sideways to face the large one.

'I get very tender, specially at certain times of the month. I don't get periods but I still get cranky, and I get sore here.'

They both have their hands on their sore breasts, hand on heart. They exchange the following information: the large one has a prolapsed bowel and bladder; the small one a prolapsed womb.

At that moment my eyes were drawn to a sentence at the bottom of the page: something about the prelapsarian world, and I tried to imagine these women in Eden, thirty years ago.

Now the two talkers pass on to how many kids they've reared, and what their husbands do, and where they live. The small one said a six-lane highway had been put in, right outside her bed-room window. She thinks they might sell up; she's had enough.

'Of the rat race,' the other one said.

The small woman had taken off her shoes, and was rearranging them with her stockinged feet. She noticed my silver vinyl sneakers and my black-and-silver striped lamé socks, and she nudged the large lady. I kept my head in the book.

The door of Cubicle 3 swung open and the tall woman with bracelets, dressed in a blue surgical gown, leaned out and told us confidentially that the X-ray would hurt. 'The mammogram is so painful,' she said, 'they put a balloon on you and press.' A nurse called her from the room on the other side of the cubicles, the door to our side shut, she disappeared.

The talkers agreed that they were both used to a lot of pain. The small one said her third child took fifty-six hours. 'They should have done a Caesarian, the doctor said after the prolapse. When they took my uterus out, they were amazed. They said it was the smallest thing they'd ever seen.'

The tall woman with bracelets reappeared, dressed in street clothes. 'All that squeezing could *give* me cancer if I haven't already got it.' The Spanish lady looked up from her book and clucked her tongue. As the tall woman left, she called over her shoulder: 'Get out your tissues!'

'My daughter didn't say it hurt,' the small one said. 'I'm sure *she* would have said.'

The voice from the other side of the cubicles called out a foreign name and then a curt, 'Take everything off down to your waist.' The Spanish lady, despite her bulk, leapt up from the seat and made several trips to the cubicle with her things. The three of us remaining stared at the bulge of her shopping bags under the door. She was taking off her shoes.

This reminded the small woman of her own shoes, which she now put back on. 'They say anything worthwhile hurts, don't they.' She smiled at me, and at the large lady. Her neck was full of tiny creases, her face peaky and bright as a bird's.

Both women crossed their legs and sat in silence. After a time, they re-crossed their legs, as if by some agreed on symmetry.

'My doctor called it a mammeograph,' the large one said, 'and yours calls it a mammogram. I wonder why.'

'You wonder about doctors,' the small one replied.

My book was now describing how Samuel Beckett came to visit James Joyce in Paris, 1933, and how he courted Joyce's mad daughter, Lucia.

> The room is comfortable, is sordid in the middle-class way. There are chairs everywhere. Two men, tall and lank, sit together, legs crossed, toe of the upper leg under the instep of the lower. They do not speak. Joyce is sad for himself, and Beckett sad for the world.
>
> Lucia is not in the room. Beckett has not really come to see her. Her infatuation with Sam will pass into madness. Jim and Sam continue in silence.

'Cotton country,' the large woman said to a new arrival, 'Wee Waa. So I hope I don't have to come back, it's a long way. We're staying over on the north side. We got all the red lights, coming here.' We have all moved up one place on the bench.

In the machine my breast was flattened by two plates, one from above, a clear perspex one, and another from beneath. I saw my breast flattened to a triangle. Two curved black-dotted lines on the perspex showed against the white flesh, and now my breast looked like a chart in the butcher's shop.

'Come back in two hours', someone said.

I went to see my mother who had forty minutes between trains at Central. She was on her way to visit my sister, who had had a baby the week before. It was a boy called Conrad. I wanted to give Mum something to take to the baby, but the shops at Central sold only souvenirs, and that didn't seem appropriate.

'I told Dad I was entitled to my own opinion,' she said. The train was leaving in six minutes. 'I told him I thought his behaviour at Christmas was . . . what did I say now?' (she looked around the train for her word).

We had been to the cafeteria and eaten bread rolls with a boiled egg and pickled onions.

'How is your writing?' she asked.

'Difficult.'

I gave her a thermos of coffee and some sandwiches and dried figs for the trip: she was going the long way, taking the train to Yass and then a bus to Canberra. 'Enjoy your adventure,' I said as we kissed goodbye. She put back her head and puffed out her cheeks. It was the first time she had gone on a trip on her own.

When I got back to the hospital the Sister said they would need to take another X-ray, but the clinic didn't open for half an hour.

I sat in the doctor's waiting-room and a woman said to me: 'She's all right, they said. It's just hormonal. Something to do with the change.' I looked up: it was the large Wee Waa cotton farm woman with her handbag still upright like a small dog on her lap.

'You mean the woman from Narrabeen,' I said.

'Yes, she's gone now. All OK.'

I felt I ought to be pleased, but I couldn't form a smile and I couldn't sit through any more difficult births, prolapses, cancer scares. I read in my book that Joyce and Beckett divide language between them, but at that time I couldn't see how they had done it.

I crossed the road to the main section of the hospital and went into a shop which sold aftershave and slippers and teddy bears. I spent fifteen minutes looking at all the bears, one by one. In the end, I chose the one which looked most like a bear, and paid the man on the till $18.95. The man kissed the bear on the nose before he wrapped it: it was his favourite of the lot, too, he said. I asked if he had any Panadol. 'We're not allowed to sell it in the hospital,' he said.

I took the bear to the cafeteria next to the shop. People were standing in the queue and asking themselves, 'What do I want?' There was a choice of products containing sugar, salt, food additives, preservatives, artificial colouring and flavouring, and there was nicotine. No, they didn't sell headache tablets. They weren't allowed. There was a chemist in Newtown, only three or four blocks away. I looked outside at the heat rising off the bitumen.

I sat down with a ginger beer and lit a cigarette. Then the Aboriginal woman noticed my tobacco and came over and asked could she roll one, so I pushed it across the table to her. I looked around for the kid with the stick, but he wasn't there.

All this time I had the teddy bear under my arm, and although it was wrapped in brown paper which crackled, I realized I was holding it to comfort myself. My parcel. I made a note to post it that afternoon. I suppose it was fear. I didn't feel fear, only the headaches.

Back at the waiting-room, two doctors, a woman and a man, wheeled in a huge machine and took it up in the lift. So many machines to find out about the body's diseases. A blue nurse and a white nurse walked past in step, one behind the other. When they came back, still in step, I asked the blue nurse whether she might find me a Panadol. 'I'll get the doctor to write you a script,' she said. 'We have our own pharmacy here.'

At o'clock I went back to the clinic and the radiologist who must have seen every size and shape and colour of breast which exists in the world, put me in the chair and manoeuvred the machine again. 'lean right into it. I won't break your ribs, don't worry. Turn your head this way, lean in now.'

The doctor was younger than me. He admired my shoes and socks and told me to take off my blouse and bra. I took off my blouse, which was a three-second operation, and stood there in my trousers and fancy shoes. I tried not to look at him; he had the soft glowing skin of a twenty-year-old. My mother had laughed at my shoes: 'You always liked weird shoes,' she said, 'and gumboots. There was a whole year when you'd only wear gumboots, and I had to buy them for the other five. Do you remember that?' I didn't remember then, but standing in the doctors's office now I remembered a photo of the girls, all in a line wearing gumboots.

I lay on the examination bed and closed my eyes. The doctor felt carefully for lumps. Where the pain was, no lump. An unexplained pain. 'How did you notice it?' he asked.

'The car,' I said, 'this is where the seatbelt crosses me.'

'Yes,' he said, 'a lot of people find it that way. But I can't feel anything.'

He rang the X-ray clinic while I was getting dressed. As the radiologist spoke, the doctor covered the mouthpiece and smiled at me. 'Nothing on the X-rays,' he whispered. Beckett, I thought, 'How it is by confessing that it wasn't.'

My headache thumped against the walls of the corridor *whump*, and came back to me. 'Any luck getting me a Panadol?' I said to the nurse. 'X-rays clear? Yes, we can always tell by your faces. That's good, you're one of the lucky ones.' On my behalf she breathed a sigh of relief. I drove home in the heat, the bear in brown paper on my lap, no sensation of relief, just the mirage on the road, and the seatbelt crossing me.

Gerard Windsor

REASONS FOR GOING INTO GYNAECOLOGY

She keeps mincing through the room. Her heels, stupidly high for the house, clatter backwards and forwards, spitting out pique and inarticulate frustration and intense dislike. The mood could, of course, be transformed in a moment. But I'm no longer interested in doing so. She goes from bathroom to suitcase to cupboard to suitcase, unnecessary, reduplicated journeys most of them, brandishing her departure in front of me. She hopes, transparently, that I'll stand up, yank her by the wrist as she goes past, tell her to stop the nonsense, and to sit down. But I'm watching porn, fairly soft porn, on the video, and I'm not even tempted to dwell on her pathetic charade. I imagine she looks at the film when she's behind me. She would say it's only curicsity. I would say that's crap. I would say she's a little tramp and would make a sly grab for whatever she can get. But she's cute enough not to let her step falter.

'Instructions for the nappy wash are on your desk,' she says on one of these ghost-train irruptions.

I refuse to acknowledge her. Tomorrow she goes to LA – it would have to be LA of course with her – and straight into the pants of this stud she's picked up.

'The cats are due for their operation,' she tries. 'Unless of course you're going to do it yourself.'

I'm impervious. I should get close to six months' peace. As the Puerto Rican rooster loses his appeal, she's likely to discover her maternal instincts again, and head for home. The children will bring her back. Even she knows she's in an exposed position, flouncing out on us like this. Silly, stupid woman, there has never been any prevision in her life, just a flailing around in all the emotional surges that eddy inside her. And when she returns she'll be in no stronger a position: her record of desertion will be against her. Whims all flutter home to roost in the long run.

'Would you mind turning down that nauseating rubbish,' she fires at me.

I let her go through, she disappears briefly, then clatters out again. I throw my arms over the back of the sofa and slide further down.

'If only your colleagues knew . . .' she trails through the exit.

She has a simple-minded view of my colleagues. They're gynaecologists precisely because we all made the same choice at the same age and for much the same reasons. We all plumped for the same option in the full flesh of our virile mid-twenties. Only a complete stranger to commonsense would believe a young man chooses women as his professional concern for purely, frigidly, scientific reasons. 'Your colleagues . . .' she says, and she's never dropped to the plumb obvious fact that my colleagues' libidos have directed their lives in the most palpably comprehensive way possible. Idiot of a woman. If I tried to point this out to her, she would mimic a feeble parody of scorn, reducing my view to sex mania.

The nymphet on the screen is doing her workout and has just bent right forward to touch the ground between her legs and her tights have ridden right up over her cheeks, so far that there's really just a delicate strip of tense material running into her crotch, and it seems it's just waiting to snap and fly open.

'Don't let me delay you,' she says. 'I know you have things to do.'

As a matter of fact, in spite of her stodgily unoriginal irony, I do have things to do. Babysitting's going to be a problem, and I might as well seize this last opportunity. It's all very well having a mother nearby, but there are limits to their usefulness. They can't live with you if you're going to have other women passing through the house, least of all if it's in any sort of volume. We may be great friends, mother and I . . . In fact she's the unassailable contrary evidence whenever I'm told that my relations with women can't be substantial. But there are some things, if known, mother might not find it easy to cope with. There's a limit to what you can expect of another generation. Still, she always sees through the likes of this one soon enough.

I'm lucky to have her. In fact a little meditation upon the subject of gynaecologists and their mothers would do all women good. The pattern of intimacy is quite striking. Even more striking is the evolutionary fissure that opens up between the two lines of descent from close bonding between mother and son. On the one side gynaecologists, on the other gays. And, most impressively, the two streams never meet. There are no gay gynaecologists, but within the profession is the greatest concentration of all those qualities that women most admire in the gay sector – the delicate touch, the urbane sophistication, the aesthetic flair, the interest in personality – but without any of the spoiling features, the cruel wit, the unscrupulous gossip, and all the rest of it. The ideal gynaecologist – and it might be surprising how frequently the average comes close to that ideal – is disconcertingly the female cynosure. Not smug. Just true.

The couple on the screen are pretty whacked, but I'm not, so I'll take up the jibing suggestion. 'Don't wait up for me,' I say to her as I pick up the keys from the hall table.

She had the dinner ready when I arrived. She's efficient like that, adaptable, practical. She has a sense of what's needed, and isn't always looking to be treated and wowed. She'll make a good mother.

'Is she really going?' she asks me, once we're halfway down the champagne.

I lean across and brush her fingertips with the fleshy parts of my palms.

All the perfumes on the table mingle. 'Yes, it's all over completely,' I assure her. 'It was long ago.' Then I hasten to add, 'But the door is locking behind her now.'

'I can't have her ghost, much less the shadow of her real physical presence, hovering around,' she says. 'I've had far too much of that.' There is real pleading in her voice.

'I know you have,' I say. My fingers apply just the slightest pressure to her wrist. I've heard all about these half-married men that have insisted on cluttering up her life. I want to reassure her that she's not getting more of the same. 'You must move in as soon as you can. You'll make a wonderful mother to the girls. They'll so desperately need someone just like you. You have so much love to give,' I add. Her face, which has been searching mine, seems to capitulate, and she drops her eyes, and entwines her fingers through mine in mute gratitude. I hesitate to say anything more to her; it wouldn't be sincere or honest. She must make do with what is available to be offered. And she is willing to do that, at least for the moment, and I can feel the responding warmth in that pressure of her hand, and I know she wants me to enfold her, and take her to bed.

It is an emotion, at least the essence of it is, that I see again and again, and my own chemistry responds willy-nilly. There is a feeling of warm, effusive, vulnerable gratitude that wells up in the patient towards the doctor after a gynaecological examination. Just for a start there is the relief that it is all over. The threat of indignity, of violation, has been averted by the sensitive manner, the paternally coaxing murmurs, and the sure touch that is as far removed from the gesture of a liberty as it is from that of distaste. A woman, inspired to feel that she has neither disgusted a man nor been invaded by him, can hardly control the quite hormonal rush of relief that overwhelms her. She is far more vulnerable then than ever she was as she lay exposed on the man's couch. I see the reaction hour after hour, day in day out. I have only ever had one rectal examination myself, and I recognised the reaction at once. I had been more than half expecting it, and, insofar as I had any attention left over from the discomfort of the moment, I had tried to steel myself against it. But the emotion burst out in a way I clearly had no control over. Given the correct handling, women will always respond that way. And there is something immensely satisfying about being the object of the response.

I stand at the bedroom door and dangle my keys. 'Is that young English protegée of yours due back from the country yet?' I ask. I see the tremor of apprehension pass across her eyes. 'If she wants a bit of pocket money while she's here, she might as well do a spot of babysitting. It'd be useful to me.' I watch her tucking the duvet in around the empty spaces beside her, and I know she feels it unwise to protest; she wants to show trust in me and to be helpful to me at the moment, but, career woman that she imagines herself to be, she is not going to clamour after babysitting duties herself.

'She's due back tomorrow actually, but I'm not sure that she'd really be interested in babysitting. Eighteen going on thirty that she is, I doubt whether she'd be too keen on spending her nights that way.'

'Well, I'll leave it to her,' I acquiesce. 'If she's interested at all. Otherwise . . .' My bleeper goes. I raise my eyebrows very slightly.

'You poor thing,' she says.

I nod, partly in acknowledging agreement, partly in farewell. 'I'll be in touch.'

Dishing out clichés is what the constant practice of most professions is. Clichés to the practitioner, that is. The sensitive man wearies himself with their reiteration. But this profession provides its own best antidote to that hazard. My practice is largely amongst younger women, and they, more than anything else, represent to me the cartwheeling kaleidoscope of life. Unpredictable, direct, autonomous, and quite sharply desirable.

I think of myself as having some style, some finesse, but on this occasion I really did just burst in. The moment she arrived I said, 'Use all the facilities. Make yourself at home. There's a pool downstairs.' She followed the instructions, without any reticence at all, but with that mix of effusive gratitude and giggling coquettishness that seemed to be partly her age, partly the English in her. I was never sure what the message of it all was, and although I took a plunge, I would not, even now, say I got it right. But the risk was worth it.

She kept up, almost to the end, the facade of the child, oscillating to the motions of temptation and reluctance. Hell knows what the rules and the objects of her game were, but she didn't lock the bathroom door, and she didn't immediately and peremptorily order me out. And let me tell you, she was quite criminally luscious. Ripe and juicy, and with a kick in the tail, or whatever it was, that would leave a snowman howling.

'Could I ask you something?' she says.

I'm running the electric shaver over my chin again before I go out. She's standing in the bedroom doorway, awkwardly, not quite knowing her place. She's playing with the tail of her long straight hair that is held back simply by a rubber band. She shuffles about, and gnaws, in a picking way, at the mane in her hand.

'Of course. Go ahead.'

'It's just that I don't know anyone else out here.'

'Go on. I'd love to help.'

'I think I've got something wrong with me.'

In the mirror I catch her looking up, then dropping her attention again to the hair ends.

'What sort of thing?' Her manner makes me just very mildly uneasy, though I have a perfectly clear conscience. I turn off the shaver, and turn to face her, and give her a light tap of encouragement on the arm. She is not talking about a scratch, I know. More than any other field of medicine, gynaecology involves us with the total human being. An odd paradox that. The whole genital bag of tricks is the machine in the machine – a set of organs that is quite irrelevant to the healthy functioning of that individual. Extraneous really, in the way not even the little toe is. But, touch the sexual organs, and you find yourself responsible for a whole quivering human life. This is real intimacy. In case after case we're sucked into sprawling, often chaotic, personal dramas. And the success of our treatment demands that we intervene and exert control over those dramas. Very humbling.

'I've got an itch I haven't had before,' she says.

'When did you notice it?'

'About a week ago,' she shrugs.

'Just an itch?'

'No . . . it's a bit . . . yukky too. Something's getting onto my knickers.'

'Come on, we better have a look at it.' I hesitate a second. 'I didn't notice anything there before.'

She shrugs again. 'I didn't have my knickers on. And I'd just had a shower.'

I bite my lip. 'You should have told me earlier.'

'You didn't ask me.' And all the time she keeps chewing on her hair, and her face is set with the mild but intractable sullenness of the young adolescent.

The phone rings. There's one beside the bed, but I prefer to take it out in the lounge-room. 'Just sit down there,' I point to the bed. 'I'll be with you in a sec.'

When I return I ask, 'Any chance you could have picked up an infection?'

She pouts and shrugs, and then changes tack and says, loudly and aggressively, 'I suppose so, but I don't see how.'

'Why not?'

'Well, there haven't been many, and I don't see how it could have been any of them.' She waits, and then asks, as much out of interest, I suspect, as of any wish to change the subject, 'Who was that?'

'Your duenna. Just as well she rang before we had the whole of this conversation. She would not have been pleased.'

'What did she want?'

'She just rang to say we wouldn't be going out tonight. She doesn't feel up to it,' I add. I'm given a quick glance, and I'm sure there's something sly, even mocking, in it.

'Well, Miss, why couldn't it have been any of them? All virgins, were they? Cutting a swathe through colonial maidenhood, are you?'

She misses my irony. 'No, not all of them. At least they can't have been.' She was giving a passable impression of being flustered. 'One of them was a gym instructor, and what I mean is that he'd be careful about being healthy and all that.'

I let this pass. 'Where else have you been, Miss?'

'Nowhere really.'

'Well, where not really?'

'Well, just my cousins, but they don't really count.'

'Why on earth not?'

'They're only sixteen and seventeen; they're still at school.'

'But they're your first cousins?'

'But I've only ever met them once before, when we were all little.'

'Where was this?'

'Where was what?'

'How did all this happen?'

'I was staying with them. It was natural. It was fun.'

What about your uncle and aunt? I mean, where were they? Do you think they would have approved?'

She actually digs her heels into the carpet. 'I came to you for some help. What's all this got to do with it?'

She's wrong, of course. I'm a total kind of person. The notion of holism has always appealed to me. By its nature, my calling allows a complete unity of private and professional life. I'm one of those men of whom it really can be said that their work is their hobby. In this case such a claim could seem crudely adolescent, but my rather more refined meaning should be obvious. I'm a man. Nothing that has anything to do with woman do I find at all alien to myself. I find myself slipping from one role to another as the situation and instinct prompt, until my distinctions become quite fuzzy. I loosen the tie that I no longer need and sit down beside her on the bed.

'I'll give you a scrip for some antibiotics. We'll pick them up when I take you home.'

'Why not tonight?' she asks.

'I mean tonight. You needn't stay, now that I'm not going out. I'll run you home whenever you're ready.'

'I think I'll stay,' she says. 'Actually I need the money, and I don't think I'm expected home.'

Sitting beside her I can't see her expression, but I note the hand again pulling nervously at the ponytail. At least I think there's a nervousness there. I'm determined not to say anything about the money: after all, she's hardly so much as nodded at the kids. And if she hasn't done her job, I don't like the implications of her getting money for other reasons.

'Come on. Up sticks. You'll be happier in your own bed. Besides, I'd like a word with your duenna.'

She stands up, faces me, puts her head on her side, and gives a wry look. 'She doesn't want to see you. I know that. Besides, if I came home early, she'd know something had happened. And I couldn't keep it from her, really I couldn't. She's been such a sweet friend to me since I've been here. You mustn't make me go. Please.' And she twitches, quizzically, at my shirt.

All right. I'll stay put. It's a matter of balance. You have all sorts of patients – wives of prime ministers, actresses, bordello hostesses – and that's simply healthy and sensible. All you don't do is get them mixed up. Keep the surgery discreet and the waiting rooms separate. They all know they're getting the best from me. And I only charge the common fee.

Tim Winton

SECRETS

Out the back of the new house, between the picket fence and a
sheet of tin, Kylie found an egg. Her mother and Philip were
inside. She heard them arguing and wished she still lived with
her father. The yard was long and excitingly littered with fallen
grapevines, a shed, lengths of timber and wire, and twitching
shadows from big trees. It wasn't a new house, but it was new
to her. She had been exploring the yard. The egg was white and
warm-looking in its nest of dirt and down. Reaching in, she
picked it up and found that it *was* warm. She looked back at the
house. No one was watching. Something rose in her chest: now
she knew what it was to have a secret.

At dinner her mother and Philip spoke quietly to one another
and drank from the bottle she was only allowed to look at. Her
mother was a tall woman with short hair like a boy. One of her
front teeth had gone brown and it made Kylie wonder. She
knew that Philip was Mum's new husband, only they weren't
married. He smelt of cigarettes and moustache hairs. Kylie
thought his feet were the shape of pasties.

When everything on her plate was gone, Kylie left the table.
Because the loungeroom was a jungle of boxes and crates inside
one of which was the TV, she went straight to her new room.
She thought about the egg as she lay in bed. She was thinking
about it when she fell asleep.

Next day, Kylie got up onto the fence and crabbed all around it
looking into the neighbours' yards. The people behind had a

little tin shed and a wired-up run against the fence in which hens and a puff-chested little rooster pecked and picked and scruffled. So, she thought, balanced on the splintery grey fence, that's where the egg comes from. She climbed down and checked behind the sheet of tin and found the egg safe but cold.

Later, she climbed one of the big trees in the yard, right up, from where she could observe the hens and the rooster next door. They were fat, white birds with big red combs and bright eyes. They clucked and preened and ruffled and Kylie grew to like them. She was angry when the piebald rooster beat them down to the ground and jumped on their backs, pecking and twisting their necks. All his colours were angry colours; he looked mean.

Inside the house Mum and Philip laughed or shouted and reminded her that Dad didn't live with them any more. It was good to have a secret from them, good to be the owner of something precious. Philip laughed at the things she said. Her mother only listened to her with a smile that said *you don't know a single true thing.*

Sometime in the afternoon, after shopping with her mother, Kylie found a second egg in the place between the fence and the tin. She saw, too, a flash of white beneath a mound of vine cuttings in the corner of the yard. She climbed her tree and waited. A hen, thinner and more raggedy than the others, emerged. She had a bloody comb and a furtive way of pecking the ground alertly and moving in nervous bursts. For some time, she poked and scratched about, fossicking snails and slugs out of the long grass, until Kylie saw her move across to the piece of tin and disappear.

Each day Kylie saw another egg added to the nest up the back. She saw the raggedy hen pecked and chased and kicked by the others next door, saw her slip between the pickets to escape. The secret became bigger every day. The holidays stretched on. Philip and her mother left her alone. She was happy. She sat on the fence, sharing the secret with the hen.

When they had first moved into this house on the leafy, quiet street, Philip had shown Kylie and her mother the round, galvanized tin cover of the bore well in the back of the yard. The sun winked off it in the morning. Philip said it was thirty-six feet deep and very dangerous. Kylie was forbidden to lift the lid. It was off-limits. She was fascinated by it. Some afternoons she sat out under the grapevines with her photo album, turning pages and looking across every now and then at that glinting lid. It couldn't be seen from the back verandah; it was obscured by a banana tree and a leaning brick wall.

In all her photographs, there was not one of her father. He had been the photographer in the family; he took photos of Kylie and her mother, Kylie and her friends, but he was always out of the picture, behind the camera. Sometimes she found herself looking for him in the pictures. Sometimes it was a game for her; at others she didn't realize she was doing it.

Two weeks passed. It was a sunny, quiet time. Ten eggs came to be secreted behind the piece of tin against the back fence. The hen began sitting on them. Kylie suspected something new would happen. She visited the scraggy, white hen every day to see her bright eyes, to smell her musty warmth. It was an important secret now. She sneaked kitchen scraps and canary food up the back each evening and lay awake in bed wondering what would happen.

It was at this time that Kylie began to lift the lid of the well. It was not heavy and it moved easily. Carefully, those mornings, shielded by the banana tree, she peered down into the cylindrical pit which smelt sweaty and dank. Right down at the bottom was something that looked like an engine with pipes leading from it. A narrow, rusty ladder went down the wall of the well. Slugs and spiderwebs clung to it.

One afternoon when Philip and her mother were locked in the big bedroom, laughing and making the bed bark on the boards, Kylie took her photo album outside to the well, opened the lid and with the book stuffed into the waistband of her shorts, went down the ladder with slow, deliberate movements. Flecks of rust came away under her hands and fell whispering a long way down. The ladder quivered. The sky was a blue disc above growing smaller and paler. She climbed down past the engine to the moist sand and sat with her back to the curving wall. She looked up. It was like being a drop of water in a straw or a piece of rice in a blowpipe – the kind boys stung her with at school. She heard the neighbours' rooster crowing, and the sound of the wind. She looked through her album. Pictures of her mother showed her looking away into the distance. Her long, wheaten hair blew in the wind or hung still and beautiful. It had been so long. Her mother never looked at the camera. Kylie saw herself, ugly and short and dark beside her. She grew cold and climbed out of the well.

It seemed a bit of an ordinary thing to have done when she got out. Nevertheless, she went down every day to sit and think or to flick through the album.

The hen sat on her eggs for three weeks. Kylie sat on the fence and gloated, looking into the chookhouse next door at the rooster and his scrabbling hens who did not know what was happening her side of the fence. She knew now that there would be chicks. The encyclopaedia said so.

On nights when Philip and her mother had friends over, Kylie listened from the darkened hallway to their jokes that made no sense. Through the crack between door and jamb she saw them touching each other beneath the table, and she wanted to know – right then – why her father and mother did not live together with her. It was something she was not allowed to know. She went back to her room and looked at the only picture in her album where her smile told her that there was something she knew that the photographer didn't. She couldn't remember what it was; it was a whole year ago. The photo was a shot from way back in kindergarten. She was small, dark-haired, with her hands propping up her face. She held the picture close to her face. It made her confident. It made her think Philip and her mother were stupid. It stopped her from feeling lonely.

Philip caught her down the well on a Sunday afternoon. He had decided to weed the garden at last; she wasn't prepared for it. One moment she was alone with the must, the next, the well was full of Philip's shout. He came down and dragged her out. He hit her. He told her he was buying a padlock in the morning.

That evening the chicks hatched in the space between the sheet of tin and the back fence – ten of them. At dusk, Kylie put them into a cardboard box and dropped them down the well. The hen squawked insanely around the yard, throwing itself about, knocking things over, creating such a frightening noise that Kylie chased it and hit it with a piece of wood and, while it was still stunned, dropped it, too, down the dry well. She slumped down on the lid and began to cry. The back light came on. Philip came out to get her.

Before bed, Kylie took her photograph – the knowing one – from its place in the album, and with a pair of scissors, cut off her head and poked it through a hole in the flyscreen of the window.

Ania Walwicz

HOUSE

i was born in my house in top room on bed wet midwife said to
me said you were a little mohican with black hair you were you
were you were once little indian with a red face and long hair i
was a little indian once i was i really was big house my house is
on a hill we are there four such a big place i am rich i am a princess i own the park in the back i own the front garden we have
the first car in the world this is my palace i used to want to shine
the parquet push the polisher up and down in a trance i get into
a daze house you are enormous i am a huge house with no end
to it park with no end outside winter i hear branches no leaves
hit one another in winter snow cover then leafy green in the
park through the backgate i tell children you can't pick leaves
here it is my park this belongs to me all this house born in had a
hole in the floor near the window at night my sister plays the
piano downstairs i can hear faint tinkle a black man stands
there i know he does i turn my face had another rooms and
rooms seven rooms eight rooms nine rooms ten rooms such a
big wood fill in house ceiling coffer palace build house german
sawmill own house wood panelling he built himself a house
they say there was a bed there like a boat swimming with lights
but someone took it away i was born in a german house pantry
with porcelain containers salz for salt salz for salt salz i am in
my house now i stand outside on the street this is swidnica i
walk up the brick road path i stand at the bottom of the stairs i
climb up step by step pink wall outside had a little waiting
space stone floor ribbed tiles door glass green knock on the door

how i open vestibule mirror wood walk in i have the most beautiful house in the world i did door through a sea of parquet and people's voices i have a party we clean up maid father study bookcase smell books how books smell blue wallpaper this room is too dark said my mother in the dining had yellow walls she had made another more one more window put in the wall open painted wall pattern with my roller lit up light in big in all light in window me i sit there and i write shiny floor all this shiny floor all this shiny floor all this shiny shiny floor i am rich i am a princess i drink from a silver coffee pot i do i really do i am special i am better here this is my house had a house i have my house now smells coffee smelt of coffee walls are yellow i am a rich princess i live here someone said they had a boat like a bed but i didn't see it they had a bed like a boat in my house i go upstairs had carpet but my mother took carpet off i like a lot of space i like a lot i want another window i want more than i have i want a window and i want my house i want my house again just how it was to my pantry to my kitchen in and inside the sun sets on my wall i go upstairs this is here where i dress dressingroom in built cupboard i play with my father's navy uniform i go into the bedroom now where i am born.

Ania Walwicz

NEONS

light me bright me match me cigarette me bright city turn on be
loud tell everybody switch yes sing red pencil tick me to on centre mid town go go glow sky lit lines wire buzz me to see ring on
me in neon on heady excite me thrill me hold me to tight rush
rush be big loud go right through now leap nerve me beat
drums loud louder fast run fast right now once go places all the
time eat more restaurant flash me show me lively dance put
lipstick on neons all colour zap me power lines shine letter light
big n me blow me put high fast see me watch zing my string
best bouncy tube glow in me get ready do it now don't wait
hurry get it right first time do it once no again switch me on i
travel fast light switch me on pink candy say words loud-
speaker my microphone leap high as can big city centre city big
very buildings whole wide world hot lights on stage line my
eyes breathe deep all revved up fast car go fast car go fast good
kill somebody dress to top fashion strut get them wiggle pink
face daze me amaze me shine me neons on sweet buzz meter
front room seat skip dance non stop favourite flower colour
allans sweets on river shine thrill me thrill me rise in a loop get
up early do lots the more better fast faster lit light on me in such
show glow me ania it's now don't wait hurry up top tip they
clap they whistle stomp yell out aloud more on high want more
and more fresh new dare do do new do now very it just here
spot lit wear shiny glistony get tight tonight darling neon
electric buy me eat sweets almonds go places every day get
money work now just right dare do do new flash me up bow

come out lit shine me coca cola i don't sleep seven up fun city
pin ball parlour amusements ride sky mid night click throw me
bright lines whirlwind wake up little susy break dark venture:
fling adventure red bulbs around my lights stage mirror my
name bright around and around light up found this does me out
aloud each letter after neon thrill lights wonderful to wonderful
stop my breath split thrill me delight move me collect thrills one
be brave live now don't go back again have ones big thrills
lights above red town break out fast do once twice glow shine
me see me what's what glow colour in dark tyger put sugar gold
eyes on bright lights lively now lively up fix me up lips dance all
night loud band hot pepper bite me on the highway lights jewel
see get to glow just do did it cinema lit flash sign best form top
push you can see me now shake spout give me a thrill burst
aureole spangles boots with spurs lips ruby glass red fluores-
cent lit light tubes shine me vinyl head on neon high city red
fingernails look at me curve shine lines easy do see me show
gas blow me light up shine up shape up pull my socks all up me
neon can't miss spiv can't take my eyes curve arc shine me
night best in dark stick me up stand out sparkling fresh hit triple
whisky pink angle centre lights dance dancing can do anything
switch me on zag zig sky glow bulb ready whole sky shine get
on up

Serge Liberman

SEEDS

Nearly empty, the house. Mere odds and ends remain, earlier necessities become ephemera which we – Mother, Father, I – toss higgledy-piggledy into boxes, into cartons soon to be taken away. The other wares already lie outside, deposited on the nature strip, on the pavement, in Father's station-wagon, themselves to be delivered to charity or to be thrown away at the local tip as junk, all the accumulated now-redundant bric-a-brac of years cluttering Zaida Zerach's home – the usual chipped dust-encrusted peeling picture-frames, old suits with the fustiness of mothballs choked, mottled mirrors, a rickety table, precarious chairs, an outworn sofa with pouting springs, his violin.

His violin. Solace to his solitude, succour to his soul.

Not overly pious, far less observant, yet does Zaida Zerach ever like to talk of souls.

'Do you know,' he says as his fingers sift melodies, wring tremolo from that varnished frame of pinewood and wire, 'there is a *dybbuk* in these strings and a *dybbuk* is a soul and that soul dances like a *shikker* across space across time as tum-ta-tum-tum it leaves one human body to enter another?'

Raisins and Almonds, he plays; *Margaritkes*, he plays: *The Little Town Belz*, he plays.

'Not music is this,' he says as strings oscillate and tremble beneath the bow, 'not music, don't be fooled, but the soul of a people through the centuries passing down from Jubal and King David through me on to you. So open up your soul Raphael

86

mine open your soul let the souls of others of your people continue and live and abide through you on to generations and to generations yet to come that their greatness *our* greatness brilliance light may yet be given unto the nations as was the charge given to our father of fathers Abraham our Father whose seed was to be as the stars of heaven and the sand upon the shore.'

'Three levels of creation define a man,' he says, plucking at strings that resonate on pine. 'What he does what he thinks what he feels. In this a man is deed a man is mind a man is soul.'

Zaida Zerach, if mother I am to believe, is intoxicated with soul.

But his own soul, Zaida Zerach's, where, where is it now to be found?

The rooms, under our tread, reverberate. Our voices, however solemn, however subdued, echo in the expanding camphored emptiness of the house, metal rings against metal, wood clatters on wood. Neither Mother nor Father seems to hear, but Zaida is playing. He stands before the window, as I do now, looks out upon the porch, the street, the terraces and the cottages as their shadows lengthen this side of the sinking sun, and makes the strings hum, the soul that customarily rides on the music not dancing now as on occasions past, but rather easing to rest, tamely, wearily, resigned. Twelve months have witnessed his metamorphosis into a reed; his pancreas has cannibalised his flesh; that which was once colour, fullness, health, is now sallowness, transparency, decay.

'When I die,' he says, 'may my body be cremated and may my ashes be thrown into the wind.'

His eyebrows, as he peers at me, pucker into folds. His are the unslept eyes of one desperate for sleep.

'For one thing, that is what happened to your Zaida Ephraim, your father's father, when Europe was a furnace, a charnel-house, a gas-chamber. And for another, no man with a navel born belongs to himself alone. Neither during this life, nor after.'

There is an occasion when Zaida Zerach sees fit to buy me an atlas. I have just completed first form creditably well. He, a man who has journeyed through Poland, Russia, Germany, Italy, France, Egypt and Ceylon entertains the notion to tell me of his travels, to teach me history, geography, current affairs, *life*. Over city, village, wheat field and steppe, I follow his finger as he traces out his route, moving from one page to another on which he creates, re-creates Siberian frosts, Uzbekistan mosques, the DP camp at Ziegenhain, the Champs Elysees, the red Suez sands with Bedouin sheltering under palms, pineapple-sellers scaling his ship at Colombo, the spectre of the new land he is approaching become form, become reality housed and paved and railed as he nears slowly, slowly, the Port Melbourne docks.

Listening to him as he plays out the life that is the stage before kaddish, it is the map of the world's rivers I remember most clearly. They are all there traversing the beaten terrain of his scalp – rivers, rivulets, tributaries – their blue not truly blue but violet, purple, inky in a topographic expanse run to austere denuded dessicating tawny waste.

'Before his death and after it,' he says, watching his own fingers at play upon the strings, 'not a wet ugly wretched hole in the ground is his home, but the world itself, the space out there, all of it, in the clouds, in the sunlight, in the mist, the fog, and with the very dust from which the man has been formed. While soul born into the universe remains forever its citizen, wandering for all time on earth to touch, to move, to enter into others.'

But Zadia Zerach, asking for that which the law of the Rabbis, the Law, enshrined in Torah, the Shulchan Aruch and Talmud, cannot sanction, is brought to his final recumbency and repose in just such a hole, in the wind-lapped surface crust of Springvale, among the tombstones that sprout, monthly, weekly, daily, like . . . like . . . like the tomatoes on his porch.

Through the grimy glass of the window I see them, his tomatoes, their stems struggling through the dense grey soil in deep aluminium cylinders, the fruit still green or ripening, or ripened to lush edibility. What gall must have been his from them to be taken, and what chagrin at being so hastily interred, the finality of it so all-annihilating, no rein in the slightest given to his soul that would wish to roam, whatever the balm flowing from Rabbi Faigen's solacing words by the grave.

'A Jewish soul has departed,' he says, Rabbi Faigen, the man of God short and young and bearded and visited with a lisp. 'Returned to its Maker that soul, the soul of a man who, like the brothers and sisters of his unhappy generation knew what it was to suffer, to lose family, to be uprooted, for years to wander about the Siberian wastes while Europe burned, for years to struggle, in Russia, Paris, Australia, and yet to endure all without harshness on his lips or hatred in his heart. A *lamed vavnik* was he, a saint among the highest, his memory forever to shine in the hearts of his dear ones.'

The first fat drops of rain fall, yielding a hollow patter against the pine of Zaida's white unvarnished coffin. The gathered mourners draw into themselves. Rabbi Faigen glances upward.

'May his memory shine,' he says. 'His memory. For after all his travails on earth, what else is left of a man? . . .'

He would say more, I swear, but instead steps back a pace, gives a signal with his brow and his chin, and with apt solemnity watches as, first, Father, then the socialist printer Levenberg, the fruiterer Norich, his partner Solinski, and Eckstein the tailor-poet shovel wet brown loam into the pit. Mother gasps, sobs, heaves, weeps, as Zaida, in the rain, body-mind-soul Zaida disappears, his friends making him vanish in a mere five minutes of dogged shovelling into a plot of earth twelve thousand miles from the leaking draught-bitten cottage in Lodz where, a lifetime before, he has been born.

Yet, though neither Mother, nor Father sees him – indeed, in taking out the chattels of his former home, they pass him by, if once, then a dozen times – he is kneeling on the porch, with a battered kettle evenly watering the roots of his tomatoes, binding the stalks to uprights with ribbons and twine, touching the leaves, fondling the soil. He wears again his tattered green sweater, wipes his hands in his baggy pants, and strains the buckles of the sandals he wears without socks.

'In the *sovkhoz*, there, too, I grew tomatoes when the frosts thawed and let the seed ripen to fruit. Because cold it was. To clean ourselves we rubbed our bodies with snow. Water we pumped up and carried from wells a kilometre, two, three away. And as for *hot* water. Hot water! Who, even Ziegenhain knew what that was, or up there on the fifth floor in the eighteenth arondissement in Paris, or even here, in this house, Raphael mine, in Carlton, in this paradise that in your atlas is called Australia . . . Even here, my blood, my heir, earthly bearer of my soul, have you ever seen your Zaida use hot water for the pampering of his flesh?'

I shake my head. No; I have never seen Zaida Zerach use hot water for the pampering of his flesh.

'After Europe,' he says, scraping with a knife the clay impacted to solidity beneath his nails, 'a man can in Australia take the very worst. And after that, still worse. Hot water turns the skin to jelly. Dissolves the pils and makes it soft and weak and wrinkled before its time. Just as softness, clover, feather-beds – may no evil eye fall upon the nest-egg your father-mother have here built up – make the soul soft and weak and wrinkled, while for the seed of Abraham with an arduous eternal mission unto the nations charged, no softness can be permitted, nor clover, Raphael mine, nor feather-bed. These only dazzle, where they are the sons of Abraham that must forever be the brightest light; these become the end of all striving, when perfection is the truer end and purity of the soul; they thwart the coming of redemption, of sanctified peace, and of the glorious and triumphant consummation of our task for which your zaidas and zaidas' zaidas found the strength yet to cherish breath and to hold to faith, even when their necks were bared beneath the sword, their bodies tied like lambs to the stake, their flesh turned to violet in the poisonous vapours let into the zyklon chambers.'

Carried on crests of resolve billowed by Zaida Zerach's proud capacity to endure, I step under a cold shower in my home, my own home, my tiled and carpeted, wall-papered upholstered immaculate home locked in a cul-de-sac on the statelier, leafier, balmier edge of Kew. Under that lashing glacial cataract, my teeth bite lemons; goosepimples clamp my every pore. I gasp, breathe fast, inhale, exhale, hold my breath, and lock my knees and stamp my feet and dig blue nails into my palms. But in the end, I escape, must escape, as, draping towels about my shoulders one, two, three of them, I stand there hunched, contracted, as near to rigor mortis as living will allow, shivering and shuddering like a storm-tossed dog. And if that is a lapse, yet do I lapse again, and yet again – first, when, in emulation of Zaida Zerach's mastery over hunger in times to wintry history now relinquished, I pledge myself to starvation rations and to fasting, compelled finally to yield to the griping sleep-depriving cramps of a stomach to emptiness unaccustomed; and further, when, in the glorification of labour such as Zaida Zerach once sweated over, grappled with, and overcame, I dig up a far corner of our garden in preparation for a vegetable patch, only to succumb to the clawing throb and stiffness of biceps, calves and back that made me abandon that plot to weeds, until Father, saying, 'Well, so much for our home-grown provider of pumpkin, carrots and beans', calls in the gardener to lay down lawn once more, my ecstasy, resolve and exertions to extinction so annihilated, no testimony remaining, no face, no name, no redemption to be salvaged.

Void, then, is testimony to my efforts: Zaida Zerach's house to emptiness now stripped, what remains for him?

'Have we left anything behind?' Father says from the doorway.

'Nothing else we can give away?' Mother says.

'Nothing,' Father says. 'We can go now. Give the place to the wind till the next people move in.'

I look about. Eerieness consumes the vacuum that has now usurped the room, the house. No more hang there the curtains, or stand the chairs the second-, third-hand, fourth-hand buffet, the table at which Zaida Zerach over Russian tea and almond bread long ago argued with Becker, Levenberg, Winkler and their wives about socialism, Marx, Pilsudski, Stalin, Israel, the messiah, God. Only smells remain – of mice, naphthalene and mould, and of dankness corroded with grime and walls bronzed and blotched with rust. I wish I could hear again his violin that might at least once more restore a touch, a memory, of warmth, however fleeting, before departing, but coldness, too, and unfamiliarity, have already stolen into every corner. Called by Father, I turn to leave, but catch sight of a slender pile of photographs on the mantel above the fireplace in which, in Zaida's time, no fire ever burned. It is Mother who has found them in the buffet, but diverted by another task, has left them behind, forgotten. I take them now and, looking back no more – all that there has been left to see, I have seen; all that there has been left to hear, I have heard – I go outside, I go outside into the openness, into spaciousness, into the light, there, where there is life both living and lived, there is also freshness and movement, direction, purpose, dispute, marvel, thought and industry.

Out there in the street, I take deep breaths again, rid myself of the mustiness and acerbity that, for decades past, have swathed Zaida Zerach, and, given the audacity, might crow out my liberation from that house become a tomb like a rooster.

To my left, on the porch against the wall, are Zaida Zerach's tomatoes. Each time I have visited him, he has plucked one for me, rendering it as an offering with the formula, 'At least you do not forget your Zaida like so many other boys, so here take this enjoy it is ripe and rich and juicy suck from its heart its very soul.'

There is another ripe and rich and juicy tomato weighing down its stalk. It, too, I now pluck. Zaida Zerach would not mind, I know. Even if he were there, not in the least, I know. But it is not to eat it, to suck from it its soul as Zaida calls it that I sunder it from its source, but rather to toy with it, manipulate it, toss it, polish it, dandle it as I would a ball, this opportunity the last as I say goodbye forever to the home that was for so long my Zaida's. And all this I do, toy with it, manipulate, polish, dandle it, and toss it, toss it high, toss it once, toss it twice, and a third time, and a fourth, on the fourth seeing it rap the spouting skirting the roof, from there to return more swiftly than my hand beneath poised to catch it, in that instant, not only the tomato slipping through to strike the ground there in turn to split and splatter, but all the photographs as well that, in my bungle, I also drop, these dulled greying fraying relics scattering, face up, face down upon the path, Zaida somewhere in Poland with his mother, his father, Zaida in the Urals with Buba Sarah, Zaida outside barracks with his brothers, his sisters, Zaida with his daughters. Mother among them, Zaida in streets, in stores, in kitchens, in fields, all different Zaidas and yet the same, not the yellow hallowed Zaida now lying in the clay of Springvale, but other younger, sturdier, darker Zaidas who hewed up soil and grew tomatoes, who dealt in draperies and, on his violin, stirred up music, stirred up souls. My Zaidas all are they, of whom Mother, as if by duty driven she too bends to salvage the photographs so sacrilegiously dispersed, chides, 'Is that how you treat the memory of your Zaida?', adding more gravely then, 'After all a man's been through, that this is all that should remain', of whom Father, ever the wry one, says, 'Well, there are his tomatoes, too, that are still over there'; my Zaida, Zaida Zerach who over his violin once said, 'There is a *dybbuk* in these strings and the *dybbuk* is a soul', who said, 'A man is deed is mind is soul', who said, 'Not music is this but the soul of a people through the centuries passing down through me on to you', who . . . who . . .

Not in the photographs does he remain, Zaida Zerach as Mother infers, nor in his tomatoes even if one allows for seriousness in Father's wry remark, nor even, as Rabbi Faigen at the funeral said, in memory alone is he. How can a man supposedly as learned, as wise as a rabbi not truly see?– As I gather up the photographs, some of them smeared and stained with the juice so rich, so red of that shattered tomato, I am pulled up to a dizzying halt. As if struck, I stand up. Around me are trees, flowers, cottages, shrubs, plantations, fences, lamp-posts, wires, grass and concrete, common things all, things I have climbed and touched and walked upon and plucked times innumerable, and yet now so acutely, peculiarly, dazzlingly different. It may be the wind skirting about the eaves that animates the vaulting revelation or the mellowing lilac light, the warmth now come to possess pricking nipping teeth, or the suddenly-leaping smells of lavender or lemon rising piquantly and headily from Zaida Zerach's neighbours' gardens. All these are – everything about me – of one unit, united in the vastness of space that, as I look about, dawns on me for the first time as so wholly and awesomely limitless and of which, solitary as I am standing on that minuscule infinitesimal spot of soil, I am yet a part. But not even this is what has startled me to near-immobility. Those seeds, those seeds! The seeds of that tomato now pulped and demolished on the path Zaida Zerach is playing his violin. They may not hear him, Father, Mother, but he is giving life to souls, and on those strings that oscillate and tremble beneath the bow, those souls dance, and they dance like *shikkers* across space across time, dancing from Jubal and King David down the generations through Zaida Zerach on to me. 'Open your soul, Raphael mine', he is saying, 'open up your soul,' and, following his bidding, I open my soul and through that opening his own soul enters into me and with his soul, he brings still more, hosts of souls, generations of souls, the ever-surviving souls of my people that through me they may continue and live and abide and that their greatness, *our* greatness brilliance light may yet be given unto the nations as was the charge given to our father of fathers Abraham our Father whose own seed was to be as the stars of heaven and the sand upon the sea.

Zaida Grandfather
dybbuk a soul transmigrated from the body of one who is dead to that of a living person
shikker drunkard
lamed vavnik one of the thirty-six righteous men of the world on whose account the world is preserved
sovhoz a Russian mechanised farm owned by the state
Buba Grandmother
Torah The Pentateuch
Shulchan Aruch literally, a prepared table; a code of Jewish Law
Talmud the main authoritative compilation of ancient Jewish Law and tradition

TRANSGRESSIONS

David Malouf

THE EMPTY LUNCH-TIN

He had been there for a long time. She could not remember when she had last looked across the lawn and he was not standing in the wide, well-clipped expanse between the buddleia and the flowering quince, his shoulders sagging a little, his hands hanging limply at his side. He stood very still with his face lifted towards the house, as a tradesman waits who has rung the doorbell, received no answer, and hopes that someone will appear at last at an upper window. He did not seem in a hurry. Heavy bodies barged through the air, breaking the stillness with their angular cries. Currawongs. Others hopped about on the grass, their tails switching from side to side. Black metronomes. He seemed unaware of them. Originally the shadow of the house had been at his feet, but it had drawn back before him as the morning advanced, and he stood now in a wide sunlit space casting his own shadow. Behind him cars rushed over the warm bitumen, station-wagons in which children were being ferried to school or kindergarten, coloured delivery vans, utilities – there were no fences here; the garden was open to the street. He stood. And the only object between him and the buddleia was an iron pipe that rose two feet out of the lawn like a periscope.

At first, catching sight of him as she passed the glass wall of the dining-room, the slight figure with its foreshortened shadow, she had given a sharp little cry. Greg! And it might have been Greg standing there with only the street behind him. He would have been just that age. Doubting her own percep-

97

tions, she had gone right up to the glass and stared. But Greg had been dead for seven years; she knew that with the part of her mind that observed this stranger, though she had never accepted it in that other half where the boy was still going on into the fullness of his life, still growing, so that she knew just how he had looked at fifteen, seventeen, and how he would look now at twenty.

This young man was quite unlike him. Stoop-shouldered, intense, with clothes that didn't quite fit, he was shabby, and it was the shabbiness of poverty not fashion. In his loose flannel trousers with turnups, collarless shirt and wide-brimmed felt hat, he might have been from the country or from another era. Country people dressed like that. He looked, she thought, the way young men had looked in her childhood, men who were out of work.

Thin, pale, with the sleeves half-rolled on his wiry forearms, he must have seen her come up to the glass and note his presence, but he wasn't at all intimidated.

Yes, that's what he reminded her of: the Depression years, and those men, one-armed or one-legged some of them, others dispiritingly whole, who had haunted the street corners of her childhood, wearing odd bits of uniform with their civilian castoffs and offering bootlaces or pencils for sale. Sometimes when you answered the back doorbell, one of them would be standing there on the step. A job was what he was after: mowing or cleaning out drains, or scooping the leaves from a blocked downpipe, or mending shoes – anything to save him from mere charity. When there was, after all, no job to be done, they simply stood, those men, as this man stood, waiting for the offer to be made of a cup of tea with a slice of bread and jam, or the scrapings from a bowl of dripping, or if you could spare it, the odd sixpence – it didn't matter what or how much, since the offering was less important in itself than the unstinting recognition of their presence, and beyond that, a commonness between you. As a child she had stood behind lattice doors in the country town she came from and watched transactions between her mother and those men, and had thought to herself: *This is one of the rituals. There is a way of doing this so that a man's pride can be saved, but also your own.* But when she grew up the Depression was over. Instead, there was the war. She had never had to use any of that half-learned wisdom.

She walked out now onto the patio and looked at the young man, with just air rather than plate glass between them.

He still wasn't anyone she recognised, but he had moved slightly, and as she stood there silently observing – it must have been for a good while – she saw that he continued to move.He was turning his face to the sun. He was turning with the sun, as a plant does, and she thought that if he decided to stay and put down roots she might get used to him. After all, why a buddleia or a flowering quince and not a perfectly ordinary young man?

She went back into the house and decided to go on with her housework. The house didn't need doing, since there were just two of them, but each day she did it just the same. She began with the furniture in the lounge, dusting and polishing, taking care not to touch the electronic chess-set that was her husband's favourite toy and which she was afraid of disturbing – no, she was actually afraid of *it*. Occupying a low table of its own, and surrounded by lamps, it was a piece of equipment that she had thought of at first as an intruder and regarded now as a difficult but permanent guest. It announced the moves it wanted made in a dry dead voice, like a man speaking with a peg on his nose or through a thin coffin-lid; and once, in the days when she still resented it, she had accidentally touched it off. She had already turned away to the sideboard when the voice came, flat and dull, dropping into the room one of its obscure directives: *Queen to King's Rook five;* as if something in the room, some object she had always thought of as tangible but without life, had suddenly decided to make contact with her and were announcing a cryptic need. Well, she had got over that.

She finished the lounge, and without going to the window again went right on to the bathroom, got down on her knees, and cleaned all round the bath, the shower recess, the basin and lavatory; then walked straight through to the lounge-room and looked.

He was still there and had turned a whole quarter-circle. She saw his slight figure with the slumped shoulders in profile. But what was happening?

He cast no shadow. His shadow had disappeared. The iron tap cast a shadow and the young man didn't. It took her a good minute, in which she was genuinely alarmed, to see that what she had taken for the shadow of the tap was a dark patch of lawn where the water dripped. So that was all right. It was midday.

She did a strange thing then. Without having made any decision about it, she went into the kitchen, gathered the ingredients, and made up a batch of spiced biscuits with whole peanuts in them; working fast with the flour, the butter, the spice, and forgetting herself in the pleasure of getting the measurements right by the feel of the thing, the habit.

They were biscuits that had no special name. She had learned to make them when she was just a child, from a girl they had had in the country. The routine of mixing and spooning the mixture on to greaseproof paper let her back into a former self whose motions were lighter, springier, more sure of ends and means. She hadn't made these biscuits – hadn't been able to bring herself to make them – since Greg died. They were his favourites. Now, while they were cooking and filling the house with their spicy sweetness, she did another thing she hadn't intended to do. She went to Greg's bedroom at the end of the hall, across from where she and Jack slept, and began to take down from the wall the pennants he had won for swimming, the green one with gold lettering, the purple one, the blue, and his lifesaving certificates, and laid them carefully on the bed. She brought a carton from under the stairs and packed them in the bottom. Then she cleared the bookshelf and took down the model planes, and put them in the carton as well. Then she removed from a drawer of the desk a whole mess of things: pro-pelling pencils and pencil-stubs, rubber-bands, tubes of glue, a pair of manacles, a pack of playing cards that if you were foolish enough to take one gave you an electric shock. She put all these things into the carton, along with a second drawerful of magazines and loose-leaf notebooks, and carried the carton out. Then she took clean sheets and made the bed.

By now the biscuits were ready to be taken from the oven. She counted them, there were twenty-three. Without looking up to where the young man was standing, she opened the kitchen window and set them, sweetly smelling of spice, on the window ledge. Then she went back and sat on Greg's bed while they cooled.

She looked round the blank walls, wondering, now that she had stripped them, what a young man of twenty-eight might have filled them with, and discovered with a pang that she could not guess.

It was then that another figure slipped into her head.

In her middle years at school there had been a boy who sat two desks in front of her called Stevie Caine. She had always felt sorry for him because he lived alone with an aunt and was poor. The father had worked for the railways but lost his job after a crossing accident and killed himself. It was Stevie Caine this young man reminded her of. His shoulders too had been narrow and stooped, his face unnaturally pallid, his wrists bony and raw. Stevie's hair was mouse-coloured and had stuck out in wisps behind the ears; his auntie cut it, they said, with a pudding-basin. He smelled of scrubbing-soap. Too poor to go to the pictures on Saturday afternoons, or to have a radio and hear the serials, he could take no part in the excited chatter and argument through which they were making a world for themselves. When they ate their lunch he sat by himself on the far side of the yard, and she alone had guessed the reason: it was because the metal lunch-tin that his father had carried to the railway had nothing in it, or at best a slice of bread and drip-ping. But poor as he was, Stevie had not been resentful – that was the thing that had most struck her. She felt he ought to have been. And his face sometimes, when he was excited and his Adam's apple worked up and down, was touched at the cheekbones with such a glow of youthfulness and joy that she had wanted to reach out and lay her fingers very gently to his skin and feel the warmth, but thought he might misread the tenderness that filled her (which certainly included him but was for much more beside) as girlish infatuation or, worse still, pity. So she did nothing.

Stevie Caine had left school when he was just fourteen and went like his father to work at the railway. She had seen him sometimes in a railway worker's uniform, black serge, wearing a black felt hat that made him look bonier than ever about the cheekbones and chin and carrying the same battered lunch-tin. Something in his youthful refusal to be bitter or subdued had continued to move her. Even now, years later, she could see the back of his thin neck, and might have leaned out, no longer caring if she was misunderstood, and laid her hand to the chapped flesh.

When he was eighteen he had immediately joined up and was immediately killed; she had seen it in the papers – just the name.

It was Stevie Caine this young man resembled, as she had last seen him in the soft hat and railway worker's serge waistcoat, with the sleeves rolled on his stringy arms. There had been nothing between them, but she had never forgotten. It had to do, as she saw it, with the two forms of injustice: the one that is cruel but can be changed, and the other kind – the tipping of a thirteen-year-old boy off the saddle of his bike into a bottomless pit – that cannot; with that and an empty lunch-tin that she would like to have filled with biscuits with whole peanuts in them that have no special name.

She went out quickly now (the young man was still there on the lawn beyond the window) and counted the biscuits, which were cool enough to be put into a barrel. There were twenty-three, just as before.

He stayed there all afternoon and was still there among the deepening shadows when Jack came in. She was pretty certain now of what he was but didn't want it confirmed – and how awful if you walked up to someone, put your hand out to see if it would go through him, and it didn't.

They had tea, and Jack, after a shy worried look in her direction, which she affected not to see, took one of the biscuits and slowly ate it. She watched. He was trying not to show how broken up he was. Poor Jack!

Twenty-two.

Later, while he sat over his chess set and the mechanical voice told him what moves he should make on its behalf, she ventured to the window and peered through. It was, very gently, raining, and the streetlights were blurred and softened. Slow cars passed, their tyres swishing in the wet. They pushed soft beams before them.

The young man stood there in the same spot. His shabby clothes were drenched and stuck to him. The felt hat was also drenched, and droplets of water had formed at the brim, on one side filled with light, a half-circle of brilliant dots.

'Mustn't it be awful,' she said, 'to be out there on a night like this and have nowhere to go? There must be so many of them. Just standing about in the rain, or sleeping in it.'

Something in her tone, which was also flat, but filled with an emotion that deeply touched and disturbed him, made the man leave his game and come to her side. They stook together a moment facing the dark wall of glass, then she turned, looked him full in the face and did something odd: She reached out towards him and her hand bumped against his ribs — that is how he thought of it: a bump. It was the oddest thing! Then impulsively, as if with sudden relief, she kissed him.

I have so much is what she thought to herself.

Next morning, alone again, she cleared away the breakfast things, washed and dried up, made a grocery list. Only then did she go to the window.

It was a fine clear day and there were two of them, alike but different; both pale and hopeless looking, thin-shoulded, unshaven, wearing shabby garments, but not at all similar in feature. They did not appear to be together. That is, they did not stand close, and there was nothing to suggest that they were in league or that the first had brought the other along or summoned him up. But there were two of them just the same, as if some *process* were involved. Tomorrow, she guessed, there would be four, and the next day sixteen; and at last – for there must be millions to be drawn on – so many that there would be no place on the lawn for them to stand, not even the smallest blade of grass. They would spill out into the street, and from there to the next street as well – there would be no room for cars to get through or park – and so it would go on till the suburb, and the city and a large part of the earth was covered. This was just the start.

She didn't feel at all threatened. There was nothing in either of these figures that suggested menace. They simply stood. But she thought she would refrain from telling Jack till he noticed it himself. Then they would do together what was required of them.

Ted Colless and David Kelly

THE LOST WORLD: SIGNS OF LIFE

Is it, by any chance, the last world? Is it the last throw of the dice? What matter, it remains, the only game in town: any way you play it makes no difference. And in these last days what is it that matters, really, but the immaterial fabric of investment that fashions this absorbing history of finality, passing bids when everything and

> All this is interesting, to excess, but also of a gloomy, black, unnerving sadness, so that one must forcibly forbid oneself to gaze too long into these abysses.
>
> – *Nietzsche*

nothing is wagered. There is no time left when all our time is occupied by the game: when there is no time to agonise, to resolve, to move, that has not already played its part. There is nothing to do when every move is already employed, contracted to the game: no need to ask where the action is when everything is animated. Apparently a stage has been reached where the game can no longer be viewed as ludicrous, where contestants and stake collapse into a singular agonistic figure whose loss entails neither martyrdom nor sacrifice, but disillusion. The tempo quickens through the trick of conjuring that figure which forestalls disillusion, ensuring that this play deals in passion. It can only be a failure of passion, a neglectful indifference, that suspends animation. Implicated in the game, however, everything acts towards the inducement of deferral which, paradoxically, putting everyone at stake, installs risk rather than allaying it. By this gambit the subject is constituted as a generation of moving differences, cast as victim to that which moves: the common and unexceptional face of crisis, the New Victim, wrought in the history of finality, phenomenalised as decadence monotonously rehearsing the end. There can be no endgame, only its deterrence stockpiling subjectivities before the burnout: it cannot be a question of the last cast of the dice – the last world, always, remains.

This new articulation of the real, executor of the critical sense of an ending, might become known as Victimality. Not an option, for there are no alternatives, nor a movement but rather an englobing tableau of passionate denunciation: the still life of

> The least miserable among them appear to be those who turn to dotage, and entirely lose their memories.
>
> – *Swift*

apocalypse. Compelled to remain in the twilight zone of

subjectivity, suspending disbelief in a homeostatic imaginary, that still discriminates. The impossible energy of particularities forestalls the inertia of massification, the absolute zero of subjectivity. When it goes to mass here it is always critical mass, the explosive dialogue of entropy and negentropy redeeming the pledge to difference before the absolution of the subject. At the stage of Victimality the agonistic exchanges will always ignite the mass in a fabulous productivity, separating and burning out its elements. A steady state of fission and displacement secures a distance for contestation, a distance miraculated on the space effected in the catastrophic dimension.

Victimality monologises these fabulous energetics, exciting the critical faculty of the burnt out case deleriating at the guilty party. A carnival of complaint, a lament without loss when every accusation confirms, the gain of the New Victim as subject, seriously undertaking its catastrophisation in fabulous and inflammatory memoirs that are no more than alibis of recollection, mnemonics of a necessary past framing a biography of grievance. But this itinerary of the subject can only hover at the brink of burn out, buying time to establish the case with the proceeds of conviction. Prior to a burnout that would render it speechless the subject is a dreary memorial to the ludic delirium of Victimality in the history of closure, sustained at its final stage as pure effect of a denunciatory mode. It's not a matter of replacing the 'cogito' with an 'accuso': for the New Victim incandesces at the horizon of accusation and only appears in protest, occasioned by the solemnity of its charge.

It is a profession of responsibility that answers to the grave urgency of the critical moment, a time-consuming but vital occupation. A generation of victims in the passionate fabric of the social. At this stage Politics – a saturation of space at the ignition of critical mass – is the last word, quickening

> It was his custom, indeed, to speak calmly of his approaching dissolution as a matter neither to be avoided nor regretted.
>
> – *Poe*

the articulation of the real, before the meltdown. As the social eventuates in the exchanges of prosecution across the critical distance a political appointment of space takes place. This dramatic appearance of Politics is the effect of its explosive inflation: everything is conditioned by relationality in this prolific and antagonistic firmament; and everything is liable to confirm the subject's assignment. The persistence of the world in its final but interminable throes is secured with this renegotiation of the social contract as pure relationality, still insistent upon the subject, always extorting vital signs in a triumph of life.

What is beyond twilight? What is beyond the monologue? This must be the zone, without qualification; the unoccupied drone, irresponsible, incommunicado. And what is beyond the horizon?

> Then I just let go and swung off into space.
>
> – *Bardin*

What could be beyond the shimmering stage of non-events, disquieting apparitions; simply the blankness of the uneventful. Delivered from accusation, what remains? Inert, immemorial, object. No longer the victimised outsider but the continuum of the insider, disillusioned, dispassionate, left alone in a world well lost. What is beyond the last world?

A moment of true feeling. A sorrow beyond words.

David Brooks

THE MISBEHAVIOUR OF THINGS

All day outside my bedroom leaves have been falling. This in itself is usual for this time of year, and does not disturb me. It is one leaf, just one – not the first to fall, but nearly the first, and not because it has fallen, or because it has not, but because in a way, it has done neither.

Outside my window this morning, after the alarm had rung, I saw it depart from its branch. The break was clear. One had no reason to suspect abnormality. But then, after the first few inches it stopped, or nearly stopped: there was at least a marked deceleration, as if it had changed its mind or the laws of gravity had been somehow suspended. Instead of increasing as it drops the rate of its fall has diminished as the day has worn on, so that now I begin to doubt whether it will reach the ground at all – so that now, when I say, as I just did, that all day outside my bedroom leaves have been falling, the statement contains another and quite different one, that all day one leaf has fallen, in a most extraordinary way.

Over and again throughout the day I have returned to it, but nothing has changed. Each time that I look through the window I can see that it has dropped further, but always a little less further than before. Everything else in the garden seems normal – or did this morning when I went out to look. Now, with all else that has happened, I'm not so sure that I would risk it.

I have been used, for a long time, to a certain unpredictable malfunction in the things around me; days when my car cuts out in mid-traffic or when pens refuse to operate at crucial moments, when a knife or razor cuts one despite all reasonable care, or a sheet of paper slices one's finger. The failure of a toilet to function properly for example, can be a shameful admonition, and a car that, parked outside while a man visits his lover, releases its brake or spontaneously starts, leaping a gutter and breaking through a neighbour's fence, can seem a most vindictive thing. But, for all that I am wont, at such times, to refer to the Malice of Inanimate Objects; this is often but tripping, stubbing one's toe against the Real, and the true causes, if I could trace them, would as likely prove to be within me as without. Such events have their purpose. Warding off complacency, guarding thus against larger neglects that might otherwise prove disastrous, they assist in a kind of balancing, and have about them a periodicity that is almost predictable. But what has been happening today – what has, I fear, only just begun to happen – is something more sinister, an abdication, an unmistakable Misbehaviour of Things.

It is not all things, mind you. Just one or two. But the number is gradually mounting. In a way, I admit, it may not be so much wilful misbehaviour as a carelessness, a lack of attention. A thing is not where I think it is – or rather, *is* there, but is also in a strange way not. I see it and it acts as if I don't, as if it isn't, or as if, somehow, *I* am not – at least, not in the way I am used to.

One mirror, one only, of all the seven in the house will not reflect me. I passed through its room with a cup in my hand and had, as I approached the far door, the unsettling feeling that something there had not been normal. It took me some moments to discover what was wrong, but soon I realised that, whenever I passed the wide, reflective surface above the sideboard, the vivid green of the lawn that it reflected – the white garden furniture, the grey paling fence – remained undisturbed, refused to acknowledge that I had walked between them. At first I thought that this was an optical illusion, some freak blind-spot in my own retina or in the arrangement of the light, but this had never happened before and the mirror's failure persisted even when I pressed my face against it. I checked my reflection in several others, and all attested my corporeal existence: the abnormality, it appears, is not in *me*, but in the thing itself.

Temporarily reassured, I spent the morning in other tasks, trying to resist like an incipient neurosis the temptation to revisit the sideboard and the bedroom window. I prepared and ate a leisurely lunch, it being Sunday, and encountered no

problem. The fillet was as rare as I intended; the salad behaved;
I could see my reflection on the knife-blade, the white rim of the
china plate. Everything proceeded normally until the wineglass. With this, however, within a very few minutes, I found
myself engaged in the strangest and least explicable tussle of
the day, a misbehaviour – if that is what it is – more subtle, more
complex than the rest.

As is my custom, in moods of particular indulgence (perhaps
this time it was consolation), I had opened a wine of my
favourite variety and region, though of a year and vineyard I'd
not tried before. On such occasions I prefer to drink after, rather
than during my meal, so that the flavour of the wine can come
to me uninterrupted and stay with me into the afternoon. My
meal finished and cleaned away I sat again at the table, poured
myself a glass and, having for a few moments savoured its
colour and bouquet, lifted it to my lips to experience what can
only be described as an abrupt hiatus, an inexplicable absence
only vaguely approximated by saying that no taste occurred,
that no wine entered my mouth. The phenomenon was
momentary, but there followed a set of astonishing transforma-
tions. I lifted the wine again, and it – the fluid – seemed to stay
where it had been, a few inches above the table, shaped as if
still contained within the glass. Attempting again, I managed at
last to taste it and, relieved that for once it seemed to behave,
took more than a sip, yet when I replaced it on the table the
level in the glass had not diminished. Intrigued, I went to lift the
glass a further time only to find that, while it appeared to be
there, surrounding its parcel of dark red fluid, my fingers
encountered only the glass-shaped wine and returned to me
wet and shiny, as if they had squeezed the grape itself. Now
wanting a draught, I did not know which part to place my hand
upon; which thing – the fluid or the glass – might next give
way; hoping that it might be the fluid, wondering, when at last
the glass and fluid came again together to my lips and again I
tasted the rich oaky fluid, that they could at the same time
remain untouched, the light on the delicate meniscus unbroken
by the slightest ripple of my presence.

Sometimes I wish that, instead of the tales of romance or
intrigue that appear so constantly on the new book stands, I
could find a Book of Ordinary Things and Gestures, that could
show us how extraordinary they really are. There is a part of me
that is dying to rush out and catch the leaf and thrust it to the
ground. There is a part of me that wants to go to my nearest

neighbours with the wineglass and beg them to witness its misbehaviour. But somehow, now, there is also a part that knows that if I were to do these things, nothing would be received, nothing would advance at all, and a gap that is here already would become only wider.

Damien Broderick

I LOST MY LOVE TO THE SPACE SHUTTLE 'COLUMBIA'

'Jane, you simply cannot marry a dog. The idea is ridiculous.'

I continued to unfold my trousseau, putting the linen neatly to one side and the silk undies to the other. With determined patience I said, 'I will brook no obstacle in this matter. I shall not be opposed.'

My mother wrung her hands, staring into the afternoon's gold glow, framed against the handsome proportions of the bedroom window. 'You always were a dreadfully wilful child, Boojum.'

'Boring, Mother. Boring. Really.' Some of the linen was from my father's new or current wife or spouse; we had not yet, in fact, established my step-parent's gender, due to the postal strike.

'It's all very well for you to take that attitude, my girl. But the fact remains that it is we who must live with the neighbours.'

I began to grow angry. 'Damn the neighbours, Mother. If I cared what the Fosters deemed proper, I should still be wearing a veil.'

'You are being hysterical, dear,' Mother told me in an etiolated tone. 'You know as well as I that you have never worn a veil in your life.'

'A figure of speech.' She can be perfectly exasperating.

'Nor a yashmak,' she said, ploughing on heedless of my raised eyes and muttered imprecations, determined to have her say, 'nor a garden hat. And I cannot imagine that this terrier gentleman –'

113

'Kelpie, Mother. Do try.'

' – this kelpie fellow is without a degree of social sensitivity of his own. Don't deny it; I know you, my girl, we might differ on some things but I trust your instincts to that extent. This dog of yours will feel uncomfortable in our circles. He will find himself expressing an interest in Mr Percy's peahens only to be misunderstood; and how will you feel about that contretemps?'

Glacially I told her, 'It is our intention to emigrate to Australia.'

Mother uttered a ferocious bray. 'I see. He's found an opening on a sheep station, then?'

'That's not even remotely funny.' I closed the lid of the heavy carved Chinese glory box, and crossed the room to the mirror. My hair had lost some of its gloss. I found part of a dry leaf tucked in near my ear and quickly crushed it between my thumb and index finger, crumbling it, letting the fragments sift to the carpet. Try as one might, running through the park is a dusty business in late October. 'There is scarcely any call on a sheep station for a theoretical nuclear physicist.'

'God forbid that I should belittle his mathematical skills. In regard to this grotesque proposal, Jane, it's clear enough to me that Bowser has calculated to a nicety –'

Seething, I let my brush fall to the floor and turned on her, cheeks so flushed I could feel their heat. 'His name is Spot, Mother, as you know. I will *not* have –' My breast heaved; all the words whirled in my brain. 'As you know because we have conducted this tedious argument sufficiently often and with such a plethora of redundancy that I am heartily sick of it.' I looked around blindly for the brush, took up a silver-backed comb instead. Mother held her tongue but I was not appeased. I watched her reflection. 'Bitch,' I muttered.

She gave a satirical snort, and left the room. I could have kicked myself.

I was not totally without sympathy for her qualms, though I'd have died before admitting so. On the other hand I judged her objections fundamentally reactionary. In this age of moonshots and dime-store hand calculators, it seemed to me not merely ignoble but rather trite to find some course of action offensive simply because it was not hallowed by family tradition.

The fact is, Spot is the brightest dog I have ever met. He entered college under a special program, endowed by the Chomsky Institution, and was a wild fellow, made for poetry

and drinking all night, and the theatre. He swiftly discerned
that culture as such is problematical, over-determined, quixotic,
that its appeal is essentially to the intellectually lightweight. He
dabbled in painting for a time, creating a small stir with his
innovative brush stroke. But it was the endless wonder of
science which spoke to his heart of hearts, and led to his
specialising first in chemistry and finally in the application of
Sophus Lie's groups to that previously intractable poser, the
'periodic table' of elementary particles and their resonances.
Much of his work was awfully abstruse and beyond my modest
attainments, yet Spot retained a sense of primal joy in his
assault on the universe. One might come out into the yard with
a bone from the table (for he was then living at our house under
an exchange arrangement) and find him gazing raptly at the
moon, his lips parted, inflamed with an innocent intoxication so
much purer than his raunchy nights backstage with the Royal
Shakespeare Company. I was struck then, fondly, by his ardent,
wistful expressions, like Carl Sagan's. Any comparison I might
make, however, is bound to be misleading. I'd never met
anyone, man or woman, who affected me so piercingly. Before I
knew it, I was head over heels in love with a dog, and I am prepared to confess that at first I was just as astonished and taken
aback by this discovery as was my dear bitter mother a few
months later when Spot went in to announce our intentions.

I suspect that what brought Mother around in the end was
the flamboyant song and dance my father laid on when the
word reached him in Hollywood, or wherever the banal
location was where he was shooting his latest depredation. My
desire to marry he found innately disagreeable, as who would
not who had entered that singular state fourteen times, yet
Randy discerned a redemptive quality in my choice of spouse.

'Just so long as it's not one of those godawful boys next door,
sweetie,' he told me when the company finally had the
telephone lines operating in the correct manner.

'He's nice,' I said in the high light voice with a giggle at the
corners of it that I use with Randy when I want something out
of him. 'You'll like him. Tee hee.'

'Ah, your laugh's a tonic, Jinny.' He paused and became very
serious. 'Just assure me on one score, sweetie. I can appreciate
his interest in quantum mechanics, but I must be certain . . . he
doesn't bite, does he?'

Strange question, from the father you love. Dote on. When
you're trying to con him. (His wife was in fact, it had

eventuated, a woman, though only just. Had the rules of entry been a hair more stringent, she might easily have graced the hippo category. Still.) After all, it wasn't as if Spot had rabies. I decided to treat the matter as a rather coarse attempt by Papa to protect his pocketbook while pretending at levity: i.e. that by 'bite' he was employing the demotic locution for 'seek undue financial advantage through abuse of personal connections'.

Coolly, therefore, I told my father, 'He has money of his own these days. His work on the correction of pitting in nuclear power containment vessels has brought us a comfortable stipend from Con Ed and certain other sizeable corporations.' No need to tell Randy everything. 'Rest assured, Daddy. He won't bite you.'

'No, no, nothing like that,' my father said, 'perfectly all right. No, pet, it's just that in that case I hope his quark is not worse than his bite.' And the terrible man began to shout and shriek with mirth at his own excruciating silliness. Marcia must have told him about quarks, because I know for certain that Randy is no intellectual giant. His talents lie instead in the direction of making money, large amounts of which he expended to make my wedding the happiest day of my life.

Spot rose to his feet at the reception, lurching more than somewhat, and replied to the toast. The cantors smiled, and the mullahs, and the officiating Cardinal applauded, with all his enclave of nuns and monks and a brace of castrati if I'm not in error.

'Acknowledgements,' cried my husband, who had been smoking.

'We wish to thank the musicians. All that sawing and smiting, bowing and puffing and groaning, and why? Why, only to soothe the guests into gaiety. Here we go. Lift those ankles and prance.

'The magicians. Tumbling, whipping endless purple, red, gold scarves through the spanking musical air, glorious. Fowls from eggs, great tails lofting under the high crystal-broken whiteness, green feathers, hard green, soft green. Sawn in half. Out of large bolted brass-and-leather boxes, proven empty moments earlier. Sheer magic. Good work, team.

'Some people find the libretto obscure. Not us. We're polyglot. And grateful for the poet's drawn face and crabbed manner and song, song.

'Who else? The lighting people, sure. Beams like harsh metal poles furring, fogging where they splash into astonishing scales of peals of tinkles of gongings of lightning blue, satin pinks, crimsons, purples, and all the whites, and the rest.

'There's food on every table, here and there in silver porcelain wooden platters slipping from plates into bowls of dip and sauces laid on the tables and marble waiting surfaces: birds, slabs of crusty meat oozing juice, the moon curves of mandarins, oranges, grapefruit, the gold and purple of passionfruit, slimy on the tongue but cut by tart, and tarts all slithery in berries and apricots, pale peaches with sugar crusting, melting cliffs of eggwhite meringue. So here's one for the chef, the cooks and helpers, the serving staff. Good eating, no doubt, no question there.

'The vintners fetched wine fit to make you drunk, smooth on the tongue and rufous, rough as dog's rasp at some abdominal cavity which finds gentility a bore, but fairly innocent of histamines, thank Christ. We'll drink a round to you lads, gladly.

'Company. The guests. Did your bit, swarmed about, chattered and nattered, and spoke in adopted accents and bellyached just enough that we'd know you were taking the business seriously and giving no quarter out of love of Randy and Joan and the lovely lass herself.'

The microphone made spattering noises from this point on, for Spot was salivating with delirious stoned intensity, laughing his fool head off and biting from moment to moment at his own flanks. Bruce Garbage (the punk crooner whom Randy had flown in from San Antonio) tried valiantly to wrest away command of the public address system, but was clearly in terror of having his leather Savile Row suit nipped. Balked, he brought up his fists and swung them down in the gesture which was later to be featured on the cover of *Time*, and his ensemble seized up their instruments once more and heaved themselves into a bout of interactive slam dancing. I was keeping my eye on the mullahs, and at last caught one furtively quaffing a small but wickedly illicit potation. When he found my eye on him he hoisted his skirts and scurried around the table, which was a happy ploy as it turned out; both castrati had passed out, sliding completely from their seats to lie curled like delicious pussycats beneath the wedding table. The guilty mullah did what he could to ease their discomforts.

And the sun poured down like honey and all the wild meadows of my body ran with long-eared hares and does and quail for my love to chase and bring down in his soft, sharp mouth, and my soul bobbed like a woolly cloud, all my education rising from my loins to the choking of my throat with my breasts all perfume yes and yes I said yes I will Yes.

'Arf,' said Spot, forgetting himself.

I felt equally rueful, as you might imagine, when the gentlemen from the government called by to announce that we might not emigrate after all. Their arguments were Byzantine and sturdily documented with sheafs of paper each of a different unusual size. Their case for refusing our exit gave every indication of hinging on Spot's deficiencies as a human being, a bigoted and unpopular stance; carefully masked, therefore, by technicalities of a veterinarian nature. It quickly came home to me that these machinations in turn were intended to deflect attention from the true reason for our durance, namely, Spot's peerless gifts as a nuclear theoretician. The government wanted my husband to make bombs for them.

'It's the diquark hypothesis,' he told me. We had no secrets from one another. Although I wasn't certain that I followed him in every detail, it seemed that rather big bangs could be caused from rather small amounts of fairly rare stuff using another variety of extremely unlikely fizzy material, which failed to add up to zero when you checked the niobium spheres.

Father interceded at once, bless him. An entire battery of lawyers worked around the clock with the opposite numbers in the Administration. Randy had lost his entrée to the Pentagon, unfortunately, following the release of that film.

Possibly with a view to comforting me, Mother called by. She patted my hand. 'Rover will be just fine, you'll see.'

I kicked her ankle. She hobbled out.

For some days we hid out in a Lina Wertmüller festival. Without disrespect I must reveal that she is not my ideal *auteur*, but Spot always made taking in a movie fun, and I was terrifically excited when he told me how much I had always put him in mind of Mariangela Melato, whom Lina employed with some wit.

'Hang in there, baby,' Randy told me from the West coast, his voice oddly interspersed by bleats of telemetry from the space shuttle mission. 'We'll have the kid back on the bomb bay floor by New Year.' For a fleeting moment I wondered if father's lawyers had misunderstood the quandary facing my husband, and were in fact directing the enormous resources of the studio to the task of getting Spot into rather than out of the weapons research program. Such things had been known to happen.

To relax, we stayed in Daddy's apartment in Washington Heights, and strolled every day to The Cloisters to view the Unicorn Tapestries, for which I have an abiding passion. So sad and limpid. Spot put his ears back and growled, which made me reconsider. The high point of the day, its unmitigated delight, was our romp through Fort Tryon Park, where one step carries you from endless megalopolitan Upper West Side to genuine woods, and a further five minutes shows you the Hudson. By this time the shores were past their highest colours, but reds burned like coals in the midst of all the turning hues of green and yellow and russet. I say unmitigated, but in all honesty I must grant that I never relished the business with pooper-scooper and leash. Joan had given us an elaborate device with plastic bags and a heat-sealer, a sentimental relic of our squashed poodle Phiphi, but while that was to be preferred to the fold of ScotTowel favoured in the Heights it never seemed to me altogether dignified. One was forced to admit, though, that the menacing glances of elderly folk walking their own Dobermans and Borzoi, pan or towel dutifully in hand, were ample deterrent to a more insouciant delinquency.

On the evening of our last day together, Spot and I ventured into Puerto Rican midtown. Drug dealers conveyed their wares and their opinions to others of their kind on every corner. Dilapidated French restaurants struggled to sustain identity and solvency on one in every four of these corners. Young men struggled past us under the load of their gigantic quadrophonic portable sound systems. Spot danced with pleasure; this milieu was not alien to his roots. It pleased him to strut beside me, a street-wise kelpie in Hell's Kitchen.

'Ghetto blasters,' he told me, as one kid bopped past in a drench of Cuban pop. The acoustic values were extraordinary. 'Third world briefcase,' he said with a yip of amusement. The Walkman craze had not yet reached the *barrio*; it seemed to me that these unfortunates needed the combined benefits of conspicuous consumption and enhanced personal presence. A news report roared in our ears, simulcast from two swarthy youths passing us in opposite directions, creating a disturbing illusion of dopplered spin. Whining abruptly, Spot crouched with his ears pricked, swinging his head from side to side in a manner which recalled (I say with some shame) the mascot on His Master's Voice recordings.

'Los astronautas Joe Engle y Richard Truly visitaron ayer el trasborador espacial *Columbia* y dijeron que todo luce "bellisimo" y en perfecto estado para el lanzamiento de mañana,' the reporter said rapidly, 'siempre que el tiempo lo permita.'

My breast became suffused with awful foreboding. I had seen that look in Spot's eye before, under a dust of stars hurled into heaven with a mad jeweller's abandon.

'Space,' he cried. 'Boojum, the final frontier.'

'Please don't call me that,' I begged him, down on my knees on the broken, urine-dank sidewalk, arms about his straining neck. 'If you must employ a diminutive, I much prefer "Jinny".'

'The spirit bloweth whither it listeth,' said my husband as he quivered and shivered in the ephiphany of his hunger, and I knew that I had lost him at last, lost to the call of the wild.

Patrick Cook

NOT THE NEWS

THE SCENE: High on a verdant, parrot-infested mountain situation squats the presidential palace of Il Bistro del los Americanos, the verdant, parrot-infested, blood-spattered fiefdom described by President Crockett as ' . . . the last place south of the border where you can get a real hometown situation McDuffburger with just the right amount of cheese'. Deep in the high-tech dungeon random peons are writhing under the bastinado, screaming as their cartilage is systematically smashed with iron bars; contorting at the voltage applied to their genitals.

Enter a proud General Porcaramba and his distinguished guest.
    Barry Ullage: Nice place you got here.
    Porcaramba: *Si*, tiny fat gringo weeth garbage can wedged on shoulders. *Muy* nice. *Muy* quiet.
    Barry Ullage: These people must be terrorists.
    Porcaramba: But of course. Why else would they be here? Think carefully before the answer, hey?
    Barry: Some of them want to come to Australia.
    Porcaramba: *Si*. That is how we know they are terrorists.
    Barry Ullage: Just as I thought. They laughed at me once, you know.
    Porcaramba: People can be very cruel.
    Exit stepping over National Guardpeons dicing for clothes.

Have you ever tried to clear a blocked effluent conduit,

rolling up the sleeve, plunging in the arm up to the shoulder and scooping out unmentionable coagulations, only to find a further excrescence, putrescent, nasty and brown, just around the U-bend?

So it is when attempting to follow the thought processes of the glabrous Mr Ullage through the plumbing of the body politic. Still smarting from the refusal of the Government to extend de facto expenses to day trips around Queanbeyan, still unable to alert the community to the terrible threat posed to civilisation by the opening of the Beige Peacock Yum Cha Emporium in downtown Launceston, the malodorous little oik has turned his porcine gaze to the main chance offered by the arrival of refugees from Porcaramba and others of that ilk.

It is wearisome to reflect, as we must, on previous litters of Ullages, standing squatly on the appropriate headland with large misspelled banners demanding Irish Go Home, soapboxing a mob to secure the immediate lynching of the Tolpuddle Martyrs, scrawling anti-Jewish slogans along the wharves by moonlight. He really missed his calling, there, the incumbent Ullage.

How easy it is to see the well-suited carpetbagger, lights glinting from the snug-fitting refuse container under a massive candelabra as he clinks a bumper of Krug or two, with a Ribbentrop or two, toasts the lawful government of his hosts, deplores the anti-social elements which the Germans are forced to tidy up and assures every uniform in sight that this riff-raff will not sully his Antipodean breed.

Unhappily, the Ullages of the parish are as ignorant of history as they are of irony. So, apparently is Lord Peacock, who is yet to learn that even in an age of television he is more likely to be judged by the cabal he keeps than by the little man who came over in '38, was it? from Poland or somesuch? and who hand-tailors his socks.

HOME
AND
ABROAD

Barbara Brooks

SUMMER IN SYDNEY

The time. When you're not working, the days stretch and float. Swimming in the mornings, reading in the afternoons, going out to restaurants at night. Getting up late and reading the paper. What day is it, and what do I have to do? People come and go, from London, Tennant Creek, Brisbane. Postcards and letters slide under the door.

Summer heat passes over quickly, wilting the garden but leaving some corners of the house untouched. At the beginning of summer it rained a lot.

The unemployed could go on beach crawls, all summer. But couldn't afford the trimmings. We sit around all morning eating croissants and watermelon in gentrified poverty, and go to Bronte at two in the afternoon. By then the sun has gone. There's a storm, hailstones drop out of a green sky. We put ice down each other's backs and shelter under the eaves of the dressing shed. The water is a kind of oily grey with a strip of sunlight along the horizon. All summer long the water is cold; the currents flow in from out in the Pacific, where the French exploded their bomb.

In Europe, it's the new ice age, not to be confused with the new cold war. In Scotland, a man is found with his lips frozen to his car; he was blowing into the doorlocks to thaw them. Peter's plane froze to the ground in Manchester for three days at 27 below. Here in the southern hemisphere this doesn't make sense, but we have already agreed that staying sane fifty per cent of the time is a good average. Down at Bronte on Friday afternoon, we take his jetlag for an airing; it floats in green water, along with a faint slick of suntan oil and the soft touch of well being, or is it cold water? We eat pies and hot dogs and the sun turns us pink and happy:

A postcard from Italy: We're in smog-clouded Venice, but Marian thinks it's Vienna (we must go to the opera). This is the rapid transit method of seeing Europe, concerned with: railway timetables, hot showers, art galleries, cheap restaurants, what day of the week is it and where do we go to keep warm? Culture comes by osmosis; we drift across Europe as the clouds gather – smog, snow, fear? A limited nuclear war for America, he said as we sat at the dinner table, could mean total devastation for Europe. Another glass of wine? What's the rage in Paris and London? Cocaine, herpes, the economic malaise; two million in anti-nuclear marches.
In the supermarket of Europe
what exotica they buy,
the travellers, like the Cruise missiles,
flying high.

We make love, joined at mouth, breast, genitals. I like to think of a circle, bodies looped and joined, continuity I guess. It comes in waves, like water. Afterwards our bodies are at rest, solid, still, still joined together, while our minds drift on the silver cord that ties them to us, and everything is quiet. Then somebody knocks on the door, and we get up and go downstairs.

We swim at Camp Cove on Saturday evening. There's a man on the beach with a metal detector, picking up the debris of affluence – ringpulls from cans, mostly, and the odd gold watch. I bought it for the kids, he says, they never use it but it's paid for itself. The lighthouse is flashing on South Head, and the fishermen are out with the mosquitoes; down below green water turns white around the rocks. We look across to Manly highrise, and back to the city. It's so quiet here, but the city is full of friction. I can close my eyes any night and see a dirt road lined with gum trees, any one of the roads I have driven or been driven along. When you came in through the heads for the first time, what did you think? Back in your past, you talk about the badlands: gold and uranium in the bluffs and buttes, Indian villages on top of them. MX missiles in the tunnels underground. There's a cannon on the cliffs along here, aimed at a paling fence. We grew up in a temporary lull, a period of relative calm and affluence.

Coming back to this country, coming back to your past, the first thing you notice is the size of the sky. Huge, open, clear as a bell, full of a hard metallic light. The country unrolls under the wing of the plane for hours and the travellers shift in their seats, preparing to arrive. Emptied out onto the tarmac in the heat, they waver, then head for the terminal. The duty-free whisky falls out of the SIA bag and breaks on the terminal floor. Watching faces separate out; coming home. Hanging on the fringes of things, backs to the mountains, everyone lives near the sea, waiting to make a getaway when the tide, or history, turns. That empty beach we took with us as our emotional refuge has gone; L.J. Hooker or the Japanese? On the east coast it's sunrise over the water through the palm trees, on the west coast it's sunset; and this summer, the blacks come to Canberra to argue their land claims. Red rocks, heat and dust, uranium mines and tailings dams; white perspex domes sending messages back to . . . Do you want to be the centre of attention? Pine Gap puts us on the map.

The tourists lie on beaches in the Deep North; nothing has entered their dreams except the smell of coconut oil and the taste of warm salt water. The B52s touch down in Darwin and fly over North Queensland on their training runs. Brown bodies roll over all the way down the east coast and the sound of planes is drowned out by hundreds of transistors playing rock music. The DJ says, it's the Clash! the B52s.

The moon is a fish that swims underwater in the daytime. A highly intelligent silver jewfish, swimming from one side of the sky to the other. What is the moon? Something that goes down, in the dark, and is forgotten. In the morning there will be blue hills round the rim.

We are just mooning around this summer, swimming through the weather like fish.

In Brisbane, it's 35 degrees in the shade, and we're flat on our backs. We lie around all day, and get up for the action at 5 in the afternoon. We sit on the verandah and make desultory conversation. Muggy, isn't it? Feels like a storm. We watch the storm pass, listen to rain on the iron roof, try to tell the difference between the sound of toads and frogs. Do you know that smell that comes from the backyard after rain? This is the edge of the storm, somewhere there are high winds, and as usual the power goes off. We sit on the verandah while it gets dark. The electricity workers have a rolling strike against anti-union legislation. Should have gone to the drive-in, Lloyd says, and goes out to the fridge for a beer. We eat fish and chips, drink beer, light mosquito coils, turn the radio on and off. Lloyd goes inside to read the paper by kerosene lamp. We crack nuts by torchlight, sitting on the back steps, and boil the kettle on the Primus. The lights are back on in the morning and so is the heat. The grass is two inches longer. At 5 in the afternoon it's cool enough to start the mower. Dozens of little grasshoppers decamp from long wet grass.

'The last I heard of Julie she was in an ashram, I thought she looked OK. I can't talk to her about it; it's one of those circular things where everything is explained by a belief that can't be explained. She says it's not the way for everyone, but it is for her.' There are posters at the Oxford Street bus stops saying 'He sees God', and the graffiti underneath says, but only when he's drunk, or, and he smokes Marlboro. 'I will consider anything – acupuncture, yoga, herbal tea – but it must have a rational basis.' Rationality is only half of it; there is nothing to be counted on as a prop. 'I said, you know there is nothing to believe in that justifies the mind suspending its questions, but even so you are always slipping up.' We came out of the church after the wedding, someone was playing the flute. There were white moths around the cabbages in the market gardens, and flies around our faces. We were thinking about love.

The way change happens, it's more like a slow sliding than anything you can put your finger on.

Peter is driving through the hot flat country of western New South Wales in an old Holden with a blanket over the seat and uncertain brakes. Heading for Adelaide, Washington, London and the political life again. We were sitting in the pub looking at brochures on Tahiti. What's happening in Australia? It's hard to find out in summer, seasonal adjustment. The other night, when the heat got worse than the mosquitoes, we went out to sit in the garden; and a voice from the dark on the other side of the table said, summer is a good time for a coup, no one would come back from the beach for anything. The first day of the trip your mind keeps racing, but after that the thoughts begin to untangle.

On the wall of the Casablanca Furniture Factory, over the road from the pub, someone has written: The workers united will never be defeated, and some intellectual has changed it to 'would'. The TAA posters along Moore Park Road have a woman in a bikini on a beach with the caption: Worker's compensation. Ripped off all year, and fucked on holiday. Everyone is reading a novel called *History*.

'I have this feeling that everything is irrelevant, and I'm falling apart at the seams. Don't know if it's objective historical circumstance, some life crisis, lack of sleep or the weather. I wish it would pass, it's disturbingly convincing to experience.' It does, and you're off to the bush with friends, kids, bottles of white wine, to lie on air mattresses in the dam and wait for the cool change. You could always go bush and you might find out you were right; summer is a good time of year. Later, surrounded by books and papers, empty coffee cups: 'It's beginning to make sense'.

There are the floating mornings, and the times at the end of the day when the light changes and the cicadas start, and someone has a radio on, very quietly, so that the sound fades in and out; outside of this sometimes things fail to connect. Sometimes it helps if you stop reading the papers, but even that is a kind of addiction, and it depends what you do for a living. Five days on Stradbroke and you find yourself after the morning swim waiting for the *Courier Mail*; after a few weeks I guess you'd stop worrying, a mind full of salt and blue glaze.

Jane is in the kitchen, insulting us the way only an astrologer can, tracing the planets over our heads. She's written a song about the economic cycle and sings us the chorus: it goes boom depression boom depression boom boom BOOM.

It's the middle of the night in Annandale, dogs barking, someone trying to start a car. We are lying in bed in a weatherboard house, like frozen moments in the yellow room. You are talking about conspiracy theories (What really happened in 1975?) and while I listen I can hear beyond you what the body and the heart say, the old harmony, mystery, short-circuiting logic; there are these moments when you put out your hand and nothing is said but everything is there. In the morning the room seems familiar, there are noises like a tin roof creaking in the heat. You wake up and ask, did you have any dreams? Then you go downstairs and bring the papers, oranges, cups of tea. I am standing at the window, but nothing outside has any significance; I am still interior, and the shape of the room protects me. Did you know this window has a flaw in it, like water?

Do you remember, when you were a child, watching dust moving in the bits of sun that came into a dark room? I used to think about atoms and electrons, stars and moons, other worlds. There always seems to be another door opening. Often, it seems, we go through it alone.

At the State Emergency Service, they have pamphlets: what to do in case of nuclear attack. Don goes to classes at the SES, but all he can tell me is that when it's about to happen we should head for the hills. We are standing in Woolworths at the time, I notice philodendrons, parlour palms, weeping figs, ferns, a spider plant in a teapot on special. I can hear a rumbling, but it's only the trains underneath us in Town Hall Station.

Apart from the new ice age, and the new cold war, there's the New Age. Down the road in Darlinghurst there's the Satprakash Meditation Centre, where they say, don't just do something, sit there. When the mind stops its questions, this is Nirvana. Is this worth serious consideration? This was the summer the orange people moved in, or out; the bagwash is orange, terracotta and red, and the colours are all down Oxford Street, the vegetarian restaurant, the boutique, the orange vegetable trucks, the building teams. Bhagwan is in trouble again, the Rolls is bogged in the Oregon mud. This was the summer Billy Graham asked us to forgive Richard Nixon because he didn't know what he was doing, and several people renounced Christianity in its more obvious forms. There's the

Natural Healing and Personal Development Centre and a galaxy of delights for mind and body, colour therapy, yoga, massage with exotic oils, psychotheraphy for the mind subject to pressure. It's possible that even here there will be therapy sessions where you can articulate your fears about nuclear war and 'come to terms' with them. Meanwhile you might be cut off the dole. You can buy tapes of dolphins and whales, pay to change your posture, major in Zen, donate money to save the rainforests. Over the road there are books that will change your life. Is this part of the process of evolutionary change, or just a momentary confusion? This is the street of Middle Class Fantasies. It's just near the bus stop, and St Vincent de Paul is over the road. It's the street of All Australian boys, party drugs, gay bars and coffee houses. There isn't a decent supermarket for miles. Something is wrong but you're not quite sure what. Sometimes it occurs to us, like a kind of bad dream, that we live in the shadow of war and can't do anything about it. 'So you think you can tell/Heaven from hell/Blue skies from pain . . .' Are we being conned again?

Tomorrow will be full of possibilities. You can ring up work and say you're sick, drink cafe latte at the Roma, cut off your jeans, take the kids to the park.

Down in George Street, the story is the sound of cash registers, the relatively innocent rustling of paper and money, as the crowds come and go, looking for something to justify the occasion. Money leaps out of your purse like a fish every time you open it, this time of year. Christmas is the silly season; office parties, flights home, cases of mangoes, hams and turkeys. It's late night shopping, the Thursday before Christmas week, Myers' windows full of animated fairy tales, just like the newspapers; somewhere above all this the moon slides through a sky the colour of deep water.

And so you say, this is the political life, faint light at the end of the tunnel, and what can I say I have accomplished? There are moments when I think how happy I am, in a car going down the hill to the beach, then the muffler falls off and everything changes. 'We don't live in isolation; the relationships between people can be just or unjust, on the smallest scale or the largest.'

While we are down at the beach that afternoon, in Brisbane it's several degrees hotter, he's working in the sun all day, and when he comes in something happens; something stops functioning for a moment and an inconsistency spreads through the veins and the muscles. Something shifts; it happens quickly and is out of control. Does it make any sense? It's been a hard life, someone without money has to make his body and his strength his capital, working from early in the morning till late at night, seven days a week at times. Some people act on the world, with others you can see they could be crushed. But the heart goes on. What do we know about the heart? When we were twenty we thought the answer was to love someone and make them happy; stuck with love and rebellion for several years we wondered why it didn't work the way we expected. One, we were women, trying to change. Two, we were gullible. Three, we had no context that made any sense – not that you can ask for one.

Inside the train, there are small sleeping compartments. The nightlights are faintly blue, and the sheets on the bunks are starched and ironed. The train goes into a mountain and comes out on the other side and we have crossed a border; we wouldn't have known, that feeling of being stretched tight between different things comes and goes, at random it seems. The landscape passes: still water, rain, paddocks with cows, and houses with lighted windows, empty platforms on country stations, then factories and railway yards. Coming into the city late at night, we've lost the moon, it was somewhere over to the left just before.

At Palm Beach at 6 in the evening there are people playing football, flying kites, rolling around on the sand in an inner tube. We wonder if they're Christians; very few people hang around in large groups looking lively these days. They don't come from Darlinghurst. But we're tourists ourselves. The water is warm, and there's very little undertow, but there's a slight drift north. Half an hour ago when we went into the water the swimmers were south of us, now they're right in front. In another hour or so they might all disappear behind Barrenjoey into the mouth of Broken Bay, shouting and laughing, while we have moved over to the Pittwater side of the peninsula, and are eating chips and drinking beer, watching the windsurfers and the sun going down behind West Head. This is the life.

This was the summer of early rain, when the roof leaked in two places after the storm. The paper dropped on the doorstep every morning and it all went on, Poland, Ronald Reagan, the nuclear buildup, the blackouts. Everywhere we went someone was listening to the cricket. So what's the story? What's the deal? There were stories, political thrillers with speculative endings, love stories with whatever is a happy ending now – they decided to live together, or separately, he left, she became a feminist, they agreed who would have the kids. There was a revolution, a coup, a large amount of US aid, a 'free election'. This is just what happened; the plots are all different now. Forget the moon; those little lights in the sky were Air America, shuttling money between here and Hong Kong.

Some of this is already in the head. There were times when the mind drifted, weightless, in certain moments, the slanting light in the afternoons, the long blue evenings. We had a good time, mostly, then we packed it in and went back to work. The pages fill with names and 'facts' and the pile of newsprint grows in the corner; there is no one thing that will tell you, but we wait for something still under the surface that meets inbetween the words. When we touch each other we imagine that we are part of something, but still whole on our own. Do you feel my history, and its tricks, when you run your hand over my skin? Sometimes we don't understand, sometimes we do but it's not quite possible to speak or act directly out of it. 'It may not be as clear as you wanted, but it's there.' Say it: this is what we are, this is what is going on.

Ron Blair

McBride's List

These days the managements of theatres prefer a small cast and my cast was small: four – five if you count the housekeeper. And Florence, a small city, is not a small set. The theatre's play reader will smile and say, 'I'm afraid your story is really a film. Besides what about all those extras, the people wandering the streets?' But despite the set, what happened on the Via Soderini was not cinema, but theatre.

One should always travel alone in a foreign country. All the senses are sharpened and appetite is pitched against uncertainty. That tip you gave, that handful of coin which was weighing you down but won you only a snarl of disgust you later learn will buy the recipient fully the left eye of a sardine; to make up for it you give a waiter, later that day, a tip in another denomination which – to judge by his smothered surprise – was enough to pay your hotel bill for a week. In the market place you ask for a piece of fruit but clearly use the wrong word, or pronounce it wrongly, and the woman's look tells you that if her husband were still alive or if his brothers were real men, you would not be still standing there grinning like a fool.

Trains plunge through mountainsides or wind you around coastlines of unimaginable beauty. Gradually, you have lived so long without words one day you hear people approaching you, tourists like yourself, but speaking in an extraordinary way. It's a whistling, twittering, dental, spitting tongue, a language bent on breakage by saliva. Ah! Then you know it at last. You have been so long alone that even good mongrel English sounded absolutely foreign for thirty seconds.

To hear your own language and not know it, even for thirty seconds, was a shock. To walk past a former mistress, once so held and prized, and not know her would be as great a cause for dismay. It was then I took out the list of names McBride had given me when I left Australia.

'I was taking some stills for a travel commercial,' he said, 'and I met some nice women. If you feel like it, look them up. They all speak English.'

'Pronto,' said Gabriella, in that curious way Italians have of giving every telephone conversation particular urgency. I told her McBride suggested I ring. McBride, the Australian photographer. Australian. Photographs. Yes, visiting Florence. Here now, yes.

I was to go around there straight away. Did I understand? Straight away. I had no idea McBride had such a way with his ladies.

A short walk along the river – Dante's cursed and unlucky ditch – and I was outside Gabriella's boutique which sold very smart modern furniture, exactly the sort of high-tech stuff to catch McBride's eye. I leaned on the heavy glass door and made it move inwards. The two women looked up.

'Gabriella?'

One of the women stood. Tall, skinny, good looking, well dressed.

'Mac-bride!'

Before I could say more she swept towards me, wound her arms around me and kissed me on each cheek.

'Caro,' she whispered, 'you have been so long away.'

Mistaken identity has a long and honourable history in the theatre. Perhaps like the twin brother in *Twelfth Night* I would be swept off to sudden marriage by a delicious mistake. The only trouble was that I looked nothing like McBride. He is small and balding and has eyes like a bull. He had a moustache then, I a full complement of facial fur. My head is long, McBride's like a cannon ball. Didn't her hand, now touching my ear, remember?

'Nicola,' she turned to her friend, 'this is the famous Australian photographer Mac-bride.'

Nicola had heard so much about me. Was I in Firenze to take more photographs? Or purely pleasure? Gabriella told Nicola that in my case pleasure and work could not be distinguished because what I did for pleasure worked miracles for others. I took photographs and as if by magic, people came from all over the world to buy her beautiful things.

There was such teasing and laughter, such warmth. And it was wonderful to speak in English again and about things that weren't to do with menus and train fares and hotel bills.

Then Gabriella turned to me and asked:

'You have brought the photographs with you?'

Now was the time to tell her.

'The ones you took when you were here last time?' she asked.

'Gabriella, I'm afraid – '

'You are afraid?'

'No. I mean – there has been some mistake. A misunderstanding.'

'You did not bring the photographs?'

'No. You are mistaken.'

'Mis-taken?' She said the word through an etymological mist.

'I am not McBride. I told you on the telephone. I am a friend of his. Another Australian.'

At dusk in Florence the shutters on all the shop windows come down with a clatter curfewing all the boutiques and show-rooms. I was not McBride. The shutter came down.

'Ah,' she said lightly, 'all you Australians are so handsome it is difficult to tell one from the other.'

Nicola gave a quick pout of sympathy. As far as Gabriella was concerned, it was dusk for all Australians. The most tactful thing I could do was to turn into twilight and disappear. Pronto.

On stage, it is sometimes an amusing problem to see how two characters can get rid of a third, particularly if that third is an insensitive lump. The restriction is simple: no force can be used. I took a seat and smiled.

'You sell beautiful things.'

'Would you like a coffee?' asked Gabriella.

She lifted the phone and ordered three coffees from a cafe nearby.

'Why are you in Firenze?' asked Nicola.

I told her that as a tourist, I was there to see the usual things. It was a beautiful city. She shrugged off the platitude. I smiled vacantly at them and nodded. Then the two women switched to fast Italian, shuttling the sounds between each other. As they spoke, each one looked at her own image as it was reflected in the black glass which made a near wall of the shop. Nicola corrected a recalcitrant curl while Gabriella cast a long look into her own face, poised before the gleaming wall waiting, as it were, for a sacred prediction, an utterance from an obsidian sibyl.

A neighbourhood handmaiden brought the coffee into the temple and placed the tray discreetly near the chief priestess. Each of us in silence tore open the sachets of sugar and in silence stirred it in. Only the sound of lips and gullets broke the silence as we each drank.

I finished mine first. After replacing my cup I moved to a more comfortable chair, a deep leather number with buttons concealed in the armrest, the kind you find on planes. One of the buttons made the chair move in whispering circles. Another tipped me back and a leather pad shot out to take my feet. By pushing several buttons at once, I found the chair both circled and bucked. Then the chair itself began to move across the floor.

'What is your work?' asked Gabriella, trying to conceal her panic.

'Theatre,' I shouted from the far end of the shop. I managed to make the chair turn back but could not somehow control its wretched bucking.

'There is no theatre in Firenze. You will have to go to Prato.' Gabriella caught up with me and pushed a button. The chair stopped. 'In Prato there is much theatre.'

'This is a great chair. I could spend all day in it.'

All day! Gabriella seized the phone and began dialling. In the taut seconds before her call was answered, she quickly searched her profile in the black glass wall for signs of distress. She began speaking. In the torrent of Italian I managed to pick up 'Australian' and 'theatre' and then the word 'young'. Then she slowed down. She was creating an image for someone. Because she was speaking so carefully, so temptingly, so caressingly, it was easy to hear the word: 'belissimo'. Then she was listening. So was I.

'Si . . . si . . . si . . . molto giovane . . . un bel'uomo.'

I was young then, but not very young, and whatever else I was, handsome I was not. Not anywhere and especially not in Italy. Gabriella smiled as she hung up. She looked over at me.

'There is a woman who knows all about the theatre. She loves the theatre. She would like to see you.'

Nicola handed her a pen and as she wrote, she continued speaking. 'This is her address. You will go there straight away.

She waits for you.'

Gabriella wrapped my hand around the piece of paper and her fingers pressed urgently.

'Go now. She wants you. She is very beautiful and very rich.'

Then I was out in the street. So that's how you get rid of people! I looked at the paper in my hand. It simply read: 'Contessa Barbardori – Palazzo Barbardori – Via Barbardori.'

I had been on the road for months and in all kinds of cities and towns. My retinas were bruised with cupolas and chapels. Today, I had had something like a conversation. With this paper in my hand, there was a good chance I might have two conversations in the one day. All I had to do was cross the Arno and knock on a door.

Knocking was pointless. The main door was huge but there was a smaller one within it and while the big door had a knocker, it was made for the days when giants walked the earth: eight feet up was a lion's head with an iron ring in its metal mouth. The smaller studded wooden door had an electric button. I pushed it.

After a time, the door opened the width of an eye. I announced my name and that I had an appointment with the Contessa. The eye was revealed to belong to a stubby, abrupt woman who, with a brisk gesture, beckoned me inside. She closed the door behind me and regarded me again without a smile. As she walked off, she indicated I should follow her. Her gesture was not quite one which might be used for a dog.

Few people, it appears, guard so jealously their private luxury as do the Florentines. From the outside, their palaces look grim fortresses built as they were to resist determined soldiery or a vengeful mob. Inside, music. The floor of the entrance room was covered with the largest Persian carpet in the world and on it were arranged an assortment of large trees which grew in pots, reaching up to the skylight twenty feet above.

The housekeeper turned and pointed to the design on the carpet where I should wait. She went on to a further room and then, from what I could see, into an office. I heard low voices. Only then did the Contessa come into the room.

Humiliation is an important ingredient in drama. The French might go further and say that not only is humiliation essential, torment is better. Torment the heroine said the nineteenth century men of the theatre and then torment her still more. But I was glad enough to settle for humiliation.

'Yes?' asked the Contessa, in an American accent, for indeed she was an American, 'What can I do for you?'

No doubt she was as rich as Gabriella had said. But if she was beautiful it must have been before the First World War, long before. She was into her eighties and her eyes were as hard as the metal studs on the front door of her palace.

'What can I do for you, sir?'

Gabriella had promised her a young man, and a handsome one. All she could see was a gaunt and hirsute bookworm.

'Gabriella,' I said as lightly as I could, 'told me you know about the theatre here.'

'I know nothing about the theatre.'

Perhaps I smiled. I think I shrugged a little.

'I think,' she said, 'that we have both been deceived – don't you?'

The housekeeper lead me to the front door and once more, I was out in the street. This time my ears were burning.

I took out McBride's list and looked at the names of the other women he had photographed in their workshops and galleries and boutiques in Madrid and Paris and Amsterdam. My pressing need to speak English had passed. I made a boat of the list and launched it onto the Arno.

Marian Eldridge

AT THE SIGNORA'S

The Signora never advertises, yet every summer guests fill the red-tiled stone farmhouse easing itself gently down the Tuscan hillside. Perhaps it is the hazy, delicate light of late summer that they come for; perhaps it is the novelty of staying in a real olive grove – in spite of its being rather neglected these days – and breakfasting on the saltless bread of this region, fruit fresh from the Signora's garden, and quark, a special curded cheese that the Signora insists is quite different from the German quark.

From miles away they come, in big cars barely scraping through the narrow medieval streets, like the Schumachers, or winding up from Florence by bus, like the Bradleys, and lurching the last few kilometers to the farmhouse in the Signora's old Fiat. 'We are your family of nations!' someone exclaims, Herr Schumacher probably, peering in the dim light of the entrance at the Signora's guest book that she keeps on a table, along with guide books and maps in a variety of languages, left over from previous guests.

Some guests arrive on foot, like young Drew who is hitch-hiking his way around the world. He says he hasn't had a haircut since leaving Australia and he's not going to have another until he returns. His hair stands up around his head in wads of curls – wasted on a boy, Frau Schumacher laughs. She has such a girlish, expectant face that when she says things like that even Drew joins in her laughter.

Frau Schumacher and the Signora find much to say to each other. The washing up water in the stone sink greases over and the weeds under the olives grow higher as they converse in part-German, part-Italian, each talking so loudly that surely neither can hear the other – but what does that matter? When she first arrives the Englishwoman Mrs Bradley, who speaks neither Italian nor German, tries out her rusty schoolgirl French, 'Savey-vous planter la pamplemousse?' but no one is listening. Frau Schumacher tells the Signora about the Schumacher's son, Volkmar, who is studying for an important exam, and the Signora tells Frau Schumacher about her husband the professor, whose work takes him to Sicily. He is so happy in Sicily. He was born in Sicily. My husband is not of this country, explains the Signora. Frau Schumacher likes to ring Volkmar every evening, she tells the Signora, just to see how he is getting along. She feels a little bit bad about having a holiday while her poor son is working so hard. The professor works hard, says the Signora, her voice growing louder and her eyes flashing. See all the things he has brought back from his work! And they look around the room at the crowds of books, papers, paintings, jugs, pinned broken plates, shards of pottery, figurines, a great terra cotta oil cask, and the shafts and tailgate of a peasant's cart so brightly decorated you can almost hear the farmer and his sons and daughters singing as they return from the fields.

The professor does not return often to the farmhouse in Tuscany, says the Signora sadly. It is the Signora's farmhouse. She grew up in it. She, like it, is of this country: Tuscany. Now it is sliding down the hillside like a rheumaticky old farmhand. Schumacher laughs at Frau Schumacher for ringing Volkmar so often – you think he is a little boy in short trousers, Mrs Schumacher? – and Frau Schumacher laughs at herself. But he is a Sicilian, that is it! shouts the Signora, her greying hair flying around her shoulders. He is not of this country! Every time he returns to my country he brings something else from his work. Soon there will not be room for one more broken plate, another old tailgate!

Maybe he stops coming then! laughs Frau Schumacher.

If Frau Schumacher is always chuckling at something, Herr Schumacher is full of jokes. They are not very good jokes, certainly, but because they are all on holiday everyone smiles. 'Molto grazie!' say the Bradleys to the Signora, practising a phrase out of their Berlitz pocket book after a particularly satisfying breakfast of bread, coffee, cheeses, meats, figs, blackberries, honey and four sorts of jam. To be sure the bread is as hard as a rock, because the Signora is convinced that it is bad for the stomach to hoe into today's bread, which arrives with tantalizing yeasty smells in a little van at daybreak. But that is just another of the Signora's eccentricities; no one really minds; it is all part of the pleasure of holidaying in an olive grove in Tuscany. So – 'Molto grazie!' mouth the Bradleys. 'Molto finito!' caps Herr Schumacher, his hand on his heart. And everyone laughs.

While the weather lasts, breakfast is eaten outside on the patio. Herr Schumacher is usually first to be seated at the old wooden trestle table under the ilex; the others dawdle upstairs, writing up diaries or postcards, or gazing at the view out the bathroom window. 'I'm giving a lot of thought to our projected joint paper,' fibs Dr Bradley to a colleague on the back of the head of Michelangelo's David. (At the postcard stand his wife, inattentive as usual, was on the point of buying a close-up of David's genitals.) 'Today I'm setting out once agen,' Drew scrawls in his dog-eared diary. 'Tho' it's tempting to stay on & do nothing, just lie in the olive grove & forget about how things are out there.' 'Dear Volkmar,' writes Frau Schumacher, who has mislaid her biro so has to push hard on the nib of Herr Schumacher's gold fountain pen that he never lends anyone. Mrs Bradley, writing a poem in her head, lingers under the shower until a pool collects on the bathroom floor and she has to swish it away with her sandal. Drew, glancing over the balcony in case breakfast is ready, sees Herr Schumacher at the table and adds, 'I don't try to discuss enything so I get on fine with everyone here tho' the German bugs me, I can't stand these heel-clicking types.' Then he throws his diary into his rucksack, pulls on his *No Nukes* T-shirt and clatters downstairs, because surely by now the Signora is ready to come running with the pots of fiercely strong coffee that is the signal to eat?

There is no sign of the Signora, however. Not liking to seem impolite to someone older than his father, even old Schumacher, Drew sits down at the other end of the table and nods man-to-man. Herr Schumacher, who has been studying a road map, pushes his reading glasses to the end of his nose. 'So . . . you are leaving us, Drew? Once more you set out on the big adventure?' he says, with a glance at the rucksack with the blue and white Southern Cross inked onto the flap. Drew nods. 'Ah yes, it is wonderful the things young people can do today,' sighs Herr Schumacher, something Drew has heard many times on his travels, like a faint rebuke. 'What a pity you did not tell the Signora sooner that you leave this morning,' continues Herr Schumacher.

'How's that?' asks Drew, but before Herr Schumacher has time to explain the others appear, Dr Bradley automatically taking his wife's elbow although she looks as fit as he to cross a few cobblestones unaided, and Frau Schumacher exclaiming as she lifts her hands to the day, 'Schumacher! Today we go to Pisa, ja?' To each in turn Herr Schumacher gives a little bow, putting his hands on the table and raising his elbows to show he would stand if he could. 'Dr and Mrs Bradley! Good *mor*-ning!' He pronounces the name carefully, *Brrad-ley*, so that Mrs Bradley, pleased, finds herself blushing as she slips onto the bench beside him. 'Mrs Schumacher! Good morning to you, too! I trust you slept well?' continues Herr Schumacher. Frau Schumacher laughs her husky, purring chuckle. 'I am saying to Drew what a pity it is he did not tell the Signora sooner that he leaves us this morning. She makes always a special dinner when a guest is leaving,' he explains to the Bradleys, who are more recent arrivals at the farmhouse.

At this mention of the Signora everyone looks hard at the covers still laid over everything on the table. Where *is* the Signora? The morning is slipping by, already the church bell on top of the hill has pealed out – jangled – as though boys on their way to confession have tugged a demure schoolgirl's plait.

'The Signora cooks – how do you say it? – something particular of this region,' explains Frau Schumacher, with a glance at her husband whose English is so much better than her own. He nods, so she continues, 'Beef – '

'Fattened to a special procedure in the valleys – '

'I've seen nothing but olives and grapes around here,' puts in Drew. 'Maybe it's really Australian beef, imported.'

'Kangaroo?' And Dr Bradley laughs at his own joke.

'In the valleys higher up,' continues Herr Schumacher. 'Fattened –'

'And cut thick, *so*,' adds Frau Schumacher, indicating with thumb and forefinger. 'And cooked on the big open fire in the sitting room.'

'But it must be with olive wood, nothing but olive wood.'

Drew says he's a vegetarian most of the time.

Frau Schumacher says she nearly is, too, after the Signora's special dinner to say goodbye to the Danes, the night before the Bradleys arrived, the meat cut *so*, and cooked a little little bit on the outside, what is the word – burned? singed? – and all the *blud* – the blood – running out on the plate and getting mixed up with the lettuce. She has to pretend she has too much on her plate and pass it on to Schumacher.

'My wife likes to eat meat if the meat is well cooked,' explains Herr Schumacher.

'Ja, and if I cannot see the form of the animal – the thigh of the hare, those quail in France with the little heads looking up from the plate – you remember, Schumacher? Brrr!' Frau Schumacher shudders, and laughs so merrily that the two retired farmhands who have rooms at the back of the house in return for helping harvest the olives, look up from chopping something on a wooden block under the clothes line.

'I guess everything's OK so long as we can't see its shape,' says Drew, in a tone that makes everyone stare.

'They say it's somewhere around here that Leonardo tried to fly,' Mrs Bradley interposes hastily, before their silence can harden.

'His assistant actually, Muriel,' corrects her husband. 'A young lad. He crashed, of course.'

'Of course!' Drew continues. 'Who else? Not the inventor – never the inventors of these things, but the assistant!'

'All the same, it would be rather delightful to try, wouldn't it, in such a lovely lovely landscape?' cries Mrs Bradley in a high false voice, frightened at Drew's words for all these young people sent out on foolish adventures. 'The grapevines you would see criss-crossing hills and valleys, and the children running to school, and in the distance the great towers of Florence!'

'Some hunter would get you,' Drew interrupts. 'Haven't you noticed how few birds there are around here? Compared with Australia, anyway,' he adds, to no one in particular.

Frau Schumacher folds her arms on the table and leans towards him. 'I think you are a little bit homesick, Drew?'

Herr Schumacher laughs. 'My wife likes to ring our home every day.'

'Last night after dinner we speak to our son,' says Frau Schumacher. 'Speak? Speaked?' ('Mrs Schumacher! Mrs Schumacher!' groans Herr Schumacher.) 'Last night we tele-phone to our home and we spoked to Volkmar. I think he would be happier out on the road like you, Drew.'

'It is a good day for travelling,' says Herr Schumacher, and they follow his gaze past the unpruned olive grove, up to the town and beyond to the cypresses, stiff as soldiers along the skyline.

Someone asks Drew about his prospects of getting a lift south quickly. It transpires that about his destination Drew has not yet made up his mind, not definitely, not finally he tells them, it depends on a few things, a phone call to friends in Hamburg, but probably he won't be travelling south, travelling home-wards, but north, to meet up with these same friends in Hamburg to take part in the peace demonstrations this coming autumn.

'A contradiction in terms, surely?' smiles Dr Bradley. ' "Peace" and "demonstrations"?'

Not at all, says Drew. There will be no violence. Everyone will have some training beforehand in passive resistance. He and his friends will form a support group for one another. That's what being friends is about, isn't it? If anyone starts acting afraid, or aggressive, or both, the others will lead them aside and talk them out of it. And it will work. Because the dem-onstrators are only putting into practice what everyone really wants. Isn't that true? (The others nod, oh yes, it's what everyone *wants*.) Of course he thinks about going south, about going straight home, it would be so much easier, but this is something that has to be done. *Someone* has to.

'When I was your age,' says Herr Schumacher suddenly, 'No, younger than you, I was at school in Dresden. It was wartime, you understand. As soon as we were old enough my whole class joined up – twenty-one of us – you know how it is, at that age, you think it is the thing to do, it is a big adventure. So off we all went. To Normandy. Five of the twenty-one returned alive.'

'And not much of Dresden left, either,' remarks Drew.

'You know about Dresden? How do you know about Dresden?' Herr Schumacher looks delighted. 'It is so long ago – before you were born – and so far from your country! Yet you know about Dresden!'

Drew hesitates. 'My grandfather was a prisoner of war – but no, that's not why I'm interested, I hardly knew him really; no, I just think about things, maybe we should all think about them'. He reddens, seeing the others exchange glances, but makes himself finish: 'Dresden was *people*.'

Herr Schumacher says excitedly, 'I too was a prisoner of war! I was captured by the Americans at Normandy. Lucky for you I want not killed, heh, Mrs Schumacher? Instead I was for many months lying in hospital. While I am recovering they discovered I have a facility for language, ja?' He beams. They all nod vigorously. 'So after I am mended I spent a year in the prison camp as interpreter for the American camp doctor. Ah, he was like a father to me, that man! I was not yet nineteen, you understand. A mere boy! And when at last I returned to Dresden I did not recognise it, no street, no home, no parents, nothing. Only as a memento of my big adventure, this – ' and thrusting out his chin he shows them a jagged scar running under his jaw and disappearing into his collar.

'There was an uncle in Hamburg – ' prompts Frau Schumacher, as the others begin to fidget, faced with they know not what ugliness patched together under the neatly pressed shirt.

' – and so I went from Dresden to Hamburg, otherwise today I would not be here and I would not have met you, Mrs Schumacher!'

'Yes, it's a terrible thing to be an occupied country,' sighs Dr Bradley.

'My friends in West Germany certainly think so!' says Drew fiercely, determined to tear at the lazy Tuscan morning so that clear light can burst through, the harsh cleansing light that he yearns for. But the others are no longer listening. They are thinking about breakfast. A surprisingly late riser for a farmer, the Signora knows that this particular day everyone wants to be off early, to galleries that open only in the mornings, to Pisa while the Tower is still standing, to the crossroads for a lift before summer disappears in a cloud of acid rain.

'Her car isn't where she leaves it by the gate,' someone observes, craning. 'She must be up in the town.'

'Talking. Talking. That's the Signora's gift – conversation.' And they smile. But they are getting awfully hungry.

'Maybe she has gone to the bus stop to meet her husband.'

'Is there a husband?'

'Of course. The house is full of his things.'

They fall silent for a moment, thinking of this shadowy husband who spends long months in Sicily while weeds spring up under the olives and the Signora warms herself with conversation.

'Maybe she has already prepared the coffee for us,' suggests Herr Schumacher, sidling past Mrs Bradley so that he can go in to see.

Yes, the coffee pots are bubbling nicely but is the coffee ready? Is it too soon? Better wait for the Signora, says Herr

Schumacher, walking up and down the patio and jerking his elbows back to stretch his shoulders.

'Oh I do hope it's a bit weaker today!' murmurs Mrs Bradley, knowing she will not dare ask again because when she said something that first morning the Signora flashed 'Huh! You like *English* coffee?'

At last they hear the Signora's car. It is unmistakable. It backfires up the drive, jerks to a stop on the patio. Out jumps the Signora, hair flying, hand to her heart. 'Sorry – so sorry I will quickly bring coffee and then something I have to say – ' head bobbing, smiling so apologetically from one to another that for a moment each guest feels uneasy. It was Schumacher's nightmare, I should have wakened him sooner, thinks Frau Schumacher. It is Muriel's long showers, thinks Dr Bradley. It is my big car, worries Herr Schumacher, thinking about his old uncle's business that provides for this annual vacation, himself at the wheel now and his wife beside him in her new crocodile shoes . . . Sometimes as we drive through these little towns children, watched by their parents, fling stones as soon as they see the number plate . . .

Mrs Bradley is watching some imaginary spot in the distance that is forced to descend because of the danger of hunters, a tiny winged figure zigging and zagging to dodge their shafts until he floats peacefully the last few yards to land by the Signora's breakfast table. Mrs Bradley moves up to make room for him (or his assistant, was it?) and of course it is only Herr Schumacher sitting down again, someone less like Leonardo she can't imagine. She glances at him sideways, this German old enough to have fought against *us*, and sees a bead of blood where he has nicked himself shaving.

Only Drew is unconcerned by the Signora's words. Already he has said goodbye, already he is out on the highway, rucksack on his back, rain biting into his neck and shoulders. 'We've been talking about World War Two,' he says as the Signora whips the covers off the table.

'Ah *war*,' cries the Signora. 'Do not talk of such things!' She gives him a quick hug, riffling his hair. 'Your own mother and father were just children then! Have you not happier things to think on, carissimo?'

'I wasn't much affected by the War,' reminisces Dr Bradley. 'I was too young, and besides I was sent into the countryside where things were comparatively safe. But that was a long time ago! If you talk about "the War" today young people think you mean the Falklands.'

'I spend the War not here on the farm but in Firenze,' recalls the Signora. 'It is not a good time – no, I cannot speak of it. But this I tell you – in 1944, while our young boys are fighting the Nazis who are in how do you call it? retreat, the Americans are in the Palazzo Pitti on the other side of the Arno, doing nothing but watch to see who will win.'

'Oh, I say!' protests Dr Bradley, who has read the military histories, and understands the logistics of battle.

'This I see!' shouts the Signora. Heads shake. Ah, these nations. America! Germany! Easier to throw stones at a passing car forty years later than keep in mind a boy with shattered bones. The Signora goes on, 'They watch and we see them watching through field glasses from the Palazzo Pitti – but no, more I do not want to remember. You go south, Drew, in the south it is warm.'

'Ja, south,' says Frau Schumacher. 'It is good for families to be together.'

'And today he sets out,' smiles the Signora. 'So! I have a surprise for everyone. That is what I wish to say. Since it is his last morning with us – ' and from the car she brings with a flourish a delicious looking cake, a slab of sponge covered with grapes baked reddish-gold in their own juice. To be eaten with quark, she says, quark of this country. Frau Schumacher describes the delicacy of German quark and in a moment the two women are laughing and shouting at each other, a barrage of jocularity.

'Give my love to Sicily! My heart is in Sicily!' cries the Signora, as Drew takes leave.

Only Mrs Bradley feels certain that he will go north. 'We send our children to fight for us while we sit here in the sun . . .'

'But is not that always the way, Mrs Brrad-ley?' says Herr Schumacher gently. 'Well, Mrs Schumacher, are you ready? Pisa! Pisa is like a woman, she leans but she never falls,' he jokes. He makes them laugh again, pulling a droll face as he says 'Today I will ask for tickets for two children and see what happens. Ja. I have tried that before, I say "Tickets for two big children, please" – but no one believes me.'

'He would make the Mona Lisa laugh,' says Frau Schumacher.

Everyone smiles at that, too.

While the two women help the Signora clear the table, Dr Bradley, claiming no respite, lights up his pipe and in a haze of tobacco smoke spends two minutes, even three, contemplating his joint paper. Soon Mrs Bradley, losing herself in her poem, wanders to the back of the house where, covertly admired by the two old farmhands, she stares into the tomatoes as she waits for the very word.

Frau Schumacher waits for Herr Schumacher.

Herr Schumacher, watching Drew getting smaller and smaller as he walks up the hill beside the olive trees, suddenly says, 'Before we go to Pisa, Gisela, don't you think you should telephone Volkmar?'

'But, Heinrich, last night I telephone Volkmar!'

'Yes, Gisela, but that was yesterday. Today is today. Don't you want to be sure that everything is all right? You put the call through, I will come in when he answers.'

And Herr Schumacher goes on watching the vanishing figure of Drew.

Carmel Bird

GOCZKA

He was red, dressed in red, and his horse was red.

My eye is looking out through the blanket. If I keep very still and stay under the blanket, I will be warm and safe, safe and warm. Still and safe and warm. I am the little boy under the grey blanket, scratchy blanket, warm and safe and scratchy. I am four now and I am under the blanket with just my eye peeping. I peep. My eye is peeping and I peep. Still, still, I am still. I am Goczka and I am very, very still. I wear the blanket like a hood, safe hood. The hood will save me from the night and the dark and the wolf. Rocked in the soft, soft swaying pink waters, womb waters, pink waters, I am the baby, safe baby, warm baby, soft baby. Wrapped in the waters, I rock and I sing, I am Goczka. The blanket, grey blanket is scratchy and safe. It is the pink waters, silk waters, my darling, my mother, my cradle, my pod. I am curled in my pod in the silver pink garden. I am curled in my pod in the garden. I peep from my pod. My eye is peeping, pod peeping. There is a smell of mould. There is a war. I peep from my blanket and I see that there is a war.

He was red, dressed in red, and his horse was red.

In Poland, there is a war. I am four years old, and here is the war. The children will be safe. Safe warm children in scratchy blankets, grey blankets, war blankets. The children are peeping from their blankets. Fifty children peeping from their blankets.

Fifty children peeping from their blankets. Fifty children peeping from their blankets. There is a smell of war, a smell of blankets, a smell of mould. I do not know these children, I do not know this place. I am four, I am sad. I am crying in the war. They have put us in a church. We will be safe in the church. The walls are stone, old stone, cold stone. We are safe in the church in the war.

I do not know these children. They are babies, they are crying. The children are crying. I want my sister. My sister in her skirt, red skirt, thick skirt, thick red skirt. There is a silver ribbon in her hair. The ribbons on her skirt are dancing in the sunlight. My sister is dancing in the sunlight. She is Yadi, sister Yadi, and she holds me and she loves me and she is my sister. Sister Yadi. I am peeping from my blanket. I am looking for my sister. I am Goczka, she is Yadi, and I cry.

With my peeping eye, I see a window. Picture window. It is glass, it is sunset, it is sunshine in the sunset. Sweet sweetie shapes of lolly glass. I see the lolly glass and I am peeping at the glass. Glass. I see the glass, glassy glass. Red glass, blood glass. Sweet glass, sweetie glass, jar of lollies, lolly glass. Yadi gives me lollies is my sister is my lollies glassy lollies sugar lollies in the glass.

We are having cabbage soup. Sit up now and drink this cabbage soup there is a war. Spilling soup slop soup yellow wee wee soup the smell of old old socks mould old socks. And incense. In the church there lurks the old incense. It is hanging in the corners, in the dust of all the corners. There is incense in the corners of the church.

When I was a little boy, little Goczka, little boy, I was sitting with my sister by the fire. Goczka, little Goczka, listen Goczka, to the stories I will tell.

This is the story, she said, of Baba Yaga. Near the house was a dense forest; in the forest was a clearing, in the clearing there was a hut; and in this hut lived Baba Yaga. She let no one near her and devoured children as if they were chickens. The trees creaked. The dry leaves crackled. And she devoured children. The door opened and Baba Yaga went in whistling and whirling. The fence around the hut was made of human bones.

Fear not. Eat and pray, and go to sleep. Night will bring help.

Goczka is lying in the church in Poland in the war and it is getting dark. He can see the stained glass window if he peers from his blanket. In the sunset, the window glows with crimson fire. It is Saint George. They tell me I am George, I am Goczka, I am George. He is killing his dragon, red dragon. Killing his dragon. There are stones. In the picture in the window, there are stones. A long thin spear, a wide red cloak, and the stones. It is bright, it is light and Goczka is killing his dragon. I am Goczka. I kill.

He was red, dressed in red, and his horse was red.

In the church with all the children, there is a woman. She looks after us. She brings us the blankets, the soup, the bread, the day and the night. Eat, pray, and go to sleep. Night will bring help. In the morning, the war will be over. It will all be over, won't it?

You have to go to sleep now. Sleep now. No more crying, no more running down the church. If you are good and go to sleep, the war will get over, and we can all go home. Be good, and go to sleep. The woman says go to sleep. I will tell you a story, she says. She says there will be a story. Once upon a time, there was a witch and this witch was called Baba Yaga.

She is telling us the story Yadi told. Yadi, sister Yadi, lovely Yadi.

And she devoured little children as if they were chickens. And if you do not go to sleep, if you do not go to sleep, the door will fly open, and Baba Yaga will come whistling and whirling down the church in her great big black cloak, and she will eat you and crunch you and spit out the bones. If you don't go to sleep. Keep quiet and go to sleep. It is the war. She said she is the teacher. She said she is the grandmother. Grandmother soup, grandmother bread, soup and bread and Baba. My Baba makes lace. She is a lady making lace. She sits in the sunshine making lace. Flicking flying bobbins pins and bobbins making lace. My Baba smells of sugar making Sunshine lace. She sometimes smells of custard and vanilla. My vanilla Baba. She sings a lullaby, lace lullaby – sleep, little baby, the red bee hums. Sloneczko, hums, the red bee hums. Sleep, sleep sloneczko, my baby, my bee.

The woman is the teacher, cabbage teacher. She is the Baba of the war. Black Baba. Big black wolfy wolfy Baba. Pull up the blanket, Goczka. It is not safe to stay awake. It is not safe to go to sleep. It is not safe. It is the war.

You will be safe in the church, with the Baba, with the children, with the blankets, with the windows. There is incense in the corner. And if you do not go to sleep, Baba Yaga will get you.

So I lie in my blanket and it is getting dark. I watch the window. The night will bring help, the window will bring help. I love the window. The window is going to save me. Lovely window loves me. All around me, I smell crying. The children are crying in the church, safe church, in the war. It is dark. If you do not go to sleep, the doors will open and she will come, Baba Yaga will get you.

Saint George is killing the dragon. There is incense in the corners. The floor is stone. There is a wind outside. Outside there is a wind, a war and a wind. Stones and the dark and a war and a great big wind. And a whirling and a whistling and a war.

I am getting cold.

He was red, dressed in red, and his horse was red.

There is still and quiet here now. We are all listening to the wind, the wind outside. The window is all dark now. Dark like snow. Some of the children have fallen asleep. Once upon a time, there were some children and they got into a boat and fell asleep. They fell asleep in the boat. It was a dark boat, the children's boat. The trees beside the water met across the water. And the children fell asleep in the boat. They floated down the river, dark, sweet river. They floated down the river in the boat.

The window is black.

I am four years old and I am Goczka and there is always a war. My sister is Yadi, and she has gone, gone with the war. Her skirt is red, her red skirt, and it is gone with her silver ribbons in the war. I am rocking in the red skirt, in the grey blanket, in the dark. There is a rustle. I hear a rustle. The leaves are crackling.

The door is creaking. It is creaking cracking open. The night is coming in. Into the church, the night is coming. Night will bring help.

If you do not go to sleep, Baba Yaga, the Baba Yaga will come and get you. I will go to sleep, I will go to sleep. I am going to sleep by the window. I am peeping and I am going to sleep.

Very high, very wide, very black, very full, into the cavern of the church where the fifty children are lying, the Baba Yaga comes. If you are asleep, you will not see her. If you are awake, she will get you. She is here. She is flapping slowly down the church. Moaning and howling, she is coming to get the children. Wild wisps of witch's hair wild wisps of hair. She is black, she is scratched, she will get you. If you do not go to sleep she will get you.

Goczka, little Goczka, close your eye, no more peeping. The Baba Yaga is here. She smells of cabbage soup. She is here with her claws. She is here.

The blanket is not safe.

There is a war. Goczka, sloneczko, there is a war.

She said she is the grandmother. She is wearing a big black cloak, wolfy cloak.

I melt into the blanket. I melt into the window. I am killing the dragon. Goczka is big, he is big inside. He is strong to kill the dragon, the dragon in the window. Quiet now, still, still. Safe in Goczka's heart, he is safe in his heart. In his heart, in my heart, there is a giant giant window. It is red and red and red. There is war, there is the Baba, there is whirling creaking crackling. All is whistling. She is flapping and whirling.

I will not go to sleep. I will not sleep. I am big and bright and strong.

I am red, dressed in red, and my horse is red.

WE
WERE
THE
LAND'S
BEFORE
THE
LAND
WAS
OURS

Michael Wilding

I Am Monarch of All I Survey

We went to see the hippy king, living in the mountains. He was in exile from his kingdom which had dissolved. And now he was like the Duke of Windsor or King Zog, in mufti.

We were not especially fond of the mountains. I lift up mine eyes unto the hills, from whence cometh my help. But that is to lift your eyes towards them, which is different from going up to them, let alone living in them. From the distance they were a calming blue, but to be in the source itself isn't necessarily the same experience; and anyway, the rocks and gum leaves are not the source of the blue, no one knows what the source of the blue is.

We got as far as Homebush where the slaughterhouses are and death lay like a miasma over flat paddocks and seeped across the roads and railway lines. That was where we realised we had forgotten to bring the address or the phone number, so we turned round and went back. And this in a petrol strike too.

He had dictated the directions on the phone.

'Have you got paper?'

'Yes.'

'Have you got pencil?'

'I've got a pen.'

'Fine. That'll do. Right. You go up the mountains to –'

And I inscribed, 'go up the mountains to –'

'And the first turning after the shops –'

'First turning after the shops –'

'Right. You don't go down there.'

'Don't go down there.'
'Then you come to the second turning –'
'Second turning –'
'Don't go down there.'
'Don't go.'
'The third turning –'
'The third turning –'
It has to be the third turning.
'Don't go down there either.'
'Don't.'
'Then you come to –'
I hold off writing it down.
'That's the one you take. You go along there to a crossroads. Disregard them. And then it becomes a dirt track, take no notice of that –'

It was like the ten commandments; thou shalt not, thou shalt not. Very Old Testament. And then Sara who was getting pissed with Sam while I took down the directions on the phone scribbled wiggly lines all down the map I'd created from the negations. 'We've already got the directions,' she said.

'This your wife? Lily?' he says.
'Yes. Well, we're not married, but –'
'But you live together –'
'Well, yes –'
'I'm just making sure of her name,' he says, 'not checking on your marital state.'
'Ah,' I say.

We go through the house onto the patio. It is a house with a patio.

We have met his wife as we go through the house. She keeps her own name. Now we meet a big bold blonde who stands on the patio like living sculpture. We are told her name but I don't catch it.

'She makes porno movies,' King Zig-Zag tells us. His wife stands by looking enigmatic.

Lily sits down with her back to the view. The view stretches across chasms to mountains. I sit and look at it. It is an impressive view if you like views. You can look at the view and not look at the people. Or you can look at the people and keep your back to the view. We don't seem to be able to do both, except jointly. Which means that one of us is always ignoring the people and one of us is always ignoring the view. I feel like one of those people who won't look people in the eye. I won't look people in the eye. Some things I cannot bear to see. I lift up my eyes to the hills, for help.

'Do you make porno movies or do you act in them?' Lily asks.

'Oh, she acts in them,' says King Zig-Zag.

'I'll put the sausages on the barbecue,' says the Duchess of Windsor.

We are given wine in crystal goblets. I drink mine and then get a can of beer I brought and put in the fridge.

'I am sick of drinking out of vegemite glasses,' says Lily, 'it's so nice to drink out of crystal goblets.'

I suck up the beer from its aluminium can. I have no commitment to aluminium cans, but I also have no commitment to crystal goblets.

Sam and Sara were going to arrive early but when we get there there is no sign of them, and we arrive two hours late. We decide not to wait for them before eating. The big bold blonde has a train to catch back to the city. So briefly flashed before us, so rapidly snatched away. Perhaps they had the orgy last night. The marinated flesh is put on the barbecue and we gaze at the view.

'When I used to smoke a lot I would spend all day just gazing at the view.'

Now he doesn't smoke a lot. Now he doesn't smoke at all it seems. They pour out these wines from bottles. None of the cardboard and foil cut-price bulk-buy wine cask here. But I only notice this when it is pointed out later. I am looking at the view getting used to the idea that there are no drugs. I wonder if Sam and Sara managed to score.

'I'd forgotten people still ate meat,' I say to Lily.

'That's because you never visit anyone,' she says.

Ah true, we are all in exile from our familiar places.

I think I eat pork chop but try not to think about enjoying eating it.

'I dropped a trip,' says Sam, behind his hand, as we walk out to his car.

'Did you get any dope?'

'Yeah, yeah, don't panic, I got some good stuff, you'll really like it. But what happened was Bob'd got this acid and he gave me a trip and so we sort of got held up.'

'Where's the dope?'

'Relax,' he says, 'it's here somewhere, it's nice stuff.'

We walk back to the house.

'Anyway,' he says, apropos the trip, 'if anything happens, any weird stuff, just you and Lily leave, just go, we'll be all right.'

Sam shuffles out to the patio with his shirt tail hanging loose and his Greek bag full of poems and books and Panadol and Serapax and antacids and a bottle of bourbon. He gives King Zig-Zag a copy of his new book. King Zig-Zag is stoking the barbecue and impaling pork chops and chicken breasts; he is preoccupied by the haute cuisine of the hills and Sam presses on his attention like a blowfly on marinated dead flesh. King Z-Z graciously accepts the book and puts it on a table. Sam stands with his cock robin stance, shuffling his feet to get the toes exactly on a line and not going over it, lined up exactly for permission to speak, for the intensity of breaking through to impermeable inexplicable self-proclaimed authority, reformatory training.

The big bold blonde picks up the book.

'Ah, poetry,' she says.

'Would you like one?' says Sam.

'They're ten dollars,' says Sara.

'Would you like one?' says Sam. 'Would you prefer to buy one or be given one?'

The big bold blonde exudes all her honey golden charm.

'I'd prefer to be given one,' she says.

'Why?' says Sam, 'why would you prefer to be given one?'

'Because it would mean more to me.'

'Then I'd have to fuck you,' says Sam.

She smiles.

She turns out to be American. She travels the world. She has been to Afghanistan, Ayers Rock, Bangkok, Nicaragua.

I roll a smoke. Nobody seems to have any dope but everyone smokes it. Sam writes an inscription in the book he is giving the American. The Duchess of Windsor is driving her to the station and sits in the car hooting the horn. Sam is in the throes of inspiration. A personalised inscription. He writes things and crosses them out, gets halfway through a word and forgets it, the car horn keeps hooting, the American keeps telling Sam she has to hurry, and it only slows him down.

In the end she gets away to meet her contact in the city.

'That's what they do,' says Sam, 'they use these attractive girls, send them round the world.'

We think of attractive girls sent round the world we have known.

'Attractive,' says Sara.

King Zig-Zag reappears in his Marcel Proust T-shirt. There is a collection of Ezra Pound's wartime broadcasts from Italy on the kitchen table we notice as we are shown round the house, the renovations, the timberwork, the matting, the tiles.

'Specially for us,' says Sam. The literary touch. To remind us of what happens to writers who get involved in politics.

We walk round the grounds. It is not all his, theirs, the land to the horizon, but a lot of it is. Some was once laid out in terraces and fountains.

It has a literary history, it belonged to someone or other, King Zig-Zag tells us.

'I think that's rather nice,' he says, 'a continuity.'

'The enemy,' says Sam.

Like Winston Churchill, King Zig-Zag has been building walls, drystone walls to hold back soil.

'It'll fall down,' I tell him. There's an art to drystone-walling. I do not tell him what the art is, how could I? All I can tell him is where it is lacking.

More fine wines are produced, more savouring of the crystal goblets.

'What they do now,' says Sam to Lily, 'what they do is at all these business things, if they want to get somebody to sign a deal, they serve special sorts of wine, or if they want them to freak out they serve something else or if they don't want the deal to go ahead they serve them something like a downer, they've got all these chemicals they use for making the wines, they've been doing it for centuries and now all the chemical companies and big business are into it, it's just like you get people pissed so they tell you everything, well this is like that only more complex, that's all.'

'The other thing they do,' said Lily, 'is coat the glasses with some chemical, then everyone has the same wine but they make sure that certain people get certain glasses.'

'Mmmmm,' says Sam quizzically, his lips a tight line, waving up and down like a French mime artist performing the line of beauty, 'mmmmm.'

The Duchess of Windsor returns from the station. King Zig-Zag disappears into the bedroom and comes out in his Dostoyevsky T-shirt. Now for the abyss.

We are herded into the company car and roar down a bush track between flashing gums and expressionist horrors. Then we stop at a point beyond which even a company car cannot be taken.

'It's not far,' they tell us, coming across like rural hippies at our urban fear of walking.

The Duchess of Windsor carries the hamper with gateaux and champagne. We file along behind her, along these narrow ruts like sheep tracks, except there are no sheep, other than us. Suddenly the ground drops away several thousand feet in front of us. About three feet in front of us. There is no warning of this horrific experience. One moment you are struggling along a bush track, head down, next there is just the abyss in front of you.

We concede it is a splendid view.

Splendid.

'Shit,' says Sam.

You could've walked right over it and never seen the view. Except momentarily at something per something feet per second.

Then she wants us to climb out on some devil's promontory and perch there eating chocolate cake and drinking sour, fizzy wine. I stand well back. They laugh, they mock. I remain immovable. Sam reacts somewhat similarly except that he is far from immovable. He stumbles around, I can see him stumbling down the devil's promontory and bowling everyone ahead of him into the abyss. He stays well back, too; but that's no good news for the people squatting between him and the abyss. I stay well behind Sam.

The gateaux are all right. They were bought in town. Where we have just come from, only a more expensive suburb. But my stomach is not quite into gateaux. The crows wheel around beneath our feet. Or their feet. I am not close enough to see the crows but I imagine they are wheeling around waiting there. I have been in a number of temptation scenes in my life, the high building number, standing up on the umpteenth floor of the Arts Council building and surveying the city beneath. But this time, on this precipice in the mountain, I cannot see what is being offered. Perhaps now we only get the sense experience, not the offer. This is less a temptation than a test, a threat; has King Zig-Zag read one of those reviews of my work that talks of recurrent images of vertigo? And ascribed it to my psyche rather than to the architecture of our times and too much TV. Like his car chase in the company car, these media images for instant excitement penetrate our consciousnesses, we believe they are our images, our perceptions, our lives. How much superman has the hippy king absorbed? But his feet are firmly planted on the ground. We can expect no jump from him.

Sam raises his hand. Can we go back now?

If he has dropped a trip I can see that all this might be rather excruciating for him. It is for me and as far as I know I haven't. Not consciously.

The boughs bleed as the car brushes past them. The soil burns as the tires spin. Oh no, don't say we have to get out and push. But we don't. Big motor, big tires, vrrrm vrrrm. The earth could open and swallow us. But doesn't.

Then we are back in the house for chocolates and more fine wines and the dope now diminishing as I roll a few numbers to relax by. One, two, three. And the Duchess of Windsor tells us about her poetic leanings and then Sam demands a record player to play a record he's brought up in his bag but they haven't got a record player, I don't believe it they haven't got a record player, well we've got a record player but it's packed away, well unpack it, says Sara, you're supposed to be the hippy king where's your record player? Well it's packed away, well unpack it. Maybe they're into cassettes, cassettes in the car, cassettes beneath the pillow, headsets for jogging, etc. It is all getting shrill now, Lily is weeping in the kitchen for some hard luck story the Duchess of Windsor is telling her, I sit in the arm chair in the living room or whatever they call it here, the library, there are a lot of books here so maybe it is a library, Sara decides the Duchess of Windsor is making a line for me so comes and sits on my lap to protect Lily's interests, now the darkness has swirled round the house, chocolates and fine wines and Sara insists Sam should read a poem, they've brought him up here they should sit here and hear a poem, hear hear says King Zig-Zag, remembering his cheer-leader days for the debating team, especially if there is no record player, I don't want to read I just want to hear this record, says Sam, read damn you, says Sara, so he reads, which means going into the preliminaries of setting the scene, the composition of place, a street in at the Cross, Sam drunk and picked up by the pigs, more prison experiences, let me tell you my hard luck story, the cell floor flowing in piss, this is real damn you, says Sara, this is what it's like being a poet. Well, I can see it's difficult, says King Zig-Zag, woof woof and other such woof-woofing, then the Duchess of Windsor reads a poem, from the collected works of Stevie Smith, against whom we have nothing personally, but it's all getting a bit like charades. Oh, I'm so frustrated, Sara suddenly yells out. And then the Duchess of Windsor suppressed a yawn and made discreet intimations of retiring, and King Zig-Zag started talking about making tracks and one last cup of coffee for the road and Sam said he'd have the coffee but wasn't ready for the road yet, it still being early in the evening, and besides he couldn't go right now and drive having dropped a trip. It didn't seem to matter whether he had or hadn't, or if he had some eight hours earlier he should be down by now, and the fact that no one had remarked anything till now showed clearly enough it wouldn't matter and no one would ever know the difference, but King Zig-Zag freaked and Sam had gained a delay. It went on for several hours. He was prised out of the house once or twice but usually scuttled back in or had other people scuttling back in for lost objects. In the end we did what he'd told me to do, just leave, and we just left them sitting in the car on the bush track, Sam and Sara, the lights coming on and off, the motor stopping and starting, and at some point Sam threw his Greek bag full of books and records and his scrapbooks into the abyss, but a bushwalker's mother phoned them up a couple of days later saying the scrapbooks had been found and did they want them back, which was good since he's just been able to sell them to the National Library for a few thousand dollars, since even poets of the most chameleon variety cannot live on air and the free lunches always turn out to have their price.

Gerald Murnane

LAND DEAL

After a full explanation of what my object was, I purchased two large tracts of land from them – about 600,000 acres, more or less – and delivered over to them blankets, knives, looking-glasses, tomahawks, beads, scissors, flour, etc., as payment for the land, and also agreed to give them a tribute, or rent, yearly.

– John Batman, 1835

We certainly had no cause for complaint at the time. The men from overseas politely explained all the details of the contract before we signed it. Of course there were minor matters that we should have queried. But even our most experienced negotiators were distracted by the sight of the payment offered us.

The strangers no doubt supposed that their goods were quite unfamiliar to us. They watched tolerantly while we dipped our hands into the bags of flour, draped ourselves in blankets, and tested the blades of knives against the nearest branches. And when they left we were still toying with our new possessions. But what we marvelled at most was not their novelty. We had recognised an almost miraculous correspondence between the strangers' steel and glass and wool and flour and those metals and mirrors and cloths and foodstuffs that we so often postulated, speculated about, or dreamed of.

Is it surprising that a people who could use against stubborn wood and pliant grass and bloody flesh nothing more serviceable than stone – is it surprising that such a people should have become so familiar with the idea of metal? Each one of us, in his dreams, had felled tall trees with blades that lodged deep in the pale pulp beneath the bark. Any of us could have enacted the sweeping of honed metal through a stand of seeded grass or described the precise parting of fat or muscle beneath a tapered knife. We knew the strength and sheen of steel and the trueness of its edge from having so often called it into possible existence.

It was the same with glass and wool and flour. How could we not have inferred the perfection of mirrors – we who peered so often into rippled puddles after wavering images of ourselves? There was no quality of wool that we had not conjectured as we huddled under stiff pelts of possum on rainy winter evenings. And every day the laborious pounding of the women at their dusty mills recalled for us the richness of the wheaten flour that we had never tasted.

But we had always clearly distinguished between the possible and the actual. Almost anything was possible. Any god might reside behind the thundercloud or the waterfall, any faery race inhabit the land below the ocean's edge; any new day might bring us such a miracle as an axe of steel or a blanket of wool. The almost boundless scope of the possible was limited only by the occurrence of the actual. And it went without saying that what existed in the one sense could never exist in the other. Almost anything was possible except, of course, the actual.

It might be asked whether our individual or collective histories furnished any example of a possibility becoming actual. Had no man ever dreamed of possessing a certain weapon or woman and, a day or a year later, laid hold of his desire? This can be simply answered by the assurance that no one among us was ever heard to claim that anything in his possession resembled, even remotely, some possible thing he had once hoped to possess.

That same evening, with the blankets warm against our backs and the blades still gleaming beside us, we were forced to confront an unpalatable proposition. The goods that had appeared among us so suddenly belonged only in a possible world. We were therefore dreaming. The dream may have been the most vivid and enduring that any of us had known. But however long it lasted it was still a dream.

We admired the subtlety of the dream. The dreamer (or dreamers – we had already admitted the likelihood of our collective responsibility) had invented a race of men among whom possible objects passed as actual. And these men had been moved to offer us the ownership of their prizes in return for something that was itself not real.

We found further evidence to support this account of things. The pallor of the men we had met that day, the lack of purpose in much of their behaviour, the vagueness of their explanations – these may well have been the flaws of men dreamed of in haste. And, perhaps paradoxically, the nearly perfect properties of the stuffs offered to us seemed the work of a dreamer, someone who lavished on the central items of his dream all those desirable qualities that are never found in actual objects.

It was this point that led us to alter part of our explanation for the events of that day. We were still agreed that what had happened was part of some dream. And yet it was characteristic of most dreams that the substance of them seemed, at the time, actual to the dreamer. How, if we were dreaming of the strangers and their goods, were we able to argue against our taking them for actual men and objects?

We decided that none of us was the dreamer. Who, then, was? One of our gods, perhaps? But no god could have had such an acquaintance with the actual that he succeeded in creating an illusion of it that had almost deceived us.

There was only one reasonable explanation. The pale strangers, the men we had first seen that day, were dreaming of us and our confusion. Or, rather, the true strangers were dreaming of a meeting between ourselves and their dreamed-of selves.

At once, several puzzles seemed resolved. The strangers had not observed us as men observe one another. There were moments when they might have been looking through our hazy outlines towards sights they recognised more easily. They spoke to us with oddly raised voices and claimed our attention with exaggerated gestures as though we were separated from them by a considerable distance, or as though they feared we might fade altogether from their sight before we had served the purpose for which they had allowed us into their dream.

When had this dream begun? Only, we hoped, on that same day when we first met the strangers. But we could not deny that our entire lives and the sum of our history might have been dreamed by these people of whom we knew almost nothing. This did not dismay us utterly. As characters in a dream, we might have been much less at liberty than we had always supposed. But the authors of the dream encompassing us had apparently granted us at least the freedom to recognise, after all these years, the simple truth behind what we had taken for a complex world.

Why had things happened thus? We could only assume that these other men dreamed for the same purpose that we (dreamers within a dream) often gave ourselves up to dreaming. They wanted for a time to mistake the possible for the actual. At that moment, as we deliberated under familiar stars (already subtly different now that we knew their true origin), the dreaming men were in an actual land far away, arranging our very deliberations so that their dreamed-of selves could enjoy for a little while the illusion that they had acquired something actual.

And what was this unreal object of their dreams? The document we had signed explained everything. If we had not been distracted by their glass and steel that afternoon we would have recognised even then the absurdity of the day's events. The strangers wanted to possess the land.

Of course it was the wildest folly to suppose that the land, which was by definition indivisible, could be measured or parcelled out by a mere agreement among men. In any case, we had been fairly sure that the foreigners failed to see our land. From their awkwardness and unease as they stood on the soil, we judged that they did not recognise the support it provided or the respect it demanded. When they moved even a short distance across it, stepping aside from places that invited passage and treading on places that were plainly not to be intruded on, we knew that they would lose themselves before they found the real land.

Still, they had seen a land of some sort. That land was, in their own words, a place for farms and even, perhaps, a village. It would have been more in keeping with the scope of the dream surrounding them had they talked of founding an unheard-of city where they stood. But all their schemes were alike from our point of view. Villages or cities were all in the realm of possibility and could never have a real existence. The land would remain the land, designed for us yet, at the same time, providing the scenery for the dreams of a people who would never see either our land or any land they dreamed of.

What could we do, knowing what we then knew? We seemed as helpless as those characters we remembered from private dreams who tried to run with legs strangely nerveless. Yet if we had no choice but to complete the events of the dream, we could still admire the marvellous inventiveness of it. And we could wonder endlessly what sort of people they were in their far country, dreaming of a possible land they could never inhabit, dreaming further of a people such as ourselves with our one weakness, and then dreaming of acquiring from us the land which could never exist.

We decided, of course, to abide by the transaction that had been so neatly contrived. And although we knew we could never truly awake from a dream that did not belong to us, still we trusted that one day we might seem, to ourselves at least, to awake.

Some of us, remembering how after dreams of loss they had awakened with real tears in their eyes, hoped that we would somehow awake to be convinced of the genuineness of the steel in our hands and the wool round our shoulders. Others insisted that for as long as we handled such things we could be no more than characters in the vast dream that had settled over us – the dream that would never end until a race of men in a land unknown to us learned how much of their history was a dream that must one day end.

Paddy Roe and Stephen Muecke

MIRDINAN

A *maban* (doctor) is living with his wife. While he goes fishing she is having an affair with a Malay. The maban discovers them and later questions his wife who lies. On further questioning she admits to the affair and her husband kills her. He leaves camp and goes to join his countrymen, where the police pick him up to take him back to Broome. Halfway he escapes by magical disappearance.

The police pick him up again and put him in the lock-up in Broome. He again escapes by turning into a cat and being chased out of the cell by the sergeant. He returns to his people.

The police pick him up again and put him on the boat to Fremantle to be hanged. At the moment of hanging he changes into an eaglehawk and flies home. He makes a song on his return.

The police and people make him drunk to destroy his power, nail him in a box, and drown him in the ocean.

Yeah –
well these people bin camping in Fisherman Bend him and his
   missus you know –
Fisherman Bend in Broome, *karnun*[1] –
we call-im *karnun* –
soo, the man used to go fishing all time –
get food for them, you know, food, lookin' for tucker –
an' his, his missus know some Malay bloke was in the creek,
   Broome Creek[2] –
boat used to lay up there[3] –
so this, his missus used to go there with this Malay bloke –

170

one Malay bloke, oh he's bin doin' this for –
over month –

so this old fella –
come back with fish one day he can't find his missus –
he waited there till late –
so he said 'What happened to my missus?–
must be gone fishing ah that's all right' he said –
so he waited and he comeback he got nothing⁴ –
'Where you bin?' he said, bloke said to him –
'Ah I jus' bin walkin' round' –
'Aah' –
soo all right next morning he start off again –
'Mus' be something wrong' this oldfella said –
oh he wasn't old but he was young –
said ' 'e must be something wrong' –
so he went fishing –
he come back from fishing –
got all the fish comeback –
so he comeback on the other road –
near the creek, Broome Creek, you know –
comeback round that way –
when he comeback 'Hello' he seen this man and woman in the
   mangroves, sitting down –
oh he come right alongside –
he seen everything what they doin' (laughs) you know –
they sitting down –

so, he seen everything –
so he wen' back –
he wen' back home firs' –
he still waitin' for his missus –
his missus come up ooh –
prob'ly half an hour's time –
the woman must have give him time you know –
'Oh mus' be nearly time for my oldfella to comeback' –
but he was about half an hour late might be, his man was there
   already with the fish he was –
the oldfella was cooking –
fish, aaah they had a talk there –
that was about, dinner time –
now he said er –
'Where you bin?' –

'I wen' fishing –
err not fishing walkin' round –
I jus' lookin' round for shells you know' he said aaah –
ah –
'You can tell lie all right' he said –
'What for' he –
'Oh I seen you –
you and that Malay man' he said (chuckle) 'Yeah' –
'No no no no I dunno nothing about these Malay p –'
'Oh yes, I was there standing up right alongside' he said
'I know what's goin' on –
so never mind' he said 'Tha's all right –
never worry' –
say 'Come on yunmi better go[5] –
see if we can get some –
we go this way bush –'

they wen' bush –
oh 'long the beach you know very close to beach –
'You bin goin' round with that Malay bloke that's right?'
he tell-im –
that man –
'Yes' he tell-im –
aah –
he had tommyhawk in his belt –
aah –
well, yeah –
'You see that one he say'[6] –
yeah that woman look –
he get the tommyhawk cut his neck right off –
with the to(haha)mmyhawk, finish –
head fall down –
then he start to chop him up then finish –
(Soft) in little pieces –
chuck 'em in the sea –
tha's the finish –

soo –
that fella wen' back –
to his camp –
pick up all his things what he had there –
pack up all his things –
an' he went straight to Thangoo Station –

Thangoo Station, there is a big camping ground there belongs
   to people too –
'Aah' –
'Aah' –
'Where you come from?' these people ask-im you know –
'I come from Broome' –
'Aah what about you missus where you missus?' –
'Oh I left-im in Broome' say –
'Oh, oh yeah –
what time you goin' to go back?' –
'Oh I go back in coupla days time' but coupla days time police
   already there (laughs) –
lookin' for him –
police picked him up –
he had brother there too –
belongs to that woman, dead woman[7] –
'Tha's the man we gotta get' he said 'tha's the bloke tha's him
   there sitting down' –
aah they come up police come up picked him up –
put a chain round his neck –
chain round his legs –
hand –
finish –

'All right' he say 'We gotta take you back to Broome –
better come with us' –
'All right' he said 'you bin kill your missus?' –
'Yes' he tell-im –
'Aha' –
now they took-im back –
they comeback –
they camp in –
no they got early there –
they comeback for dinner –
halfway –
the one governmen' well –
tha's Cockle Well –
Robuck Plain –
so policeman and policeboy was very tired you know –
they dragged that bloke all the way –
like a dog you know with a chain[8] – (laughs)
walking –
footwalk –

173

and two bloke policeboy and policeman riding 'orse –
'All right we let the horses go –
let the horses have a –
rest (exhales) you know –
let-im have a feed –
while we have our rest' –
so they let the horses go –
to take all the pack horses everything out packs –
they have their rest –
ooh till about –
three o'clock I think –
all right –
p'liceman tell his boy 'You better get the horses I think now –
nearly time –'
all right –
policeboy go and get the horses –
bring all the horses back –
policeboy comeback –
policeman was packin' up all the gear –
plate an' billy-can an' everything puttin' them all in the pack
  you know ready –
tighten everything up –
policeboy come straight up 'Hey' he said 'Where's that man?' –
policeboy sing out to police –
'He's under that tree' –
'Where?' –
they look round –
'Oh Chris' he's gone!' –
so they walked up there an' had a look –
the chain –
from his neck –
still got lock –
from his leg –
still got lock – (laugh)
'Hullo' now they start thinking 'What's wrong?' –
'Ooooh' the p'lice boy say 'Might be tha's –
that man must be *maban* man[9] –
he very clever man'' –
'Yeah?' –
'Yeah' –

so they went back to Broome –
they couldn't find him –

no track –
where he come out –
his track where he was layin' down there –
but after that no track –
nothing –
so they comeback –
Sergeant asked them blokes –
'Oh, you find the man?' –
'Yeah we found-im' – (laugh)
'Where is he?' –
'Oh we lost him again –
here's the chain' –
they show that Sergeant (laughs) –
'He come out of the chain jus' disappeared' –
(gravel voice)[10] 'Aaah doooon't' –
Sergeant never believe –
(laughs) he couldn' believe –

so next time they went back again –
lookin' for 'im –
they hear that man is back again in the same place –
'Oooh he's back there' –
so somebody grab-im over there too –
that sister er brother belong to that sister –
you know dead, dead woman –
he grabbed (laughs) that man –
and send somebody –
from there on foot right up to police –
'We got that man here we holding him' –
so police must come and pick-im-up –
they pick-im-up –
they went out for him pick-im-up again from same place –
he come with them right up to police station this time –
right up to police station –
right up –
right up to police station –
yeah –
'Here's the bloke –
tha's the murderer –
we got him now' –
'Oh good' –
'All right' he say –
Sergeant –

oh **they** got a few statement off him –
when they got the statement and everything off him they put-
   im in the lock-up, room –
oooh cemen' wall too –
old lock-up –
police station –
lock-up room –
lock-im-up –
put the key everything in –
all right –

soo –
ooooh bat –
five o'clock I think in the afternoon –
they want to give him supper –
Sergeant went there himself with the –
with the supper you know he bring supper for him –
tea –
go in there open the put the plates down and everything tea –
open the –
door –
he went inside –
have a look in the (laughs) lockup room –
he's not there –
he went all the place –
lockup you know, rooms –
nothing –
nothing –
couldn't find im –
'Aaah', *meow* –
meow –
one pussycat on top you know walkin' round –
(growl) [10] 'Aaah' Sergeant grab stick 'Shh! go on! get out!' –
(laughs) OUT he got through the door –
gone –
soon as he went other side er police station he's a man walking
   in the footpath (laughs) –
he go 'cross the creek –
Broome Creek –
oh everybody seen 'im –
all the people seen 'im –

so police went round now look –

'We lost one bloke from –
from the police station –
you people seen-im?' –
'Yes!' they say –
'Where?' –
'He was walkin' along the footpath here –
he gone –
to Fisherman Bend same place again that way' –
but that was him –
he turn himself into cat – (laughs)
an' Sergeant himself hunt him out from (laughs) lock-up room
    (laughs) –
so he went –
finish –
(Stephen: True story?)[11] Eh? (Stephen: True story?) –
yeah, he gone –
finish –
sooo, when he wen' back they grab him again –
the same people –
same people –
oooh well he was thinkin' this time –
'I think no good' he say –
'My people don't like me' –
so they send one more man –
footwalk –
they grab that bloke they hold-im there –
a place called *kibilarid* –
that's where their camping ground is *kibilarid* –
that's in Thangoo country –
all right they come back –
policeman come again –
pick-im-up –
they bring-im right up to Broome –
this time they put 'im on the boat –
straight away –
boat was there too waiting –
they send him to Fremantle –
Fremantle –
they took him right up to Fremantle on –
the boat –
he was all right –
he was still in boat –
(Softer) he was on the boat –

he wanted to go too –
have a look at the country I s'pose (laughs) he went right up to
Fremantle –
they going to hang 'im –
hang 'im straight away –
'cos those days they hang people you know –

all right they took-im right up –
must be hangin' place there too eh in Fremantle big place is it?
   (Stephen: Yeah) yeah well tha's right –
so they took-im there –
all right –
they gave-im last supper –
ooh feed anyway –
tucker you know –
after that they put-im on ah –
I dunno what –
mighta been some sorta flatform?[12] –
they put the rope around his neck –
they put-im on that one –
it's ready –
(soft) straight away before he get out you know –
they had to do everything quick –
while he was there –
you know –
(soft) all right –
(breathy) they musta count –
from ten backward I s'pose (laughs) you know –
they count –
he know too he, he know all that counting –
he was, he had the rope round his neck –
the LAST number –
the, that, flatform musta go down eh or something –
I, I dunno how they do that but (Stephen: Yeah, goes down)
   there's something, yeah –
right! GO! finish –
he fly out he's eaglehawk –
the loop was there (laughter) the hang rope you know –
an' he's gone he's eaglehawk (laughs) –
he fly away riight back to his country (laughs) –
(Stephen: Good one!) (laughs) –
(Aside to Nangan) eaglehawk *iyena* – *ginyargu* –
(Nangan: Em[13]) –

waragan[14] you know, eaglehawk (soft) he fly away –
(Softer) he was a eaglehawk then –

all right –
so when he land in his place –
he made a song –
for that one –
Fremantle –
you know –
he made a song now I gonna sing this song –
djabi, djabi song[15] –
I'll sing –
(Stephen: Mm)–

(Start high)
ah brimanta la la la wiriri
brimanta mudjaring ngalea
brimanta la la la wiriri
brimanta mudjaring ngalea
brimanta la la la wiriri (growl)
brimanta mudjaring (out of breath)
(takes breath)
brimanta la la la wiriri
brimanta mudjaring ngale
tali minma walburu ridjanala
tali minma
tali minma walbur – walburu ridjanala
tali minma – li minma walburu ridjanala
tali minma
brimanta **la la la wiriri**
brimanta mudjaring ngalea
brimanta la la la wiriri brimanta **mabu**[16]

sooo that's im –
so I'll tell you what the meaning on that one –
(Stephen: Oh yeah, yes please) on the song (Stephen: yeah) –
brimanta means Fremantle (Nangan: Fremantle, Stephen: Oh
    yeah) –
(laughs) you know but he never call-im proper, well that's
    Fremantle Fremantle *briiimanta* –
la la la wiriri 'cos this man wanted to hang him had red clothes[17]
    –

(Stephen: Wiriri) *wiriri* –

179

wiriri means red –

you know (Stephen: *La la la* just tune) yeah *la la la* just tune *la la laaa wiririii* –

(Sings) *briimantaaa la la laaa wiririii brimanta* you see he had red clothes –

that man wanted to hang this bloke (laughs) –

and *mudjaring ngalea* –

mudjaring ngalea he bin run away *mudjari* –

mudjara means run away (Stephen: Yeah) –

run away –

mudjari –

mudjaraaa mudjariii ngalea that's his –

ngalea means that's his –

he had power in his –

in him you know –

in his belly[18]–

maban maban (Stephen: *Ngalea* belly) yeah –

(Sings) *mudjariii ngaleaaa* (Stephen: Why, why belly?) yeah –

an' *tali minma, walbaru ridjanala tali minma* that's telephone everybody bin ringin' up to hang this man (laughs) (Stephen: *Minma*) on the telephone (Stephen: *Minma*, man?) eh?–

(Stephen: *Minma* is man) yeah – (Stephen: Is it?) –

(Sings)
tali minma walbaru ridjanala
tali minma andjirili irbina
njirili ibina njirili ibina

means the telephone –

njirili you know –

telephone –

poles –

(Stephen: Ya) that's, everybody been ringin' up –

this man gotta get hanged today –

telephone –

taliii minma means he tell-im everybody you know –

just like he talk little bit in English too –

telephone you know (Stephen: Yeah *minma*) mm –

(Sings)
tali minmaa walburuu ridjanala
tali minma andjilri irbina
tali minma walburu ridjanala

yeah –
they didn't know I –
they didn' know me he say I gonta fly –
gonta (laughs) turn into eaglehawk –
that's when he kept that inside here –
in his, *maban* in his belly you know –
(Stephen: Mm) so that's all (Stephen: That's a beauty that one)
  and that man name is[19] –
(Stephen: I got 'im – Mirdinan) ahh Mirdinan (Stephen: Yeah,
  Mirdinan) Mirdinan yeah –
huncle too –
my uncle I call-im uncle (Stephen: Oh!) (Nangan: Mirdinan
  ngadja) *mirdinan ngadja* his name –
mirdinan ngadja –
this one[20] call him *djambardu*, grandfather (Nangan: Mm
  djambardu) *djambardu* yeah grandfather –
call-im huncle –
(Stephen: That story's in your family!) (laughs) yeah yeah –
oh yes he's a family –
he belong to this country too (to Nangan) *ginja marda?* he
  belong to this country (Nangan: Yeah yeah) yeah he's our
  people –
seaside –
yeah –
he mix with (Nangan: Aaaall what Njigina) –
Nyigina Yaour Garajderi everything he's –
we all one –
so he's one of our people too that fella –
you know this country people seaside –
ooh yeah[21] –
that's not the finish yet –
of the story –
that one (Stephen: Mm) –
but then people still –
when he come back –
now these people ask him –
'How did you come back? Where you come back from?' –
'I come back from Fremantle' say –
'Fremantle?' –
'Yes' –
'How you come back from Fremantle?' they said –
'I fly –

I bin turn meself into eaglehawk –
I fly from there right back to my country' (laughs) –

and –
he come back from his country, that's from bush –
to these people where policeman used to pick him up all the
    time you know –
but these people didn' like him –
they still want the –
gibim to the police²² –
if the police can' do anything well they ought to kill that old
    fella too you know his own people –
(Stephen: Yeah) they ought to kill him –
same way like how this woman but they gave him –
they didn't want to get trouble –
from the police, they had to give-im back to police –

so they gave him back to police one more time –
and everybody gave him a drink, policeman gave him a drink –
made him drunk – (laughs)
and they put-im on the boat and nail-im-up in the box –
you know they made a box for him nail him up inside –
chuck-im on the boat –
when they got halfway –
this bloke was drunk –
inside –
so he lost himself –
(Stephen: Mm) –
and they chuckled that –
they chuck-im overboard –
in the middle of the sea (Stephen: Oh) –
with the anchor –
or some sorta weight anyway (Stephen: Mm) –
so the box won't float –
so that's the finish of him (Stephen: Mm) –
he's dead –
that way –
they had to make-im drunk (laughs) –
and the poor bloke –
they bin make-im drunk eh (Nangan: Yeah) –
yeah, an' he lose himself –
but he coulda come out of that box too if they didn't –
give-im drink –

182

(Nangan: Take-im outside Broome) –
yeah outside Broome, oh the middle of the sea –
(Nangan: That deep hole there) –
in er steamer passage you know –
in the middle of the sea –
but they put weight too so the box won't float –
so they got him that way –
but they had to give-im drink before they can (Laugh) –
before they can beat-im you know –
that's the only way they can beat-im the some other ways they
    couldn' beat-im –
he was a very clever man –
this fella –
oh everybody know this story you know[23]

NOTES

1. *Karnun* is the local Aboriginal name for Fisherman's Bend.

2. This could be translated as 'his wife knew a Malay man who was on a boat in the creek'. The story refers to events which probably occurred in the early 1920s when many Malays, Japanese and Chinese were working in the booming pearling industry.

3. The pearling luggers were flat-bottomed and would be left dry in the creeks at low tide.

4. 'Coming back with nothing' is a motif in these stories which indicates that something has gone wrong.

5. *yunmi* means 'you and me'.

6. Mirdinan points to something to avert her gaze.

7. 'belongs to' means they were in a certain relationship, brother and sister in this case.

8. Many Aboriginal prisoners were brought into town in this way.

9. A *maban* is an Aboriginal 'doctor'. These are men or women who are well-trained in Aboriginal law and have special perceptive skills or fighting skills.

10. A 'growling' voice used in disbelief, or to admonish someone, disperse dogs, etc.

11. A 'true story' is like a legend. It is about identifiable people and events in the not-too-distant past. This classification is opposed to *bugaregara* stories (stories of the 'dreaming'). The interruption also occurs at a structural break in the story.

12. 'Flatform' is a linguistic hypercorrection. Since Aboriginal languages lack 'f' sounds, these are mostly pronounced like 'p'. Somebody over-correcting their 'p's' will therefore produce words such as this.

13. Butcher Joe Nangan.

14. *Waragan* is the word for eaglehawk in Nyigina.

15. *Diabi* is a type of 'popular' Aboriginal song, found also throughout the Pilbara.

16. *mabu* (Nyigina) means 'good', 'finished'. This song was sung in unison by Paddy Roe and Butcher Joe Nangan. The bold lettering indicates their singing together, while the single underlining indicates Butcher Joe alone.

17. The judge.

18. The 'belly' is seen as the location of personal power and personal feelings.

19. The listener is being tested to see if he remembers the name.

20. He is meaning Butcher Joe.

21. A certain amount of text, concerning the kinship of Mirdinan to Broome people was edited at this point.

22. 'gibim' is 'give him'.

23. The narrator is pointing out that this is a public rather than a secret story.

Moya Costello

BRIAN 'SQUIZZY' TAYLOR

Hey, I must tell you what happened the other day.

You know how we went up the coast, um, with that young guy. He was like, ah, a self-styled punk. Yeah. Only about fourteen. Well he got involved in London, he was staying there for a while, with these working-class kids; you know, like real punks. They wrecked football trains and he got hooked on cough-mixture and god knows what, dog pills. Well, he came up the coast with us to dry out, and it's just rife with hippies, you know, blonde hair, Balinese gear, god! They went crazy over Richard Clapton, he had a concert there, when he sang 'I've got those Blue Bay blues', you know, about Byron Bay. I mean, that song must have been written ten years ago. Well, o god, he wore a heavy German overcoat, like a military one, and heavy boots, like these great clumping things and he had black pants, and short spiky hair dyed red and he walked onto the sand; I mean this is the middle of summer, the proverbial burning deserts; and I thought: what is this guy going to do? And then I thought: what do punks do in summer? No, really. What do you do in black plastic? It's nonabsorbent right? Surely you have to consider these things. Unless, I don't know punks go in for endurance tests. I mean, it's downright uncomfortable. And black, all that black. It just absorbs the heat. And try to keep looking pasty-faced. They probably raid the chemists for Block-Out. I mean, how are you going to avoid a tan? Well, you just couldn't go out, could you. I mean, punks are really out of place in Australia, aren't they? Winter is the season of the punk. They must have a really hard time in Australia. Well, you'll never guess. I was just looking at the paper the other day, and what do you think? I saw this piece about this Brian 'Squizzy' Taylor, and he's a punk-surfie. Can you imagine that? I mean it's taken an Australian to do it. Are Australians known for their ingenuity or something? 'cause this guy's got it. He's won some surfing award or something, you know, like riding a board. He's got these black wraparound sunglasses and tight pants and sandshoes, and he walks onto the beach like that, I mean isn't that amazing? It's like, well I think it was an art book, yeah, on Van Gogh, and in it his letters to his brother were quoted, and I remember looking them up and finding they hadn't been published in English, then I don't know, a few weeks later a book of his letters came out, in hardback; it's one of the few hardbacks I've bought; I bought another one, I think it was *Blood Red Sister Rose*, you know, by the Australian guy, Thomas Kenneally, that's right; or another time I'd seen a programme on Che Guevara and Tanya, his last girlfriend, and then I was just looking at some poetry in a bookshop and I saw a poem about Tanya by William Carlos Williams, or was it one of the American women poets, Anne Sexton or someone? Yeah, and then I was thinking about how punks manage in Australia and here's this Brian 'Squizzy' Taylor in the paper.

Carmel Kelly

PARK

Now. That is it. Yes. That is the point where we stopped. Where the dead black leaves circled so slowly as the trickle of water entered the small shallow depression in the rocks. The pale amber path led us to this point where the creek crossed the bush in a thin line and the rocks began. This also was the point where the Christmas bush, singing a sweet crushed pink, bloomed all summer. Such a gentle reminder. I can take this creek at any time. On a gloomy afternoon, when it might rain in the quiet that is a silence that belongs to no time, we hear the creek slowly murmuring, gurgling through the shrubs that dip low into the water. The water spiders skitter cheekily against the black mirror of the water. The sun is about to set a sure and definite red, hurting the horizon. The day is ending. Soon we will return to our warm home and have chops and fresh peas and read our favourite book. And there will be cups of tea all night with mint and honey. There is no way time can be stopped. Whatever has passed has become fiction. I have no proof that any of this existed except to say. Go there. Go to the bush. Take that path and you will see that I am right. The creek existed, where it forks the path. There may however be no trace, no evidence that I was there. But it is alright. That time is destroyed. We will see it no more. You have your turn to see and discover.

Today is the hottest day of all. We have reached the Karloo pool around midday. The ants are racing on the path. The Karloo pool today is a deep amethyst green, a forest green, the green of a dress ring, but varying from amber at the edges to a sudden plunge of cool green. The children run down the bush path. The heath is flowering and a faint perfume fills the air. The gymea lilies are in bloom this year they say. Gymea lilies flower every seven years they say. Sometimes they are called Illawarra lilies they say and they run run run in the summer heat, their faces bright. They are happy! They will eat when they are hungry! They run run run to their favourite pool and then they pause. This is a silent moment. The water is gently twirling. There is an embankment. And then a rock extends into the deep part. What you do is shift down this rock and then you are standing up to your waist, no your chest, in a silent coldness. And then you move a little further in and you are now ABOVE YOUR HEAD!!! Your feet can't touch the bottom! You can swim, however, very quickly to a rock just a few yards away on the other bank. Your hand touches rock. Your feet touch the cold rough grey rock and you look down and there are your hands, your legs, distorted in the glass. You laugh. You are exhausted. And then you look over the length, the long slow length of the silver pool to the vee where the hills meet in the valley. Shall we stay here till nightfall? Till the sun goes down and the long pool turns still and black and the black crows stop flying? Shall we sit on this rock that leans into the water and watch the amber water forever? The mother is reading, sunbaking on her back. The flies torture. She has on a big straw hat. Her long thin brown aboriginal body is lying there. What is she reading? A novel in French or German? Maybe *Voss*. The mother reads reads. She doesn't mind being disturbed by her children. Her children can run run everywhere. Take off your clothes she says. Let the sun feel your body, make you feel good. No, say the children. People will see us. Don't be silly says the mother. But the children know the boys on their bikes will come creeping down the path. Suddenly they will look up and see a scarlet bike gleaming through the gums. Mum! they will scream. People! And the mother quickly covers her naked flesh, her flat soft breasts, and looks around indignantly.

The river from this pool now begins an exploration that is unbelievable. Very shortly, just around the corner, the river arrives at a BEACH. A beach of fine white sand in the middle of the Royal National Park. And then the river begins a story that will always remain unspoken. The river turns to clear glass. All the gumtrees are reflected with a shimmer in the clear glass.

The river moves past trees and clouds. The river moves so slowly, transparently. This National Park was the second one in the world to be declared. But its beauty has never been sung. Take me to that waterway where I have tried to recreate life, unsuccessfully from memory. Take me to that shore and I will make you see what I say. Some strangers are telling me it is beautiful. And what can I say? This was once my childhood. This was where I lived. This was my territory. And once it was the tribe's. This is where my soul grew. This is the country I was made of. This was where I learnt about something so perfect, so exquisite that I cannot live for long without it.

And now the atomic reactor's perfumed breath drifts within three miles of these pools, the green crayfish crawling laboriously with one huge over-developed claw over the sandbeds, the lyrebirds, the goannas that climb the big gums and stare, the light yellow wattle, dusted with a white cream, the perfect flannel flowers, the spider flowers, blackboys.

The park is not perfect. It is wild and the flowers are tiny and sometimes obscure. It is not an English beauty. There is no abundance of emerald green. But there are very light bright green gum leaves, fresh in this summer morning.

Anna Couani

XMAS IN THE BUSH

Running along far away from the road. Along the shallow creek bed, the wide flat rocks just below the water, creamy brown. The creek is wide here and open for hundreds of yards until it makes a turn. And straight ahead above the blackberry bushes and foliage along the water's edge is the typical country house with a row of yellow pines up one side, white walls and a red roof. The mother, the father and the children are here. With friends. The adults stand on the beach made of river stones or on the big rock in the middle of the creek or on the bank, talking, talking. All day. They make sandwiches while they talk. They smoke cigarettes. They point at things. The sight of a parent's eyes following the pointed finger across to the bank on the other side of the creek or into the branches of a nearby tree. They gesticulate sometimes. The men put their hands in their pockets and take them out again. The women fold their arms or put their hands on their hips. They go for a walk very slowly while they talk. Along the road, across the ford, up the hill, round the corner. They stay away for hours, talking. The shadow of the hill falls over the creek. It grows cooler. They come back and organise dinner while they talk. The women talk to each other. The men talk to each other. The men talk to the women. They all talk at once. They set out the card table under the trees, light the kerosene lamp and play 500 while they talk. They miss tricks while they talk. The children go to sleep in the tents and wake up in the night and hear them talking. Then later they wake up and everything's quiet.

In the morning the father throws the dog in the water. The dog paddles madly to the shore. The father talks about snags in the river. They all discuss the difference between snags as in water hazards and snags as in sausages. Sausage dogs. Smoke. Children who've drowned. Bushfires. Snakes. Carpet snakes. The long grass. The blackberry patch. The tar baby. Was there such a thing as Brer Bear. The pyjama girl. Bullrushes. Flash floods. Flying foxes. The hazards of flying foxes. High tensile wires and electricity lines. Broken electricity lines hanging down into creeks. Fords with cars on them washed away in flash floods. River snakes. March flies. Bot flies. The difference between bot flies and sand flies. Maggots in sausages. Maggot stories. Meat safe stories. Ice chest stories. Milk delivery when milk was in buckets. The bread cart. The sound of the bread cart. Draught horses. Old draught horses. Horses being sent off to the blood and bone factory. Horses in the city. Sewerage. The sewerage works. Polluted creeks. The correct drinking sections of the creeks. The aeration process. Stagnant water. Boiling the billy. Billy tea. The Billy Tea brand name. The inferior quality of Billy Tea. Swaggies. Gypsies. The cleverness of gypsies. Poverty. Bread and dripping. Sausages. Home-grown vegetables. Outdoor toilets. Improvised toilet paper. The long summer nights. Mosquitoes. Marshes and bogs. Moonee Moonee and Brooklyn. The possibility of a mosquito breeding in the dew on a leaf. Bites. Bee stings. Allergies to bites. Death from bee stings. How to make a whistle from a leaf. Playing the comb. The mouth harp. The bush bass. Bottle tops. The corrosive qualities of Coca Cola. Big Business. Monopolies. Bigger and bigger monopolies. Free enterprise. Russia. The idea of women working in men's jobs. Suez. American election campaigns. The Ku Klux Klan. The colour bar. The Iron Curtain. The Cold War. The ideals of communism as distinct from the practice. China. Industrialisation. Cuba. Atheism and agnosticism. The idea of the supreme being. The church in Russia. The Jews. Israel. The world wars. The next one. The fatalistic approach. The end of civilisation. The end of the human race. The inexorable continuation of the universe in spite of the human race. Humans as microscopic and trivial beings. The frailty of humans. The stupidity of humans. The innate badness of humans. Animal life and animals' code of behaviour. The rationality of animals. The fowls of the air and other biblical quotes. And now I see as through a glass darkly.

At the end of the last hand of 500, they remember other discussions they've had and that they always concluded with politics. The father turns down the Tilley lamp.

Richard Beckett

FORTY SUSAN SANGSTERS STRIDE OUT AT THE WELLINGTON BOOT

I don't know when one of you out there last got a good look at Susan Sangster (she still goes by that name), but a couple of weeks back I crashed into about forty of her. Susan Sangster as a Barbie Doll? The thought is intriguing, to say the least. The social event was the Wellington Boot.

Now, despite the facts that the area of the Central West of NSW is served by a couple of television stations, some Sydney-owned newspapers and a sort of ragbag collection of restaurants, bowling clubs, RSLs, shooting societies and at least one certified chapter of the Hell's Angels, and that grass, snow and smack can be obtained if one knows where to go, unlike Sydney there are certain events in the social calendar that bring joy to a country person's life. The Wellington Boot is one of these.

To end the suspense: the great Boot meeting is in fact a day at the races, with a bit of steak and eggs at the end, as the late great Lennie Lower used to say with more than some enthusiasm.

The town of Wellington lies about three-quarters of an hour to the north-west of us (all times recorded in this column are by Holden ute with my crazed New Zealand partner at the wheel). In the 1820s it was the Government cattle station. Molong at that time was a sort of halfway station, and the great town of Orange was almost nothing and known as Blackmans Swamp. The iron gangs were on the road. And as I've said in previous columns, although Banjo Paterson was born down the bottom of the road, so to speak, he thought nothing of us; and Henry Lawson brought Joe Wilson and all his damned mates from

Gulgong, which unfortunately is a good hundred kilometres away over a couple of hills.

Now one would think that a country race meeting would be a fairly pristine event from the point of view of smells. A little scent of horse manure in the air, the anguished hate-sweat of a broken punter, and a scent of fear 'because this isn't my money and the boss might see me' from some renegade fencer. Not a bit of it.

I'm here to tell you that country race meetings, despite the fact that they are held in the wide open spaces under huge peppertrees (of South African origin, if anyone is interested) smell just the same as any supermarket mall that one can encounter in any Sydney suburb. To my mind the miasma is made up of a combination of whale oil and MSG on a greasy hotplate. Not a pretty nostrilful.

However, not only do the ordinary punters eat the things, but the Susan Sangster Look-Alikes positively dote upon them (at least at the Wellington Boot). They also dote upon that great old Harold Park Australian favourite. It is called a nasty mess of long red things in a huge stainless steel tub of boiling water, with wet buns on the side, and two jars – one of yellow stuff which is not mustard and another of red stuff which is not tomato sauce.

The wet red thing is put into the long white rubber thing and a knife used to put some muck on top of the lot. This year America really got at Wellington. The convict station didn't have any mustard. American salad cream had been substituted. And, so help me, given the cultural cringe, some whackers were asking for what they believed was more or less a genuine convict hotdog.

Meanwhile, the forty Susan Sangsters were more or less a-leapin' which got me into the partridge-and-a-peartree situation.

One knew when one came to Molong that one was going into a time warp. Once I believed that this warp was about 1950. I was wrong. At the Wellington race meeting, despite the fact that the Boot was won by a late 20th century horse by the name of Matilda's Waltz, in many respects both of us were back in the 11th century and the Divine Right of Kings.

For starters, there were tents for the gentry. However, the gentry were not saddling up with the great shire and clydesdale horses to take to the lists. No farriers were at their tents. The farriers were looking after King Boe (a splendid grey who won the

Bradshaw Waste Industries Association Stakes). These were not the great fields of Henry VIII. In other words, there was no cloth of gold. The tents in this instance were taken up by what appeared to me to be a splendid lot of both Double Bay Failures and Punks Gone Nice. Not a pretty sight. Fortunately, the betting ring was the usual Australian usual.

So that was the great day out in the country . . . supermarket miasma and bum horses. The Susan Sangsters walked until the dusk fell down. Some of them divested the slightest amount of clothing, but not many.

At the end of the last race a bloke turned to me and said, 'You can stuff him.' It was unclear whether he was referring to a horse or a human being. However, I thought to myself did it really matter until he turned to me and said, 'The French eat the buggers . . .'

Well, yes they do, and a grilled horse steak is slightly sweeter than a New York cut of beef. Some people, in fact, call the taste of horsemeat cloying. But not me. I think it tastes like bad goat. No matter.

You don't have to eat, only to taste at the great Wellington Boot.

(This was originally written when Susan was indeed Mrs Sangster. However this state, as with a number of other features of our lives, has been subject to change.)

FINALE

Beverley Farmer

OUR LADY OF THE BEEHIVES

Tomorrow, thought Kyria Eirini, waking as the house sighed and crackled in the dark, tomorrow I'll go to the church. To the Panagia of the Beehives. For Varvara's sake.

The Panagia *sta Melissia*, as it was known, was hardly a church at all, compared to the proper one in the town square, Agios Nikolaos, the patron saint of sailors. The Panagia's was little more than a *parekklesi*, a chapel built to honour a promise by the grandfather of the man who kept the bees now. If the Panagia would save his sons in the storm that had wrecked the fishing boats – he stood watching from the hill among the torn acacia trees – he would build Her a chapel, he vowed. He built it in the shape of a bee box, but with a small square tower, and mixed blue in the whitewash to make it the same colour as the hives. The oil lamp before the ikon of the Panagia would never go out, the old mothers of the town made sure of that.

Inside there was a rustling, never pure silence, even when no one was there; and when the lamps were lit for a *litourgeia* an amber light filled it. The candles on sale at the entrance were made of the pale beeswax, and smelled of honey as they burned. An itinerant artist, having covered the walls and ceiling with images of haloed saints, had painted the shawled Panagia Herself with a gilded Child in skirts, in a garden full of lilies and large brown bees.

Kyria Eirini, turning over on her bed in the hot house, told herself to go and light a candle to the Panagia in the morning. Two candles: one for her dead Vassili, whose sins were forgiven; and one to ask Her to do something. And this morning I won't wake Andoni to go and buy fish. I'll let him off. I'll make *imam bayildi* for lunch instead, she thought; and fell asleep again.

Barbara, in the dark beside Andoni, felt swollen all over, raw and gritty from the day's sun and salt and sand. Like a hard-boiled egg her body held the heat in. She had dreamt again that some great whining insect, a bee or a wasp, had stung her. In this dream she was asleep on the beach in the noon sun. Waking as the sting pierced her, she was alarmed to see darkness. The harsh slow sound she heard was not waves, but Andoni's breathing.

Vassilaki cried out in his sleep. She got up and knelt with her cheek against his. 'Mama?' he murmured.

'Nani', she said. 'Go to sleep.' But he was fast asleep.

She sighed. It was too hot to lie awake. Instead she crept into the shadows of the sitting room, switched on the hard light and tore two pages out of her diary to write a letter to her sister.

Dear Jill (she would address it Poste Restante).

I hope you arrived safely and love Athens. We're all fine here. It was great to see you and Marcus. We've just moved into a better house, the Captain's, no less, two floors furnished. The bedrooms are upstairs, with homespun sheets and lots of chairs, a table, but the rooms are large and full of heat – bare planks for floors. Downstairs we cook and eat and keep cool. We have a marble-slabbed bench with a sink and a *tap* – running water! – and a portable gas stove-top with two large burners and a little one for the coffee *briki*. (If we run out of gas a neighbour's child will run to the *kafeneion* for us and along will come the *kafedjis* with a new bottle on his motor scooter.) The Captain and family have moved next door. His wife has left us plates, cups, glasses, cutlery, pots, pans, baskets . . . There's a large round dining table, painted shiny green, and ten rush-bottomed chairs. There are spiky bundles of herbs – mostly *rigani* – hung like birch brooms on the wall, and plaits of onions and garlic, and shrivelled hot red peppers on a string: we are to help ourselves. Her yellow tabby sits on guard day and night.

And as if all that were not enough, this house has a lid!

Well, it has an indoor staircase, as well as the usual cement outside one: an indoor ladder, really, fixed into the floor and leading to a trapdoor set in the planks above. The *kapaki*, they call it: the lid. The older houses all have one. It props open on its hinges, or there's a ring in the wall to hook it into, or you can keep it shut – the sensible thing, Andoni's mother says, when there's a child to worry about. The lid looks too heavy for Vassilaki, but it's not, only awkward to lift. Besides, any one of us, being unused to houses with lids, might step into space where floor should be. (She looks on the dark side.) So we don't let Vassilaki go near it. (The Captain's wife agrees.)

It's like *Treasure Island*!

For the rest: no bath, but as the Captain said, with the sea so near who needs one in summer? And in an annexe behind the kitchen there's a cubicle with a sit-down toilet, a sewered one, a bucket of water to flush it, and a plastic waste-paper basket for the used paper which we mustn't ever flush, only burn.

As for the washing, we heat water in a sooty pan of the Kapetanissa's, kindling a fire under it in the yard with twigs and brambles, wads of newspaper and (yes) used toilet paper. We wash the clothes in plastic basins and rinse them in the wheelbarrow with the hose . . . In short, it's bliss!

I wish you could come and see, but of course you have to get back to London. Tell Marcus the whole town asks after him ('that brother of yours, is it, that Marko') and please write soon.

Much love,
Barbara.

It was not what she had meant to write, but it would have to do. In the yellow glare she flicked over the pages she had written when Vassilaki was a baby. A couple of pages, that was all, in two years. She was always tired.

He lies in my arms (she read).

To sleep he has to suck one fist and clamp the other in my hair, or in his own.

When he cries and I pick him up he sobs, pushing his face into my armpit, like our old cat.

I unwrap his heavy napkin. He has a small pink bag, seamed and ruched, and above it a pink stalk that extends itself and squirts, like some sea creature.

With a grunt he squeezes out mustard, soft lobster mustard.

He presses on the white bags that give him milk, and opens and shuts his vague eyes.

It might be a girl this time, she thought. We can call her Eirini and that will gratify Andoni's mother. Andoni would have to be told soon, when the time was right. It was a wonder he hadn't guessed. He had something on his mind.

When she sank back on the bed in the dark, Andoni took her in his arms and drove fiercely inside her. Neither of them spoke. He was slippery all over. He hissed like a dolphin surfacing, and then subsided. They drifted back into sleep.

The Captain's daughter, Voula, lying awake in her room next door, saw the gold lozenge of their sitting room light fall on the balcony, and later disappear. It was Andoni, she thought. 'I love you, Voula, my darling,' she whispered in English, though she had only ever heard Andoni speak Greek. She saw herself on the balcony again, brushing out her hair in swathes, hair smelling of rain water; and Andoni looking on. How could such a man have married a thin ginger-yellow oblivious foreign broomstick of a woman like Barbara?

It was almost as if he were not married at all.

She stood up. Her mother was snoring in the next room. She crept out of the cracking house, past other moon-white houses and along a dusty path fenced with sharp thistles to a beach out of sight of the town. The lights of the gri-gri boats were as small as the stars. She dropped her clothes on the dry sand and padded across the black suede of the wet sand with its cold pools of stars, knotting her hair in a crown as she went, to keep it dry. Then she ran straight into the thick water. The shock of it made her shudder. It was so cold it was as if she had been cut in half: she could neither feel nor see herself below the waist. She bobbed down and quickly up. Her breasts glowed, dropping glints of water. Her feet stung now where thistles had scratched them. Blood pounded in her head.

If she floated, her face lying on the water should be a mirror of the moon. But then she would wet her hair. She would be found out. A moon afloat in black ice.

The heroine of a book she had read swam alone at night. She was a sea-girl too, a fisherman's daughter, the foundling child of a mermaid; and a man watched her, watched Smaragdi in the water. But that was not why, Voula insisted to herself: I love swimming at night and I always have and I always will.

But she knew that this time she was hoping that Andoni, unable to sleep, would sense where she was and follow her.

'Who's there?' she would say, splashing to make a surface of froth to cover her.

'Andoni,' he would say. 'Did I frighten you?'

What would she say? 'No. It's all right.'

'What?' He would falter. He would not be sure.

'A little. But don't go. It's all right.' She moved her cold hands over her breasts. His hands would be dry, warm.

A whimper came from the shore. She stiffened, horrified. On the grey sand a shadow was moving towards her clothes. With a gasp she sank to her nose to hide. She could see a white body, long-legged, white-scarved: no, it was a goat. 'Meh,' it said.

With a snort of alarmed laughter Voula splashed out. *'Fige'*, she hissed, and it stared at her. *'Fige!'* She slapped its burry rump and it trotted off, its frayed rope hopping behind it. Glancing anxiously at shadows, she dragged her clothes on to her wet skin and hurried along the path. Thistles slashed her. The goat, looking back, leaped and was gone. Moonlight lay heavy and white on shuttered walls. Nothing moved. Her shadow was sharp, and at every streetlamp a dim one joined it, grew and dwindled away. It reminded her of the game she played with Vassilaki's shadow when they went to the beach; Andoni's little boy. Her step was light as the shadows falling. No one seeing her out at this time of night would doubt why.

The door creaked, but her mother snored on. She laid herself cool and dry on her bed and yawned. Bubbles of blood stung on her ankles. The moon was blue stripes on a wall.

A loud door creaked, waking Barbara, but no other sound followed. The house creaked a lot as the night cooled. She lay and thought that the air in the room was like coal in a fire, black and steadily smouldering. It would be good to walk through the grey dust of the streets now. The boats would be converging out at sea, gathering in the net. *Savridia*, she thought: *kefalopoula, marides, barbounia, fagri, sardelles*. She knew more fish in Greek than in English. It would be good to wade into cold black water flickering with fish. But there would be a scandal if anyone saw her. Besides, she was tired.

With a sigh she turned her soaked body over. A donkey sobbed, a goat gave a sudden meh-eh-eh. Soon the roosters would wake. Soon Andoni's mother would knock on the door and call Andoni to go and buy fish, unless she slept in. Soon Vassilaki would wake, waking them all.

She closed her eyes and slept.

2

Voula met Andoni coming out of the water with his speargun and flippers, pushing his mask up on to his rough hair. 'Hullo, did you catch any?' she said.

'No. None there.'

'Bad luck.'

'You're looking very beautiful today.'

'I look very beautiful every day.'

'Is that so?'

She only smiled and swung away, ruffling the surface. That he was watching her made her aware of all her colours and shapes intensified in the morning sea. In a few minutes he waded back in and floated and swam lazily some metres away. But neither of them spoke again.

This morning as usual Barbara had clothes and napkins to wash, soaking in a basin on the back *taratsa*. She wrung them out and with a grunt hurled the dirty water into the vegetable garden. Hens skittered. She poured powder and hot clean water on the clothes and pumped and kneaded them. There were ripe grapes already in the vine above her head, and flies crowded in them. The morning sun shone through grapes and leaves; she looked on the ground for green reflections, as if they were made of glass; but the shadows were black. They were sharp in the still light. Strange, thought Barbara, brushing sweat off her eyebrows, how shadows look sharper on a still day, as if a wind would blur air as it blurs water. Bubbles catching the sun in her basins of clothes were like white opals.

Kyria Eirini swept the leaves and hens' droppings off the dry earth of the yard with a straw broom with no handle, then rinsed and wrung out the clothes with Barbara and helped her hang them out. Then she went in to tidy up. When she opened the shutters and panes to air the rooms, the sun fell in thickly and whatever was inside glowed, furred with gold. No matter how often she dusted, more dust drifted in and settled. At least it's fresh dust, thought Kyria Eirini. Insects buzzed in and out.

She was glad when Barbara and Vassilaki went to the beach at last, to the same spot as always, so she knew where to find them. She would rather stay and be alone in the Kapetanissa's kitchen. She boiled rice in milk and honey to make *rizogalo*, stirred it and poured it on to plates to cool before she tapped cinnamon over its tightening lumpy skin. Andoni and Vassilaki loved her *rizogalo*. She sliced doughy eggplants and salted them, sliced onions and garlic and tomatoes. She breathed in the smell as the olive oil smoked in her hot pans. 'God be praised,' she muttered. 'Everything we need, He gives us.' She slid slices of eggplant in and the oil frothed over them.

Barbara came to life only in the sea. Her speckled body glowed, magnified, and made its green gestures metres above her shadow on the sea floor. Pebbles were suddenly large then small as the water moved. She dived to grasp one. A bird must feel like this, she thought as she dived and twisted, gasped, the bubbles pounding in her ears: a bird flying in rain. When she came up a white net of light enfolded her lazily.

When she came out of the water she lay on a towel with another towel over her to keep off the sun, and lay in a daze facing the sea. Whenever she blinked she saw a flare of red: then the green sea, then the red flare again, as regular as a lighthouse lamp.

Kyria Eirini bent over her eggplants arranged like small black boats in the pan, ladling the filling of onions and tomatoes more carefully than usual into each one: the pan would be on show in the baker's oven. Barbara would be annoyed with her for struggling down the hot road to the bakery with it, when they could have had something easy for lunch. The thought of Barbara's annoyance was almost as pleasant as the thought of how Andoni would carry it home, sucking his fingers coppery with oil when he arrived because he had picked at it on the way.

So she struggled, hot in her black clothes, down the road to the baker's, exchanging greetings as she went. She pointed out to the baker exactly where she wanted her pan, and he told her that he knew his oven as he knew his own hand. She bought a hot white loaf and went on to the Melissia to light a candle to the Panagia, which was after all the real reason she was there.

The church was stuffy and dim, with a rosemary smell of old burnt incense. The glazed faces of the saints stared. Kyria Eirini crossed herself and slipped her drachmas into the box for two candles. One she stuck in the tray of sand, for the dead: one in the iron bracket, for the living. The Panagia held her dwarfish Christ to one blue shoulder, her hollow eyes stern.

'It's not for myself,' she thought to the ikon. 'It's for my daughter-in-law. The Australian one. Fool though she is. *Aman.* Has she no pride? Enlighten her, help her, I pray. And the girl too, save her from temptation. Andoni is turning out just like his father was, whose sins are forgiven.'

As she was leaving, a bee settled on her sleeve. She shook it off. It hovered. 'Xout!' she said. They blundered together out into the sunlight.

At home she wrapped the bread in a cloth. Her dress was stuck to her. She swilled cold water from a bucket over the speckled kitchen floor to wash it. Its stones came to life, all their colours, like shingle on a sea floor. The cat that came with the house, and spent the mornings dozing under the table, sprang up on a chair and spat at her. 'Xout!' spat Kyria Eirini. The cat fled to the window sill and hunched there with a brazen scowl.

When Andoni walked in, Kyria Eirini was scrubbing spots out of the washing before Barbara got home. She started and looked guilty. 'You're home early,' she said.

'I said I'd buy the bread.'

'I bought it.'

'Why? When I told you I'd go!'

'I wanted to light a candle. It was on my way. I took a pan of *imam bayildi* as well. You can get that if you like.'

'*Aman*, Mama! You could just as easily cook it here.'

'Yes, but you like it better baked.'

'Not when it's so much more work.'

'But since it's better?'

'Tiring yourself out for nothing. It's madness.'

Andoni's reaction was all she could have hoped.

'Kyria Eirini?' came Voula's voice at the gate. Still in her bathing suit, she was hugging a pile of striped *kilimia*. 'We thought – my mother and I thought – do you need more blankets at night?'

'Ach.' Flustered, Kyria Eirini waved her soapy hands. 'Thank you. That's very kind.'

'I'll leave them upstairs, will I?'

'Yes, there's a good girl. Thank you.'

Voula, padding into the dark kitchen, ran into Andoni before she saw him, he was so dark himself.

'Careful.' He climbed up ahead to hold the *kapaki* open.

Voula laughed. 'I grew up in this house.'

'All the same.'

'My father fell through once. He was drunk at the time.'

'Didn't you ever fall through?'

'I wasn't allowed to go near it.'

'So you never did?' He followed her and shut the trapdoor.

'No, I was a good girl.'

'Was. And now you're not.'

'Is that what you think, is it?'

'I'm hoping to find out. How old are you?'

She blushed. 'Old enough.' No, this was going too far: she looked round for something safe to remark on, and saw waxy lilies in a vase of her mother's. 'Pretty,' she said.

'Take one.' He lifted one out, its curled stalk dripping.

'Oh, no.' She stepped back. 'Are they from Kyria Magda?'

'Why not? Some old woman with whiskers gave them to your mother. Her goat got out and ate half your mother's beans

last night, haven't you heard? You will. You're getting a bucket
of milk too. Your mother hates them, she says, so here they are.'
He nodded the lily at her. 'Take it, come on.'

'They make her sneeze,' she explained.

'Too big to wear.' He held it up to her hair. 'Pity.'

'How can I take it? It would look – I can't.'

With a stare he dropped the lily out the window. Shocked.
Voula ran into the sitting room with the *kilimia*. He climbed
back down to wait, letting the *kapaki* slam shut. But Voula left
the house, trembling, by the outside stairs.

Andoni trudged off to the bakery.

It was a relief when lunch was over. Barbara and Andoni
assured Kyria Eirini that the *imam bayildi* was delicious. But the
baker had burnt one edge of it, and besides she thought there
was just a little too much salt. They didn't think so. Vassilaki
refused to eat any and filled up on all the *rizogalo*.

The washing was dry by then, hooked on the barbed wire
fence among the speckled pods, green and red, of the
Kapetanissa's climbing beans. Drops of water, falling from their
bathers, rolled and were coated with dust. A shirt and a napkin
had fallen on to the red earth. They would have to be washed
all over again. Barbara sighed. Nothing seemed to dry without
its earth or rust or bird stain.

The Kapetanissa had green onions and garlic growing as well
as beans, and eggplants with leaves like torn felt, and cucum-
bers, potatoes, tomatoes, wilting melon vines. Her hens and the
rooster had squeezed through the wire and were scratching and
jabbing among the watered roots. Brown papery birds, murmuring to themselves, their eyes half-closed. Weary of summer.

Vassilaki had seen them too. He ran in by the gate to chase
them out, but they pranced loudly into hiding. 'Xout!' he
shouted.

'Vassilaki?' She had folded the clothes and was up to the
napkins now. 'Where are you?' He came padding out. She
pulled the wire over the gatepost. He was holding a long
funnel-shaped pale flower.

'*Kitta*, mama,' he said. 'Look.' His mother had different
words for everything.

'Mm. It's a lily. Where was it?' she said. Then: 'Put it down
quick! Quick! There's a bee in it.'

So there was, when he looked. A bee with brown fur was
crouched, its legs twitching, in the buttery glow at the bottom of

his lily.

'Why?'

'It wants that yellow dust, see? On those little horns? It wants to make honey. *Meli*. Put it down now.'

'Why?'

'It might bite.'

'Why?' He held it out at arm's length.

'It might think you want to hurt it.'

'Nao,' he told it.

'Just put it down.'

'*Echo melissa*,' he called over the fence to the Kapetanissa and Voula, who had come out to see why the hens were squawking, and were packing the earth back round the roots with their sandalled feet.

'Careful, she bite you!' Voula called back, but softly in case she woke the neighbours.

'*Ela*, Voula!'

'Put it *down*, Vassilaki!'

He dropped his lily. The bee flew out, made a faltering circle and then was lost among the oleanders.

'*Paei*,' he sighed.

'Yes. It's gone.'

'*Paei spiti?*'

'Yes, it's gone home.'

'*Pounto spiti?*'

'In a bee box. On the hill near the church.' He looked puzzled. '*Konta stin ekklesia.*'

'Why?'

'*Paei na kanei meli*,' smiled Voula, shading her eyes. She followed her mother inside.

'Mama?'

'Yes. It's gone to make honey.'

'*Einai kakia.*'

'Who's bad? Voula?'

'Bee.'

'No, it's not, it's good – *kali*. But you have to leave it alone. You can pick up the lily now it's gone.'

'Nao.' They left it lying there.

He went ahead of her up the outside stairs – the wall was too hot to touch – and through the empty sitting room behind the balcony. He had gone when she came up with the washing. '*Pou eisai?*' she whispered. 'Keep away from the *kapaki*.' When there was no answer she looked in the bedroom: only Andoni, asleep. She found Vassilaki in the next room, on his back on the bed beside the black heap that was his grandmother. His eyelids fluttered as she kissed his cheek; he brushed the kiss away with a loose hand. His hair was damp. 'Nani,' she whispered. He was already asleep. The room burned with a buttery glow like that inside the lily.

The floor creaked as she crept in, her soles rasped the planks, but Andoni stayed asleep, as if stunned, his mouth open. He had thrown the sheet off. He glistened, brown all over and shadowed with black hairs, barred as well with shadows that fell from the window over him. She lay down beside him in her dress: they would all be getting up soon. The rough cotton was stuck to her. Her breasts ached. Andoni muttered something indistinct. She sighed, hearing a mosquito whine. Our four bodies in the house, she thought, four bubbles of blood, and a fifth still forming, afloat on our white beds. A hollow light seeped through the shutters. Time and the sun stood still.

4

When they woke, the women always brought coffee and glasses of water up to the balcony. Andoni read the newspapers there. The shadows grew longer almost as they watched, until the street was filled with them. Sometimes a sea breeze rose: the *batis*. Ach, *o batis*, people would say to each other with relief. Sometimes – especially when there was no sea breeze – the family went back to the beach for a late swim, in water warmer and brighter, tawny-shadowed and full of reflections, different from its morning ones. Then the sun shrank, spilling its last light along the hoods of the waves.

This afternoon there was no sea breeze.

'Will you drink a little coffee?' And Barbara woke with a start. Kyria Eirini's grey head was at the door. 'Sorry, Varvara. Were you asleep? Vassilaki's awake.'

'Oh, not just yet, Mama, thank you.'

'Well, whenever you like.' She closed the door. Barbara lay blinking in the hot stillness. There was a crushed hollow beside her; she had not heard Andoni go. Her wrists and ankles itched and had red lumps all over them. She found a mosquito on the dim wall, slapped it, and was trying to wipe off the red smear with spit when the door opened again.

'Varvara, sorry. Vassilaki wants to go to the beach. Ach, not a mosquito? I sprayed too.'

'One. Look at me.'

209

'It's your sweet blood, you see. Vassilaki is insisting. Can you see any more?' They both peered up. 'Not, it was just that one, Varvara *mou*.'

Vassilaki was insisting. '*Thalassa, thalassa, thalassa*,' he chanted.

'We were there all morning,' Barbara moaned.

'*Thalassa pame*, Mama!'

'Mama *nani*,' reproached his grandmother, stopping him in the doorway.

'Let his father take him,' Barbara said.

'He go to buy newspaper,' came Voula's voice in English. 'I take him, if you like.'

'Voula, would you? Come in.'

Voula came to the doorway, a coffee cup in her hand, with the other hand gathering her hair at her nape then letting it flow free. Vassilaki pushed past her: 'Mama!' Kyria Eirini made an apologetic face at Barbara and plucked at his shirt. '*Mi Yiayia!*' And he shook her hand off.

'Come with me today?' Voula squatted beside him.

'*Pou?*'

'*Sti thalassa?*'

'Mama?'

'Mama *nani*.'

He faltered, scowling, but finally took her hand. They went downstairs to the shadowed garden to get a towel from the wire fence and find his bucket and spade. Then they came hand in hand out into the yellow evening. When he started to drag his feet, Voula dodged to make her shadow cover his, and he laughed, remembering how she always played the shadow game: and she remembered the moonlit streetlamps. 'What! You have no shadow!' she said.

'I have so!' He made his shadow escape and caper ahead.

'You have not!' Hers pounced on it again. 'You see? Where is it?'

'There!'

Families sitting on balconies looked on smiling.

Going past Kyria Magda's Voula saw from the corner of her eye that the ivory-necked lilies had gone from the pots on the *taratsa*. The white goat, tied to a post, fixed its slit brass eye on Voula and said, 'Meh-eh.'

'Meh-eh. Meh-eh,' said Vassilaki. '*Alogaki?*' If it was a horse, then he could ride it.

'*Katsika einai*,' explained Voula, not knowing the English

210

word. *'Echei gala.'*

'Pou?'

She pointed to the pink bag bouncing between the stiff hind legs; Vassilaki stooped to look, and giggled. Kyria Magda, screeching hullo, staggered across the yard with a bucket of water. 'All right then, drink, you little whore': and the goat, in its thirst, plunged its chin and ears deep, and sneezed, rearing. 'Run away, will you?' said Kyria Magda, her hands on her hips. 'I'll teach you. Yes, I'll teach her,' she told the watchers: a sour smile crossed her face.

'Kakia yiayia,' said Vassilaki when they were well past.

All the way to the beach Voula let him keep ahead of her with his shadow, making little rushes forward whenever he flagged, so that they arrived sweaty and out of breath. She dipped herself in the water, no more, not wanting to take her eyes off him for a moment; though he always paddled in the shallows and if he did stray further out there was a sandbank. Waistdeep, he was filling his bucket with water and spilling it on his head. It splashed all round him and sent ripples flickering up. From his hair, darker and flatter now, bright drops went on falling.

'Ooh! *Kitta*, Voula!'

She sprang to her feet, *'Ti?'*

'Kitta! Psarakia!'

'Pou?'

'Na!' He pointed. There were the little fish, when she looked, first like silver needles, then like black ones. He sank his bucket in bubbles to the bottom to catch them. She lay down again, resting on her elbows. In the distance the boats were tied to the pier. A small one was pulled up on the sand nearby with an octopus spread to dry over its lamps, swarming with wasps. No one else had come down to the beach. I am beautiful, Voula decided: but he's not here to see. Over the sandbank the water was a honeycomb, a golden net. Vassilaki was intent. Now with his bucket, now with his spread hands, he bent to catch fish. *'Psarakia?'* he pleaded. *'Psarakia?'*

They stayed until the sun turned the long shoals red.

Andoni, hunched over a newspaper, saw them coming home along the street, its dark patches not only shadow now but wet dust where the shopkeepers had hosed it. At the other end of the balcony his mother and the Kapetanissa sat making lace with crochet hooks, each of them ignoring her own quick fingers to covertly watch the other's.

'When it's wet it smells like coffee,' remarked Kyria Eirini. 'The earth, I mean.'

'Here comes Vassilaki,' said Andoni.

'Ach, good!' She swung round. 'Yes, here they are!' Sounding too relieved, she knew: the Kapetanissa bridled. Did they think the child might not have been safe with her Voula, did they? She raised her heavy brows.

'Are they late, perhaps?'

'No! Not at all!' They were laughing, licking icecreams. 'Look, she bought icecreams.' Kyria Eirini made her voice soothing. 'She gets on so well with him, doesn't she?'

The Kapetanissa was not satisfied. Andoni picked a sprig of basil from the nearest pot, rubbed it and sniffed at the green mash his fingers made. His mother waved to Voula and Vassilaki, who waved back.

'I noticed yesterday what a beautiful swimmer she is,' Kyria Eirini went on, making it clear that of course he had been in good hands. 'May we not cast the Evil Eye on her,' she added, as custom demanded after praise, and pretended to spit. The Kapetanissa smiled at her, appeased.

'Yes, she's a genuine mermaid. Everyone says so.'

'Who's a mermaid?' Barbara called lazily from inside, having caught the one word *gorgona*.

'Voula. They're home,' answered Andoni's mother.

'Oh, good.' Barbara went on reading. She knew she was a better swimmer than Voula any day.

Vassilaki's chest had pink trickles on it where icecream had dripped through the soggy tip of the cone faster than he could suck it. Voula flapped the towel – it had lumps of wet sand on it – and hung it on the fence. 'Have a wash?' she said, and pulled the slack hose through from the garden. Vassilaki loved the first wash, the sun-warmed water in the hose. He pulled his shorts open and squeezed his eyes shut waiting for the silver water to come coiling over him. When it did he gave a yell. Voula stooped down to swill the sand and the icecream off him. But the water was running cold now and he squirmed away, giggling as if it tickled.

'Come here.' She was giggling too.

'Nao!'

'There is sand on you!'

'Nao!'

Neither of them had heard any buzzing or seen a wasp or a bee hanging, its wings rippling the air. But now Voula felt a searing stab in her thigh. She screamed with pain and shock.

'*Ti?*' shrieked Vassilaki.

Voula was slapping at her thigh, staring round wildly. Whatever it was fell twitching in a puddle. She bent over it: impossible to tell now if it was a wasp or a bee. She crushed it with her hard heel.

'*Melissa!*' Vassilaki shrieked again. He peered at the crushed shell. Was it his bee? Would it dart up and sting him next? A hen jabbed and took it, spraying mud on him as she skipped away. '*Paei!*' yelled Vassilaki. '*Voula mou!*'

But this was not his Voula, cupping her stung thigh, her face red and twisted. Vassilaki stared. This was not his Voula. He stumbled into the kitchen. No one. '*Mama mou!* Mama!' He bolted up the wooden steps and raised the trapdoor.

'*Vassilaki!*' screamed his mother's voice. He swung round in bewilderment – where was she? and the trapdoor fell shut with a thud above him, jamming his fingers. He screamed loudly, lost his balance and tumbled down the steps on to the floor.

5

At first everyone had thought that the screams they heard were part of the game with the garden hose. Now they all came running. Barbara scrambled through the trapdoor and down the steps to pick Vassilaki up. She sat on the cold floor of the kitchen holding him against her. For long moments he held his mouth open in a silent roar, turning dark red. Then at last sobs and tears burst out. 'Oh, oh, oh,' moaned Barbara in the Greek way that always soothed him best, rocking with each 'oh'.

'*Ponaei!*' he wailed.

'Oh, oh, *poulaki mou*,' she murmured helplessly.

Andoni crouched over him and ran his hands over the wet quivering little body, the yellow mat of hair. There was a lump there and blood seeping; grey splinters showed in the plump flesh of his arms and legs; but no bones were broken. Red tangles were printed on Barbara's dress where he had laid his head.

'What happen?' said Andoni.

'The *kapaki*. He fell downstairs.'

'I know that.'

'*Ponaei!*' Vassilaki touched his head and shrieked when he saw blood on his hands.

'Oh, don't cry, no, no. It'll be better soon.' She kissed his hair.

'*Melissa*, Mama,' he snuffled.

They looked, but there was no sign of a bee sting.

'*Ma pou, poulaki mou?*'

'*Ti* Voula.' He pointed.

Voula, her face swollen with crying and as red as his, was standing in her bathing suit at the kitchen doorway. 'A *melissa* bite me and he frighten,' she said. 'And he hurt his self. The *kapaki* fall on him.' Her thigh bulged with a lump as big as a tennis ball: she had found the barb in it.

'Luckily, he's not badly hurt,' said Kyria Eirini.

'He got a fright. I'm sorry,' Voula explained gratefully, because Kyria Eirini spoke no English. With a gasp of pain she squatted on her heels to face Barbara. 'It happen so quick!' she said tearfully; and met with shock a bitter relentless glare from Andoni.

'*Kakia* Voula!' Vassilaki hid his face.

'No, no, no,' said Barbara.

'But it was an accident,' said Kyria Eirini to everyone. 'These things happen. They can happen to anyone.'

The Kapetanissa gave her a grateful look. She had warned them about the *kapaki*, but this was not the time to say so; and besides, she blamed all such accidents on the Evil Eye, but she could hardly say that either. Instead she hustled Voula home to take out the barb and dab vinegar on the sting, at the same time questioning her at length. Voula burst into more sobs, Andoni had blamed her without a word. She blamed herself, she told her mother, who stoutly told her she was being stupid. It was the Evil Eye, it was written, it was the will of God; she crossed herself.

'Yes, but they all hate me now,' said Voula.

Vassilaki, his sobs dwindling to sniffles and hiccups, was still clamped fast to Barbara on the floor. '*Ponaei,*' he whimpered now and then, when she tried to move; but it was clear that he wasn't badly hurt. When his grandmother knelt beside them with a bowl of milky antiseptic and a tuft of cotton wool, he knew what was coming: '*Ochi*! *Ochi*! *Ochi*!' he wailed, wriggling.

'Ach, *poulaki mou.*' His grandmother's eyes watered.

'I'll do it', said Andoni.

'*Ochi*! Nao!'

'Vassilaki! Vassilaki *mou*!' His grandmother snapped on the light and ran up the steps, calling. He peered, blinking in the yellow glare, from behind his wet fists. '*Da da*!' she shouted, and punched the trapdoor. '*Da da to kapaki*! *Da*! *Da*! *Da*!'

214

Vassilaki gave a wheezy laugh. *'Da da pali*, Yiayia!' he commanded; so she beat it again, and again, until her arms ached and he decided that the *kapaki* was punished enough. And by then Andoni had swabbed the blood away.

As soon as Vassilaki was asleep Andoni inspected his head with a bright torch he had found, parting the damp tufts.

'He's all right. Really,' Barbara said.

'He could get delayed concussion,' muttered Andoni.

'I don't think so.'

'It's your job to look after him. Why did you leave it to Voula?'

'She offered. Vassilaki wanted her to take him.'

'He could have been killed.'

'It was an accident. It could have happened to anyone.'

'Did you call him to go up that way?'

'No, of course not!' Barbara jumped up.

'But you called him.'

'That was after he lifted it up.'

'I hope that's true.'

'I don't tell lies, Andoni.'

'You don't do anything much any more, do you?'

'No? Do you know why? I'm tired.'

'Tired!' He turned way.

'Tired, yes. Because I'm pregnant.'

It was some time before he turned to her; the torch in his hand threw winged shadows. He stood staring.

'You're not pleased.'

'Yes, I am. Yes. Are you sure? When will it be?'

'Mid-January, I think.'

'Does Mama know yet?'

'Most likely.'

He smiled at that.

'He's sleeping normally,' she said. 'He really will be all right.'

'I might just go for a walk, then. Just down to the *kafeneion* for a while. I'll burst if I stay here.' He bent over Vassilaki, then handed her the torch and went down into the street. From the balcony she watched him appear under each streetlamp, and disappear again.

After searching all over the sitting room, she found her diary under a pile of *kilimia*, striped red and green and black, which she didn't remember having seen before: and took out the two pages of her letter to her sister. She had more to tell her. A moth flapped at the torch, its shadow rocking the gold walls.

> P.S. – Jilly, I'm pregnant. I was going to tell you when you were here, but somehow it never seemed to be the right time. They will wish me *kali eleftheria* when I tell them: it means *good freedom* – by which they mean *good* (easy) *birth*.
>
> Be happy,
>
> B.

As they did every night, Voula and the Kapetanissa watched the boats get ready to go out in a jumble of nets and crates and lamps. Half the town was wandering along the waterfront and up and down the pier by then, dressed in their best for the *volta*. The streets were very dark now, except under the lights: people tripped over stones and tree roots. The sea held its oyster colours of yellow and grey longer, even when the caique and its little boats were chugging across to the fishing grounds, lamps strung in a row over the ringed wakes.

Later they sat with the families of the crew sharing bottles of beer and ouzo and plates of *mezedes* at the *kafeneion*. Moths fell against them. Often there was no other sound but the thump of the hurtling powdery moths. At every table children insisted, to the men's satisfaction, on sipping the froth from every glass of beer; soon they fell asleep in their mothers' laps. Cats yowled under the chairs. Their fur twitching, they would put a calm paw on top of a cricket, then let it limp free, then cover it again. Their eyes flashed green. Beyond the yellow edges of the lamplight more crickets started creaking under the pines. Out at sea the boats gathered under a milky dome of colder light. A gull cried out; then another.

Voula, standing to pass her aunt a plate of *kalamari*, suddenly saw Andoni on the beach. But he looked away and walked on into the dark.

'Wasn't that your tenant?' What's his name?' her aunt asked, munching loudly.

'No. I don't think so,' Voula said. She longed to be alone. Her stung thigh throbbed.

There were no lights on next door, when Voula and the Kapetanissa came home. They went straight to bed. The house was too hot for sleep, and held its heat and silence the whole night.

In the next room Vassilaki said in English a word like a bell, but woke only his grandmother. She could see the slatted moon from where she lay. There will be dew, she thought, by morning, and the houses will look like blocks of feta straight out of the brine, until the moon sets. At dawn they will be blue. I must wake Andoni to buy fish, she decided, because once the moon is full the boats know better than to go out with their little lamps. For a week we'll be without fish.

It was too hot to sleep, and besides she was no longer sleepy, having gone to bed earlier than usual when Barbara did. They had sat in the light of an amber lamp in the kitchen and eaten cold what was left of the *imam bayildi* just the two of them mopping their plates with bread and talking quietly, almost secretively. They felt fonder of each other than they had for a long time, and they both knew this, and so were shy with each other. She thought of asking Barbara if she might be pregnant, but it was not the right time yet. When Vassilaki woke tousled and grizzling, they soothed and dandled him. They spoonfed him an egg that she soft-boiled for him in the coffee *briki* and on which Barbara drew a naughty face, a little Vassilaki. His pallor was gone. He sipped the egg greedily and then ate some bread with grainy honey and a peach like a yellow rose that she had saved for him. She wanted to read Barbara a prayer from the *Theia Litourgia* but the lamplight, heavy with moths and beetles, was making her eyes sore. They are like fish in a yellow sea, Barbara said, waving insects away. They carried Vassilaki, fast asleep, up the outside stairs to bed. She heard Andoni come up soon after.

For all she knew, good may have come of the child's fall, since Andoni blamed the girl for it; though who knew how long the good would last or what harm might come of it? In any case, it was not how she would have gone about it. The child hurt, the girl stung, the bee dead. A bee had come blundering into the sun out of the Panagia *sta Melissia*. Was it that bee? Was a bee's life of so little account to the Panagia, that she sent it to die? Thy will be done: she crossed herself. It's not for me to say. Maybe our lives are of no more account than a bee's, if the truth be known.

She must nail up the *kapaki* in the morning.

Out in the night a click of hoofs and a faint 'meh' made her sigh. There was a goat loose again. It must have come for the rest of the Kapetanissa's climbing beans; it would finish the lot off tonight, no doubt, and the Kapetanissa would talk of nothing else tomorrow. How did the Garden of Eden ever survive with goats in it? Goats eat every green shoot that pokes up. They're a ruin, goats are, though the milk makes up for it.

Is that bee alive now in the next world, she wondered; and is there honey there? Water, and milk and eggs, bread and wine? Shall we all have other forms, or none and be made of air? We boil wheat with sugar to make the *kollyva* for the dead; but it's only we, the living, who eat it. Or so it seems. For us of this world, at least, it tastes good, salty and sweet together. Like sardines fried in sweet green oil or watermelon with a slab of briny feta, or any dry cheese; honey on rough bread; grapes, rich heavy muscat grapes, dipped in the sea to wash them.

Pain is like salt, in a way, she thought: it can make the sweetness stronger, unless there's too much of it. Pain and sorrow and loss.

There was too much salt in the *imam bayildi* today. Never mind. Well.

My poor Vassili, whose sins are forgiven: that was a salty old joke he loved to tell, the one about honey. Only a man could have made that joke up. A man might even believe it, who knows?

A gypsy (he put on a wheedling voice) came to an old widow, I forget why, and said, 'What is your wish, my lady? I can give you one of two things. A fine young man to marry, or a pot of honey. Just tell me which you want.'

'Now what sort of a choice do you call that?' (And he cackled like an old widow.) 'I couldn't eat the honey, could I? There's not a tooth in my head, is there?' (At which he laughed angrily as if he knew all about old widows, and disliked what he knew.)

She breathed deeply of the shuttered air, cooler now with the dew towards daybreak, and pulled the rough sheet up over her folded throat. In the next world may we all be young again, she fell asleep wishing. All of us young and at peace by the sea for ever.

Helen Garner

POSTCARDS FROM SURFERS

One night I dreamed that I did not love and that night, released from all bonds, I lay as though in a kind of soothing death.

Colette

We are driving north from Coolangatta airport. Beside the road the ocean heaves and heaves into waves which do not break. The swells are dotted with boardriders in black wetsuits, grim as sharks.

'Look at those idiots,' says my father.

'They must be freezing,' says my mother.

'But what about the principle of the wetsuit?' I say. 'Isn't there a thin layer of water between your skin and the suit, and your body heat . . .'

'Could be,' says my father.

The road takes a sudden swing round a rocky outcrop. Miles ahead of us, blurred by the milky air, I see a dream city: its cream, its silver, its turquoise towers thrust in a cluster from a distant spit.

'What – is that Brisbane?' I say.

'No,' says my mother. 'That's Surfers.'

My father's car has a built-in computer. If he exceeds the speed limit, the dashboard emits a discreet but insistent pinging. Lights flash, and the pressure of his right foot lessens. He controls the windows from a panel between the two front seats. We cruise past a Valiant parked by the highway with a FOR SALE sign propped in its back window.

'Look at that,' says my mother. 'A WA numberplate. Probably thrashed it across the Nullarbor, and now they reckon they'll flog it.'

'Pro'ly stolen,' says my father. 'See the sticker? ALL YOU VIRGINS, THANKS FOR NOTHING. You can just see what sort of a pin'ead he'd be. Brain the size of a pea.'

Close up, many of the turquoise towers are not yet sold. 'Every conceivable feature,' the signs say. They have names like Capricornia, Biarritz, The Breakers, Acapulco, Rio.

I had a Brazilian friend when I lived in Paris. He showed me a postcard, once, of Rio where he was born and brought up. The card bore an aerial shot of a splendid, curved tropical beach, fringed with palms, its sand pure as snow.

'Why don't you live in Brazil,' I said, 'if it's as beautiful as this?'

'Because', said my friend, 'right behind that beach there is a huge army camp.'

In my turn I showed him a postcard of my country. It was a reproduction of that Streeton painting called *The Land of the Golden Fleece* which in my homesickness I kept standing on the heater in my bedroom. He studied it carefully. At last he turned his currant-coloured eyes to me and said,

'Les arbres sont rouges?' Are the trees red?

Several years later, six months ago, I was rummaging through a box of old postcards in a junk shop in Rathdowne Street. Among the photos of damp cottages in Galway, of Raj hotels crumbling in bicycle-thronged Colombo, of glassy Canadian lakes flawed by the wake of a single canoe, I found two cards that I bought for a dollar each. One was a picture of downtown Rio, in black-and-white. The other, crudely tinted, showed Geelong, the town where I was born. The photographer must have stood on the high grassy bank that overlooks the Eastern Beach. He lined up his shot through the never-flowing fountain with its quartet of concrete wading birds (storks? cranes? I never asked my father: they have long orange beaks and each bird holds one leg bent, as if about to take a step); through the fountain and out over the curving wooden promenade, from which we dived all summer, unsupervised, into the flat water; and across the bay to the You Yangs, the double-humped, low, volcanic cones, the only disturbance in the great basalt plains that lie between Geelong and Melbourne. These two cards in the same box! And I find them! Imagine! *'Cher Rubens,'* I wrote. *'Je t'envoie ces deux cartes postales, de nos deux villes natales . . .'*

Auntie Lorna has gone for a walk on the beach. My mother unlocks the door and slides open the flywire screen. She goes out into the bright air to tell her friend of my arrival. The ocean is right in front of the unit, only a hundred and fifty yards away. How can people be so sure of the boundary between land and sea that they have the confidence to build houses on it? The white doorsteps of the ocean travel and travel.

'Twelve o'clock,' says my father.

'Getting on for lunchtime,' I say.

'Getting towards it. Specially with that nice cold corned beef sitting there, and fresh brown bread. Think I'll have to try some of that choko relish. Ever eaten a choko?'

'I wouldn't know a choko if I fell over it,' I say.

'Nor would I.'

He selects a serrated knife from the magnetised holder on the kitchen wall and quickly and skilfully, at the bench, makes himself a thick sandwich. He works with powerful concentration: when the meat flaps off the slice of bread, he rounds it up with a large, dramatic scooping movement and a sympathetic grimace of the lower lip. He picks up the sandwich in two hands, raises it to his mouth and takes a large bite. While he chews he breathes heavily through his nose.

'Want to make yourself something?' he says with his mouth full.

I stand up. He pushes the loaf of bread towards me with the back of his hand. He puts the other half of his sandwich on a green bread and butter plate and carries it to the table. He sits with his elbows on the pine wood, his knees wide apart, his belly relaxing on to his thighs, his high-arched, long-boned feet planted on the tiled floor. He eats, and gazes out to sea. The noise of his eating fills the room.

My mother and Auntie Lorna come up from the beach. I stand inside the wall of glass and watch them stop at the tap to hose the sand off their feet before they cross the grass to the door. They are two old women: they have to keep one hand on the tap in order to balance on the left foot and wash the right. I see that they are two old women, and yet they are neither young nor old. They are my mother and Auntie Lorna, two institutions. They slide back the wire door, smiling.

'Don't tramp sand everywhere,' says my father from the table.

They take no notice. Auntie Lorna kisses me, and holds me at

221

arms' length with her head on one side. My mother prepares food and we eat, looking out at the water.

'You've missed the coronary brigade,' says my father. 'They get out on the beach about nine in the morning. You can pick 'em. They swing their arms up really high when they walk.' He laughs, looking down.

'Do you go for a walk every day too?' I ask.

'Six point six kilometres,' says my father.

'Got a pedometer, have you.'

'I just nutted it out,' says my father. 'We walk as far as a big white building, down that way, then we turn round and come back. Six point six altogether, there and back.'

'I might come with you.'

'You can if you like', he says. He picks up his plate and carries it to the sink, 'We go after breakfast. You've missed today's.'

He goes to the couch and opens the newspapers on the low coffee table. He reads with his glasses down his nose and his hands loosely linked between his spread knees. The women wash up.

'Is there a shop nearby?' I ask my mother. 'I have to get some tampons.'

'Caught short, are you,' she says. 'I think they sell them at the shopping centre, along Sunbrite Avenue there near the bowling club. Want me to come with you?'

'I can find it.'

'I never could use those things' says my mother lowering her voice and glancing across the room at my father. 'Hazel told me about a terrible thing that happened to her. For days she kept noticing this revolting smell that was . . . emanating from her. She washed and washed, and couldn't get rid of it. Finally she was about to go to the doctor, but first she got down and had a look with the mirror. She saw this bit of thread and pulled it. The thing was *green*. She must've forgotten to take it out – it'd been there for days and days and *days*.'

We laugh with the teatowels up to our mouths. My father, on the other side of the room, looks up from the paper with the bent smile of someone not sure what the others are laughing at. I am always surprised when my mother comes out with a word like 'emanating'. At home I have a book called *An Outline of English Verse* which my mother used in her matriculation year. In the margins of *The Rape of the Lock* she has made notations: 'bathos; reminiscent of Virgil; parody of Homer.' Her handwriting in these pencilled jottings, made forty-five years ago, is exactly as it is today; this makes me suspect, when I am not with her, that she is a closet intellectual.

Once or twice, on my way from the unit to the shopping centre, I think I see roses along a fence and run to look, but I find them to be some scentless, fleshy flower. I fall back. Beside a patch of yellow grass, pretty trees in a row are bearing and dropping white blossom-like flowers, but they look wrong to me, I do not recognise them: the blossoms too large, the branches too flat. I am dizzy from the flight. In Melbourne it is still winter, everything is bare.

I buy the tampons and look for the postcards. There they are, displayed in a tall revolving rack. There is a great deal of blue. Closer, I find colour photos of white beaches, duneless, palmless, on which half-naked people lie on their backs with their knees raised. The frequency of this posture, at random through the crowd, makes me feel like laughing. Most of the cards have GREETINGS FROM THE GOLD COAST OR BROADBEACH OR SURFERS PARADISE embossed in gold in one corner: I search for pictures without words. Another card, in several slightly differing versions, shows a graceful, big-breasted young girl lying in a seductive pose against some rocks: she is wearing a bikini and her whole head is covered by one of those latex masks that are sold in trick shops, the ones you pull on as a bandit pulls on a stocking. The mask represents the hideous, raddled, grinning face of an old woman, a witch. I stare at this photo for a long time. Is it simple, or does it hide some more mysterious signs and symbols?

I buy twelve GREETINGS FROM cards with views, some aerial, some from the ground. They cost twenty-five cents each.

'Want the envelopes?' says the girl. She is dressed in a flowered garment which is drawn up between her thighs like a nappy.

'Yes please.' The envelopes are so covered with coloured maps, logos and drawings of Australian fauna that there is barely room to write an address, but something about them attracts me. I buy a packet of Licorice Chews and eat them all the way home: I stuff them in two at a time: my mouth floods with saliva. There are no rubbish bins so I put the papers in my pocket. Now that I have spent money here, now that I have rubbish to dispose of, I am no longer a stranger. In Paris there used to be signs in the streets that said, *'Le commerce, c'est la vie de la ville.'* Any traveller knows this to be the truth.

The women are knitting. They murmur and murmur. What

they say never requires any answer. My father sharpens a pencil stub with his pocket knife, and folds the paper into a pad one-eighth the size of a broadsheet page.

'Five down, spicy meat jelly. ASPIC. Three across, counterfeit. BOGUS! Howzat!'

'You're in good nick,' I say. 'I would've had to rack my brains for BOGUS. Why don't you do harder ones?'

'Oh, I can't do those other ones, the cryptic.'

'You have to know Shakespeare and the Bible off by heart to do those,' I say.

'Yairs. Course, if you got hold of the answer and filled it out looking at that, with a lot of practice you could come round to their way of thinking. They used to have good ones in the *Weekly Times*. But I s'pose they had so many complaints from cockies who couldn't do 'em that they had to ease off.'

I do not feel comfortable yet about writing the postcards. It would seem graceless. I flip through my mother's pattern book.

'There's some nice ones there,' she says. 'What about the one with the floppy collar?'

'Want to buy some wool?' says my father. He tosses the finished crossword on to the coffee table and stands up with a vast yawn. 'Oh-ee-oh-ooh. Come on, Miss. I'll drive you over to Pacific Fair.'

I choose the wool and count out the number of balls specified by the pattern. My father rears back to look at it: this movement struck terror into me when I was a teenager but I now recognise it as short-sightedness.

'Pure wool, is it?' he says. As soon as he touches it he will know. He fingers it, and looks at me.

'No,' I say. 'Got a bit of synthetic in it. It's what the pattern says to use.'

'Why don't you – ' He stops. Once he would have tried to prevent me from buying it. His big blunt hands used to fling out the fleeces, still warm, on to the greasy table. His hands looked as if they had no feeling in them but they teased out the wool, judged it, classed it, assigned it a fineness and a destination: Italy, Switzerland, Japan. He came home with thorns embedded deep in the flesh of his palms. He stood patiently while my mother gouged away at them with a needle. He drove away at shearing time in a yellow car with running boards, up to the big sheds in the country; we rode on the running boards as far as the corner of our street, then skipped home. He went to the Melbourne Show for work, not pleasure, and once he brought me home a plastic trumpet. 'Fordie,' he called me, and took me to the wharves and said, 'See that rope? It's not a rope. It's a hawser.' 'Hawser,' I repeated, wanting him to think I was a serious person. We walked along Strachan Avenue, Manifold Heights, hand in hand. 'Listen,' he said. 'Listen to the wind in the wires.' I must have been very little then, for the wires were so high I can't remember seeing them.

He turns away from the fluffy pink balls and waits with his hands in his pockets for me to pay.

'What do you do all day, up here?' I say on the way home.

'Oh .. play bowls. Follow the real estate. I ring up the firms that advertise these flash units and I ask them questions. I let 'em lower and lower their price. See how low they'll go. How many more discounts they can dream up.' He drives like a farmer in a ute, leaning forward with his arms curved round the wheel, always about to squint up through the windscreen at the sky, checking the weather.

'Don't they ask your name?'

'Yep,'

'What do you call yourself?'

'Oh, Jackson or anything.' He flicks a glance at me. We begin to laugh, looking away from each other.

'It's bloody crook up here,' he says. 'Jerry-built. Sad. Every conceivable luxury! They can't get rid of it. They're desperate. Come on. We'll go up and you can have a look.'

The lift in Biarritz is lined with mushroom-coloured carpet. We brace our backs against its wall and it rushes us upwards. The salesman in the display unit has a moustache, several gold bracelets, a beige suit, and a clipboard against his chest. He is engaged with an elderly couple and we are able to slip past him into the living room.

'Did you see that peanut?' hisses my father.

'A gilded youth,' I say. "Their eyes are dull, their heads are flat, they have no brains at all." '

He looks impressed, as if he thinks I have made it up on the spot. 'The Man from Ironbark,' I add.

'I only remember The Geebung Polo Club,' he says. He mimes leaning off a horse and swinging a heavy implement. We snort with laughter. Just inside the living room door stand five Ionic pillars in a half-moon curve. Beyond them, through the glass, are views of a river and some mountains. The river winds in a plain, the mountains are sudden, lumpy and crooked.

'From the other side you can see the sea,' says my father.

'Would you live up here?'

'Not on your life. Not with those flaming pillars.'

From the bedroom window he points out another high-rise building closer to the sea. Its name is Chelsea. It is battle-ship grey with a red trim. Its windows face away from the ocean. It is tall and narrow, of mean proportions, almost prison-like. 'I wouldn't mind living in that one,' he says. I look at it in silence. He has unerringly chosen the ugliest one. It is so ugly that I can find nothing to say.

It is Saturday afternoon. My father is waiting for the Victorian football to start on TV. He rereads the paper.

'Look at this,' he says. 'Mum, remember the seminar we went to about investment in diamonds?'

'Up here?' I say, 'A *seminar*?'

'S'posed to be an investment that would double in value in six days. We went along one afternoon. They were obviously con-men. Ooh, setting up a big con, you could tell. They had sherry and sandwiches.'

'That's all we went for, actually,' says my mother.

'What sort of people went?' I ask.

'Oh . . people like ourselves,' says my father.

'Do you think anybody bought any?'

'Sure. Some idiots. Anyway, look at this in today's *Age*. "The Diamond Dreamtime. World diamond market plummets." Haw haw haw.'

He turns on the TV in time for the bounce. I cast on stitches as instructed by the pattern and begin to knit. My mother and Auntie Lorna, well advanced in complicated garments for my sister's teenage children, conduct their monologues which cross, coincide and run parallel, rarely touching or linking. My father mumbles advice to the footballers and emits bursts of contemptuous laughter. 'Bloody idiot,' he says.

I go to the room I am to share with Auntie Lorna and come back with the packet of postcards. When I get out my pen and the stamps and set myself up at the table my father looks up and shouts to me over the roar of the crowd,

'Given up on the knitting?'

'No. Just knocking off a few postcards. People expect a postcard when you go to Queensland.'

'Have to keep up your correspondence, Father,' says my mother.

'I'll knit later,' I say.

'How much have you done?' asks my father.

'This much.' I separate thumb and forefinger.

'Dear Philip,' I write. I make my writing as thin and small as I can: the back of the postcard, not the front, is the art form. 'Look where I am. A big red setter wet from the surf shambles up the side way of the unit, looking lost and anxious as setters always do. My parents send it packing with curses in an inarticulate tongue. Go orn, get orf, gorn?'

'Dear Philip. THE IDENTIFICATION OF THE BIRDS AND FISHES. *My father*: "Look at those albatross. They must have eyes that can see for a hundred miles. As soon as one dives. They come from everywhere. Look at 'em dive! Bang! Down they go." *Me*: "What sort of fish would they be diving for?" *My father*: "Whiting. They only eat whiting." *Me*: "They do not!" *My father*: "How the hell would I know what sort of fish they are".'

'Dear Philip. My father says they are albatross, but my mother (in the bathroom, later) remarks to me that albatross have shorter, more hunched necks.'

'Dear Philip. I share a room with Auntie Lorna. She also is writing postcards and has just asked me how to spell TOO. I like her very much and *she likes me*. "I'll keep the stickybeaks in the Woomelang post office guessing," she says. "I won't put my name on the back of the envelope."'

'Dear Philip. OUTSIDE THE POST OFFICE. My father, Auntie Lorna and I wait in the car for my mother to go in and pick up the mail from the locked box. *My father*: "Gawd, amazing, isn't it, what people do. See that sign there, ENTER, with the arrow pointing upwards? What sort of a thing is that? Is it a joke, or just some no-hoper foolin' around? That woman's been in the phone box for half an hour, I bet. How'd you be, outside the public phone waiting for some silly coot to finish yackin' on about everything under the sun, while you had something important to say. That happened to us, once, up at –" My mother opens the door and gets in. "Three letters," she says. "All for me."'

Sometimes my little story overflows the available space and I have to run over a second postcard. This means I must find a smaller, secondary tale, or some disconnected remark, to fill up card number two.

'*Me*: (opening cupboard) "Hey! Scrabble! We can have a game of Scrabble after tea!" *My father*: (with a scornful laugh) "I can't wait."'

'Dear Philip. I know you won't write back. I don't even know

227

whether you are still at this address.'

'Dear Philip. One Saturday morning I went to Coles and bought a scarf. It cost four and sixpence and I was happy with my purchase. He whisked it out of my hand and looked at the label. "Made in China. Is it real silk? Let's test it." He flicked on his cigarette lighter. We all screamed and my mother said, "Don't *bite*! He's only teasing you." '

'Dear Philip. Once, when I was fourteen, I gave cheek to him at the dinner table. He hit me across the head with his open hand. There was silence. My little brother gave a high, hysterical giggle and I laughed too, in shock. He hit me again. After the washing up I was sent for. He was sitting in an armchair, looking down. "The reason why we don't get on any more," he said, "is because we're so much alike." This idea filled me with such revulsion that I turned my swollen face away. It was swollen from crying, not from the blows, whose force had been more symbolic than physical.'

'Dear Philip. Years later he read my mail. He found the contraceptive pills. He drove up to Melbourne and found me and made me come home. He told me I was letting men use my body. He told me I ought to see a psychiatrist. I was in the front seat and my mother was in the back. I thought, "If I open the door and jump out, I won't have to listen to this any more." My mother tried to stick up for me. He shouted at her, "It's your fault," he said. "You were too soft on her." '

'Dear Philip. I know you've heard all this before. I also know it's no worse than anyone else's story.'

'Dear Philip. And again years later he asked me a personal question. He was driving, I was in the suicide seat. "What went wrong," he said, "between you and Philip?" Again I turned my face away. 'I don't want to talk about it,' I said. There was silence. He never asked again. And years after *that*, in a cafe in Paris on my way to work, far enough away from him to be able to, I thought of that question and began to cry. Dear Philip. I forgive you for everything.'

Late in the afternoon my mother and Auntie Lorna and I walk along the beach to Surfers. The tide is out: our bare feet scarcely mark the firm sand. Their two voices run on, one high, one low. If I speak they pretend to listen, just as I feign attention to their endless, looping discourses: these are our courtesies: this is love. Everything is spoken, nothing is said. On the way back I point out to them the smoky orange clouds that are massing far out to sea, low over the horizon. Obedient, they stop and face the water. We stand in a row, Auntie Lorna in a pretty frock with sandals dangling from her finger, my mother and I with our trousers rolled up. Once I asked my Brazilian friend a stupid question. He was listening to a conversation between me and a Frenchman about our countries' electoral systems. He was not speaking and thinking to include him, I said, 'and how do people vote chez toi, Rubens?' He looked at me with a small smile. 'We don't have elections,' he said. Where's Rio from here? 'Look at those clouds!' I say. 'You'd think there was another city out there, wouldn't you, burning.'

Just at dark the air takes on the colour and dampness of the sub-tropics. I walk out the screen door and stand my gin on a fence post. I lean out on the fence and look at the ocean. Soon the moon will thrust itself over the line. If I did a painting of a horizon, I think, I would make it look like a row of rocking, inverted Vs, because that's what I see when I look at it. The flatness of a horizon is intellectual. A cork pops on the first floor balcony behind me. I glance up. In the half dark two men with moustaches are smiling down at me.

'Drinking champagne tonight?' I say.

'Wonderful sound, isn't it,' says the one holding the bottle.

I turn back to the moonless horizon. Last year I went camping on the Murray River. I bought the cards at Tocumwal. I had to write fast for the light was dropping and spooky noises were coming from the trees. 'Dear Dad,' I wrote. 'I am up on the Murray, sitting by the camp fire. It's nearly dark now but earlier it was beautiful, when the sun was going down and the dew was rising.' Two weeks later, at home, I received a letter from him written in his hard, rapid, slanting hand, each word ending in a sharp upward flick. The letter itself concerned a small financial matter, and consisted of two sentences on half a sheet of quarto, but on the back of the envelope he had dashed off a personal message: 'PS, Dew does not rise. It *forms*.'

The moon does rise, as fat as an orange, out of the sea straight in front of the unit. A child upstairs sees it too and utters long werewolf howls. My mother makes a meal and we eat it. 'Going to help Mum with the dishes, are you, Miss?' says my father from his armchair. My shoulders stiffen. I am, I do. I lie on the couch and read an old *Woman's Day*. Princess Caroline of Monaco wears a black dress and a wide white hat. The knitting needles make their mild clicking. Auntie Lorna and my father come from the same town, Hopetoun in the Mallee, and when the news is over they begin again.

'I always remember the cars of people,' says my father. 'There was an old four-cylinder Dodge, belonging to Whatsisname. It had – '

'Would that have been one of the O'Lachlans?' says Auntie Lorna.

'Jim O'Lachlan. It had a great big exhaust pipe coming out the back. And I remember stuffing a potato up it.'

'A *potato*?' I say.

'The bloke was a councillor,' says my father. 'He came out of the Council chambers and got into the Dodge and started her up. He only got fifty yards on the street when BA-BANG! This damn thing shot out the back – I reckon it's still going!' He closes his lips and drops his head back against the couch to hold his laughter.

I walk past Biarritz, where globes of light float among shrubbery, and the odd balcony on the half-empty tower holds rich people out into the creamy air. A barefoot man steps out of the take-away food shop with a hamburger in his hand. He leans against the wall to unwrap it, and sees me hesitating at the slot of the letterbox, holding up the postcards and reading them over and over in the weak light from the public phone. 'Too late to change it now,' he calls. I look up. He grins and nods and takes the first bite of the hamburger. Beside the letterbox stands a deep rubbish bin with a swing lid. I punch open the bin and drop the postcards in.

All night I sleep safely in my bed. The waves roar and hiss, and slam like doors. Auntie Lorna snores, but when I tug at the corner of her blanket she sighs and turns over and breathes more quietly. In the morning the rising sun hits the front windows and floods the place with a light so intense that the white curtains can hardly net it. Everything is pink and golden. In the sink a cockroach lurks. I try to swill it down the drain with a cup of water but it resists strongly. The air is bright, is milky with spray. My father is already up: while the kettle boils he stands out on the edge of the grass, the edge of his property, looking at the sea.

Frank Moorhouse

BUENAVENTURA DURRUTI'S FUNERAL

A compilation of references and encounters, plans for a pilgrimage, a love story, notes on the problem of 'discipline of indiscipline', and two footnotes to a poem.

The American Poet's Visit. After lunch over coffee and stregas at Sandro's the poets showed their pens. Two of the poets had Lamys, another a Mont Blanc, and another a pen from the New York Museum of Modern Art which looked like a scalpel. A fifth said he thought he'd 'get a Lamy.'

They handled each other's pens, writing their favorite line from Yeats or Eliot or whoever. 'Mere anarchy is loosed upon the world,' one wrote. He had not seen poets at this before.

He then made a reluctant presentation of a book of Australian stories to the visiting American poet Philip Levine, for whom the lunch had been organised. He said the book contained the story 'The American Poet's Visit' and that he had been induced to present it by his friends as a *'joke Australien'*.

'Did Rexroth ever read the story?' Levine asked after being told that it was about the American poet Rexroth.

That wasn't known. It is necessary, he explained, to comprehend the Australian condition or what was then the Australian condition. When we here, he gestured at the table, were all younger, we wrote from a special freedom and perspective which came from feeling that we lived outside the 'real world'. For us, Europe and the US were the world. We lived somewhere else. When we wrote we did not conceive that people from the

real world would ever come to read our work. We could write
about them without fear of being read.

'That's right,' said John, 'without the fear of being read by
anyone really.'

'Further, people from the real world were, paradoxically,
people from literary history and they had a fictional gloss to
them – you were not of the world of *Meanjin*'.

'Meanjin?' asked Levine.

'Our literary world, I mean.'

'It's the Aboriginal word meaning "rejected from the *New
Yorker*",' someone else said.

'Hence our special freedom.'

Levine, or someone at the table, said that now someone else
would be able to write another story – 'The Second American
Poet's Visit.'

'Ah, there cannot be another story because we are being read
now by the people from "out there".'

Everyone fell thoughtfully glum at this observation.

'But when the first story was published, the editor thought
"Rexroth" was a pseudonym for a "real person".'

'And Philip isn't the second poet to visit – there's been
Duncan, Ginsberg, Simpson.'

'Kinnell, Levertov, Snyder.'

'Strand.'

'The Harlem Globe Trotters.'

'We are now part of the poetry night-club circuit.'

'The poets arrive – we look them up in Norton's *Anthology of
Modern American Verse* so that we can quote them a line or two
of their poetry.'

'Speak for yourself,' said John.

' "In this cafe, Durruti,
      the Unnameable
      Plotted the burning of the bishop of Saragossa." '

'Very good,' said Levine, 'they are indeed my lines from
Norton's.'

Levine said that although Norton was laboriously footnoted
for students there was no footnote for his poem 'The Midget' to
explain who 'Durruti' was or the 'Archbishop of Saragossa.'

'Do you people know?'

We shook our heads expectantly.

He wrote down the name Durruti and the name Archbishop
of Saragossa on a table napkin because of the noise in the
restaurant and we passed it around, reading the names.

A biography of Durruti is reviewed in TLS. He wrote to his friend Cam Perry in Montreal, a professor of hypnosis, and asked him to get the biography of Durruti which was published in Montreal by Black Rose Books and reviewed in the *Times Literary Supplement*.

He said in the letter to Cam, ' . . . by the way, here in Australia the reviewers are saying that I'm not "really" decadent. I didn't spend all that money and go through all those squalid situations at the Royal George Hotel to be told by reviewers that I'm not decadent. You were there – write to them . . . '

He wrote jokingly to Levine, now back in California, saying that there was a biography of Durruti and that Norton should be informed so that he could make a footnote in the anthology.

The Archbishop. The Archbishop of Saragossa was shot dead in 1923 as an anarchist act – 'a cleansing social act'. He was a key figure in the repression of that city. Popular rumor said that he held weekly orgies at a convent which in itself seemed to be something of a redeeming feature of the Archbishop. When he died he left a fortune to a nun who then deserted her order.

At the time of the shooting Durruti and the Los Solidarios (an Anarchist commando group) were blamed – 'credited'? – and while they almost certainly planned the execution the actual shooting was probably done by Francisco Ascaso, a close friend of Durruti. But it was said that Ascaso was the stone, Durruti the blade.

In Sydney they always said assassination was ultimate censorship. But things were tougher in Saragossa.

Durruti lived in Barcelona. Barcelona he knew visually from Michelangelo Antonioni's film *The Passenger* and Luis Bunuel's film *That Obscure Object of Desire* and he knew too about the Barcelona telephone exchange and Durruti from his reading about the Spanish Civil War. There'd been no real point in telling Levine or the poets that he did know who Durruti was.

In 1936 Durruti and the anarchists gained control of the Barcelona Telefonica and collectivised it. The communists at this time were plotting to destroy the power of the anarchists and the battle for the exchange was part of this power struggle. When calls came to Barcelona for 'the government' the anarchist operators would instruct the callers in anarchist theory and tell them there was no 'government' recognised by

233

the anarchists in Barcelona. Although it slowed down telephone calls the control of the exchange was useful: a 'school'
for the anarchists and their callers. And it should be mentioned
that, the telefonica aside, most functions run by the anarchists
were well run.

The Passenger was a special film for him. *The Passenger* is about
a journalist played by Jack Nicholson who is approaching forty
and who takes on the identity of a casual acquaintance after the
acquaintance dies while they are together in a hotel in North
Africa. Nicholson lives out the man's life engagements.

It is in Barcelona that Nicholson meets a young student –
Maria Schneider – who involves herself with him on his drive
along the Spanish coast from Barcelona through Almeria,
Purellana, and Algeciras. He keeps the final appointment in the
Hotel de la Gloria and meets the other man's destiny – he is
shot dead in that hotel.

The film was special because he'd been approaching forty
when he'd met a seventeen-year-old schoolgirl in Adelaide –
he'd been there for the Festival. On erotic impulse he had asked
her to drive with him to Darwin – 5000 kilometres clean across
the continent and back again. She had said without hesitation,
'yes.'

'Your mother?'

'She'll be OK.'

They had driven the first thousand kilometres at 160-180 km
an hour hardly speaking, just observation and occasional
biographical anecdote, straight across the desert and made love
at the small town of Athraroola in a motel which had not yet
been cleaned by the staff but they could not wait.

She had been transfixingly erotic for him and the silent
interplay was intricate – uniquely so, and he'd told her this. She
took the compliment and said gracefully, 'my body is young but
I know some things about its pleasures.' She said she thought
she understood 'sexual mood.'

On that drive across the first thousand kilometres his desire
for her had grown unbearable and he had stopped the car out in
the desert and suggested they walk for a little, with the
intention of making physical connection with her.

They'd stood there in the desert. He had moved to kiss her
but received no signal of permission.

'Look,' he said, 'I can't take this uncertainty, my body, my
head can't take it – you will make love with me when we reach

the next town?'

'Of course I will,' she said, 'let's go' and then moved back to the car before he could take her in his arms. He'd felt the pact should have been sealed affectionately. But then he'd thought that maybe she did not go in for 'affectionate sealing of pacts.'

In the motel they had not drunk alcohol, which was unusual for him, but he'd felt no need. After their first love-making she'd come to him and coaxed him back into her saying, 'Give me more,' and he'd had no trouble making love to her again.

Despite the intricacy of their silent interplay she'd had difficulty talking to him at times and he had had to 'make' the conversation.

Though during the drive across the desert before the love-making but after the pact, she had turned to him and asked, teasingly, 'have you read Lolita?'

'Yes,' he said smiling, 'have you?'

'Yes and I like it. I identified.'

'So did I.'

In Darwin he'd found a copy of Turgenev's First Love.

'In this book,' he said, 'the father competes with the son for the love of a girl.'

'Who wins?'

'The father. It is a book which you read firstly from the son's point of view and then later in life you read it from the father's point of view. A male does. I don't know how it reads from a female point of view.'

'I'll tell you,' she said.

A year later she said, 'you know you gave me Turgenev's First Love to read and you said you didn't know how it read from "a female point of view"?'

He said yes, he remembered.

'Well,' she said, 'it reads acceptably well from this female's point of view,' and she laughed, half privately, and he guessed he was being compared with her young boy friend.

He had continued to see her in the years that followed during her vacations from university and they'd meet in motels somewhere in Australia. They had other long drives in different places in three States. He had not been shot in any hotels. Inevitably he would be at the motel first awaiting her. She would arrive with her sausage bag, which she called her 'parachute bag,' stuffed with a few things and many books which would never be opened during the trip.

They would always refer to The Passenger and recall favorite details.

He had during one of their trips talked to her about a possible journey to Spain as a homage to the Spanish anarchists and to *The Passenger* and to Bunuel.

She had laughingly refused to take the idea of a pilgrimage to Spain seriously. 'Why should I know anything about the Spanish Civil War – except to know who were good and who were bad?' He did not know whether it was because she thought the pilgrimage unlikely or whether she didn't want to be too much a part of his fantasies.

'There are the "real" lessons of the Spanish Civil War,' he said, but she did not pick up the question and he refrained from overloading her with his preoccupations.

He on the other hand had taken the pilgrimage too seriously. He said to her a few times that they would do it the year he turned forty and she graduated.

He listed the places they would visit. Madrid University which the Durruti Column had defended and near where Durruti had been shot; the Ritz Hotel where he had been taken to die; the Hotel Victoria in Valencia where Auden and the others drank. The Hotel Gaylord in Madrid from *For Whom the Bell Tolls*, The Hotel Continental where Orwell stayed during the war. The Hotel Christian where Hemingway's *Fifth Column* is set.

'And the Ritz in Madrid is one of the twenty leading hotels of the world.'

But she would stop the conversation before it got too far.

In a motel dining room in some Victorian coastal town one night she said, 'but if we did that you'd be shot in a hotel room like Jack.'

'Do you really think that?' He took her hand.

And then a darkness passed over her face and she said she did not wish to talk about it, as if she had forebodings.

Hypnotic coercion and compliance to it. Instead of the biography of Durruti, Cam sent him a copy of one of his academic papers published in the *International Journal of Clinical and Experimental Hypnosis*. It was about the potential of hypnosis to coerce unconsenting behaviour. One position asserts that coercion is possible through the induction of distorted perceptions which delude the hypnotised person into believing that the behaviour is not transgressive. The other position asserts that where hypnosis appears to be a causal factor in coercing behaviour, the other elements in the situation, especially a close hypnotist-client relationship, were probably the main determinants of behaviour.

He read the paper with delight from the things people did with their lives and from the way these things entered his life.

Cam said the Durruti book would follow.

Up at the Journalists' Club. Up at the Journalists' Club he met some old friends from his cadetship days and following a joke about the anarchist and the Barcelona Telephone Exchange – a joke they'd been enjoying since those days – they argued over what was the last battle fought in the Spanish Civil War.

He said he was more interested in the 'real' lessons of the Spanish Civil War.

'The Spanish Civil War is not behind us,' he said suddenly, 'it is in front of us.'

'The bitch is on heat again,' Barry said.

'No,' he said, 'I mean that it is not the war with the fascists which is ahead of us but the war between the free left and the authoritarian left.'

'Poland,' said Tony.

'The real lesson of the Spanish Civil War is that in this country not everyone who calls themselves Left is Left.'

'We still have to break the haughty power of capital', Barry said.

'We are breaking capital's haughty power.'

'Oh yeah?'

Tony said that Durruti was nothing more than a pis tolero.

' "The anarchists were generous but they were still political gangsters", ' quoted Barry.

'Obscure Object of Desire,' he and Tony answered simultaneously.

'Correct,' said Barry, 'I think Tony was a fraction faster.'

'There was the defence of the University of Madrid.'

'Durruti's Column fled – proving the fundamental unreliability of anarchist formations,' said Tony.

'But they were the last days of Simple Anarchism,' Barry said wistfully.

'What of the moral bigotry of anarchism – certain unpalatable behaviour towards homosexuals and prostitutes,' said Tony.

'Admitted,' said Barry.

'Sydney Anarchism eradicated moralism and replaced it with

Higher Libertarianism.'

'Of course.' They all laughed.

'Go to the communes for moral bigotry.'

'I am still a Friend of Durruti,' he said.

'I can't believe this,' Robyn said. 'Am I in the Journalists' Club in Sydney in the eighties and still hearing this? I can't believe this conversation.'

'Durruti was the front man of anarchism in Spain but it was Ascaso who was the theoretician. I am a friend of Ascaso,' said Tony.

'Let us drink to the discipline of indiscipline which must guide us all in every action,' he said.

'Pinch me, am I dreaming?' said Robyn.

'I drink to Cantwell who was an anarchist shot by the Viet-Cong.'

'An anarchist who worked for *Time*.'

'There are many anarchist traditions.'

Later he said to Barry that he had never quite understood all the ramifications of the 'discipline of indiscipline.'

'There is much to be said on that subject,' Barry said, but did not elaborate.

The Tide is High. He received a letter from her saying that in her final vacation she was working with the Elcho Island Aboriginal Crafts centre. 'I have been thinking of you big mobs – as they say up here – and the tide is high, as Deborah Harry says, and I have a feeling that it is getting close to that trip to Spain you talked so much and so often about. And you'll be turning forty soon. I'm planning my Grand Tour now that I'm nearly finished.'

He was deeply pleased that she had raised the trip to Spain. He wrote to her asking who was Deborah Harry?

He joined her on Elcho Island and they fished for parrot fish and speared mud crabs and cooked on hot coals.

In a motel in her home city after their return they'd made love, she had said that she had to go soon because her boyfriend was waiting. She had looked at him with her childlike eyes and said, 'will you want me again before I go?'

'Yes, I will – now that you have asked me – it was the asking which aroused me.'

'I thought it would arouse you,' she said, smiling with knowingness.

Searching for Durruti. He wrote to Levine in California, 'I'm really writing to pursue the subject of Durruti. I have been planning a pilgrimage to the Spanish Civil War and would like to include an anarchist pilgrimage. My guess is that the poem "The Midget" is set in a cafe that "could have been" the cafe in which Durruti plotted? Or is it a well known cafe? (I guess I sound like an MA student).'

A curious day. He wrote to her, 'It looks as if our Spanish pilgrimage may then be shaping up. I had a curious day. I was working on the Buenaventura Durruti story (which is dedicated to you). It is a long way from finished but it is a collection of references about Durruti, Barcelona, *The Passenger* and you. Last night I met some old mates from my cadetship days at the Journalists' Club and we argued about the Spanish Civil War – today your letter came saying that you might be ready to go to Spain with me. I did not think that you ever took the trip to Spain seriously . . . '

The Discipline of Indiscipline (1). The next week in the *New York Review of Books* he read a reference to the problems of Durruti and the discipline of indiscipline. Bernard Knox who had been in the International Brigade said, 'Madrid in the winter of 1936-37 was a remarkable place. The word epic has often been used of the events of that time but there was also a surrealist quality to it. I have often thought since that Luis Bunuel, if he had been there, would have felt quite at home.'

Knox said that Durruti created the idea of 'a discipline of indiscipline'. He had once talked with the Durruti Column to discuss passwords and patrol routes. Knox said he was plied with cigars, chorizo sausage and wine ' . . . needless to say the passwords we had arranged were quickly forgotten and they fired on our supply column that night . . . and when Durruti led his men back into the line he was shot dead and the Column disintegrated . . . the Anarchist columns . . . had shown almost superhuman courage in the fight in Barcelona but facing experienced troops in the field they were soon outmanoeuvred and outflanked, whereupon they ran like rabbits . . .'

William Herrick took issue in the next *New York Review of Books.* 'There isn't a fighting force on earth whether communist, anarchist, fascist or whatever, that has not at one point or another run like rabbits.'

Knox replied, 'Mr Herrick is quite right about running like

rabbits; as anyone who has lived through a war or two has done so more than once – sometimes it is the right thing to do. But only discipline, organisation and a proper chain of command will enable troops who have run like rabbits to reform and consolidate; the anarchists had none of these things, in fact they despised them.'

The People Armed. The book *The People Armed,* a biography of Durruti published by Black Rose Press, arrived from Cam.

'I have just had a real blockbuster of a paper accepted but the title was rejected. I thought the title "Dualistic Mental Processes in Hypnosis" was quite couthful. Sorry to hear that you are not considered decadent enough. Anytime you want a reference on the unmitigating squalor and depravity of your mind, let me know, I'd be delighted.'

The Discipline of Indiscipline (II). Durruti had about 6000 men in his Column. Each group of 25 had a delegate. Each four groups formed a Century. There was a Committee of Centuries made up of all delegates. A committee of Sections made up of delegates from the Centuries and finally a Column War Committee consisting of all delegates of the Sections and the General-Delegate of the Column – Durruti.

A Military Technical Council of experts made the strategic plans and submitted these to the War Committee.

The War Committee had a bureaucracy for services such as statistics, propaganda, intelligence and so on.

There were two commando units known as the Sons of the Night and the Black Band.

The Durruti Column refused to submit to military law imposed by the Republican and Communist forces.

Orwell said that the Column was more reliable than one might have expected. Bullying and abuse were not tolerated. The normal military punishments existed but were only used for serious offences.

Durruti wanted his army to be a model for the society they were fighting to create.

Journalists would sometimes question the men of the Durruti Column, 'you claim to have no leaders yet you obey Durruti.'

The militia men always replied, 'we follow him because he behaves well.'

She begins her Grand Tour. He received his first letter from her. 'I am in Bangkok wishing you were here with a hip flask full of brandy and some crooked conversation . . . I will be an experienced traveller by the time we meet up in Spain . . .'

It was fine cognac they'd drunk from his flask, not just brandy.

There was a new articulate confidence in her letters.

He remembered once chiding her for what he saw as her negativity and conversational passivity. He'd shouted at her. But then he'd read Henry James' *Watch and Ward* – a novel about a thirty-year-old man who adopts a ten-year-old girl to raise as his wife. The narrator finds the adolescent girl 'defiantly torpid' but then realises that 'her listless quietude covered a great deal of observation and that growing may be a soundless process.'

The death of Durruti. There are a number of stories about the death of Durruti – that he accidently shot himself with his own rifle, that he was shot by an 'uncontrollable' who resented any discipline including even the discipline of indiscipline. But his chauffeur said that he was hit by a stray bullet during the battle for the University of Madrid.

Durruti was taken to the Ritz Hotel then being used as an anarchist hospital where he died on 21 November, aged forty.

An anarchist funeral. Before the funeral the sculptor Victoriano Macho came with other artists of the Intellectual Alliance to make a death mask of Durruti.

Hans Kaminski, a German journalist, described the funeral. 'It is calculated that one inhabitant out of every four lined the streets. It was grandiose, sublime, and strange. Because no one led the crowds there was no order or organisation. Nothing worked and the chaos was indescribable . . . Durruti, covered by a red and black flag, left the house on the shoulders of the militia men from his Column. The masses raised their fists in a last salute. The anarchist song 'Son of the People' was chanted. It was a moving moment. But by mistake two orchestras had been asked to come . . . one played mutedly, the other very loud and they didn't manage to maintain the rhythm . . . the orchestras played again and again the same song; they played without paying attention to each other . . . the crowds were uncontrollable and the coffin couldn't move . . . the musicians were dispersed but kept reforming claiming the right to play. The cars carrying the wreaths could not go forward and were forced to drive in reverse . . . it was an anarchist burial – that was its majesty.'

In 1981 a pop group called the Durruti Column was formed in London.

The location of the graves. Levine wrote '. . . for me the place to which I make my pilgrimage is the grave of Durruti which sits between the graves of Ferrer Guardia and Ascaso. How to find it? In the Great Cemetery behind the fortress is a small Protestant burial ground. Between the bulk of the Catholic Cemetery and this little annex is a spot at the edge of a hill and there the three graves sit, the gravestones having been removed. But people come secretly and write on these dry concrete slabs 'CNT' and 'FAI', *'Viva anarquista'* and the names. It was illegal to take photographs of the graves . . .'
  Two old picknickers directed Levine to the graves.
  'Durruti,' said the man, 'I was on his side.'
  The old woman hushed him.

Francisco, I'll bring you red carnations. In Levine's poem for Durruti's closest friend Ascaso, he says that Ascaso was a stone, Durruti a blade.

  . . . the first grinding and sharpening
  the other . . .
  in the last photograph
  taken less than an hour before
  he died, stands in a dark
  suit, smoking, a rifle slung
  behind his shoulder, and glances
  sideways at the camera
  half smiling . . .

The card, 'I have fallen in love.' A card arrived from London showing 'Ulysses deriding Polyphemus' by Turner. It showed Ulysses and his men escaping in their ships from the blinded Polyphemus who, silhouetted against the sky, is throwing rocks at them (see Book IX of the *Odyssey*). They were escaping from the land of the Cyclops, 'a fierce uncivilised people who never lift a hand to plant or plough . . . have no assemblies for the making of laws, nor any settled customs . . .'
  She was now in London on her Grand Tour and the card said

with irony, 'I am sorry but I can't go with you to Spain. I have fallen in love and decided to "settle down", I am, after all, 21 now.' She had written in as a second thought 'physically yours as ever, please do not communicate.'

Once he had bumblingly tried to describe their relationship to her, to give it shape. She had stopped him, saying, 'It is a love without definition but not without art.'

He studied the card. Was she escaping from him, a blinded Polyphemus?

Spanish Refugee Aid. Anarchists fought not only in the armies of the Spanish republic but also in the Second World War. Some in the French resistance others as regulars in the Division Le Clerc. Some of them are still refugees unable or unwilling to go back to Spain after all these years. The old and the infirm are looked after by an organisation called Spanish Refugee Aid. Contributions can be sent to SRA Inc, 80 East Eleventh Street, New York, NY, USA, 10003.

How did the card affect him? He had often tried to describe to her the distinction between his attraction to her as a 'person' and his attraction to her as an 'archetype'. She had been a perfect example of 'the beautiful young girl.' And he had seen her growing as a person. She was probably right that the archetype was now left behind. She was right to have had forebodings about him dying in the Hotel de la Gloria. They had talked about suicide. When he had discussed the pilgrimage with her he had thought but not said, that he really might die there in the Hotel de la Gloria, that that might be a good point to conclude it.

Now she had diverted him from that appointment with the Hotel de la Gloria.

Compensation for angst. He had told her once on a beach during one of her depressions that he'd found a lot of good things in life which compensated for angst. She'd said, 'oh yeah, what are they?'

He'd told her of the surprises and serendipity of the life of inquiry, infinite, unimaginable twistings of sexuality, about the infinite imagination and its works, about the weary exhilaration of negotiation, the elegancy of the deal, and about the revelations of hunting and of the camp.

'But you once said volupte was the only solace!' she said,

laughing at him.

'That too.'

What would he be able to tell her now, now that he was forty.

He'd have to say that while all those things were still true, on some days it was only a tepid curiosity and a tired-hearted buccaneering which carried him on. But maybe they could explore the discipline of indiscipline together. And he could show her how their relationship had become two footnotes to a poem.

ACKNOWLEDGEMENTS

The following stories have been published previously in the sources mentioned: 'Mirrors', *Meanjin*, No 4, 1983 and *Billy Blue*, January, 1985; 'The Bathroom Dance', *Overland*, No 92, 1983; 'The Book', *Scripsi*, No 3, 1983; 'The Heraldry of the Body', *Westerly*, No 2, 1983; 'Conrad's Bear', *Southerly*, No 4, 1984; 'House', *Network*, 1983; 'Neons', *Aspect*, No 1, 1984; 'Seeds', *Outrider*, No 2, 1984; 'The Lost World: Signs of Life', *Art and Text*, No 12, 1983; 'Not the News', *National Times*, 14-20 September 1984; 'At the Signora's, *Australian Literary Magazine*, April 1985; 'Goczka', *Syllable*, No 2, 1984; 'Forty Susan Sangsters Stride Out at the Wellington Boot', *Sydney Morning Herald*, 9 September 1985; 'Buenaventura Durruti's Funeral', *Overland*, No 97, 1984.

The editor and the publishers would like to thank the publishers of the following pieces for permission to include them in this collection: 'Partying on Parquet', from *Vernacular Dreams*, Angelo Loukakis, UQP, 1986; 'Farnarkeling: A Typical Report', from *The Gillies Report*, John Clarke, McPhee Gribble/Penguin Books, 1985; 'Reasons for Going Into Gynaecology', from *Memories of the Assassination Attempt*, Gerard Windsor, Penguin Books, 1985; 'Secrets', from *Scission*, Tim Winton, McPhee Gribble/Penguin Books, 1985; 'The Empty Lunch-Tin', from *Antipodes*, David Malouf, Chatto & Windus, 1985; 'The Misbehaviour of Things', from *Book of Sei & Other Things*, David Brooks, Hale & Iremonger, 1985; 'Summer in Sydney', from *Leaving Queensland*, Barbara Brooks, Sea Cruise Books, 1983; 'Land Deal', from *Dreamworks*, Norstrillia Press, 1983; 'Mirdinan', from *Gularabulu*, Paddy Roe and Stephen Muecke, Fremantle Arts Centre Press, 1983;

'Brian "Squizzy" Taylor', from *Kites in Jakarta*, Moya Costello, Sea Cruise Books, 1985; 'Park', from *The Waters of Vanuatu*, Carmel Kelly, Sea Cruise Books, 1985; 'Xmas in the Bush', from *The Train*, Anna Couani, Sea Cruise Books, 1983; 'Our Lady of the Beehives', from *Home Time*, Beverley Farmer, McPhee Gribble/Penguin Books, 1985; 'Postcards from Surfers', from *Postcards from Surfers*, Helen Garner, McPhee Gribble/Penguin Books, 1985.

The photograph on page 107 is a detail from *Woman Dancing*, Eadweard Muybridge (Fotofolio, New York).